PERMANENT RECORD

LESLIE STELLA

To Nathan Hale
School Library,

AMAZON CHILDREN'S PUBLISHING

Leslie Stella

Amazon Publishing
Attn: Amazon Children's Publishing
P.O. Box 400818
Las Vegas, NV 891490
www.amazon.com/amazonchildrenspublishing

Library of Congress Cataloging-in-Publication Data is available.

ISBN-13: 9781477816394 (hardcover)
ISBN-10: 1477816399 (hardcover)
ISBN-13: 9781477866399 (eBook)
ISBN-10: 1477866396 (eBook)

Book design by Becky Terhune
Editor: Robin Benjamin

Printed in the United States of America (R)
First edition
10 9 8 7 6 5 4 3 2 1

For Caroline Stella

I owe an enormous debt of gratitude to my agent, Lucy Childs, without whose tenacity this book would not be. I am so thankful for her insight, honesty, and, above all, loyalty.

Thanks also to Molly Friedrich for introducing us.

I am grateful to the team at the Aaron M. Priest Literary Agency for their dedication to their authors.

And most of all, thank-you to my family for understanding why I have to spend so much time sitting here in front of this computer.

CHAPTER ONE

July

I guess what I hate most about going to a psychiatrist is the magazines in the waiting room. It's not that none of them appeals to me personally—I don't expect him to order a subscription to *Toxicology Today* or *Young Botanist* just for me. But *People* and the Oprah magazine? I think I speak for all the patients when I say those magazines are big fat reminders of what we're not. If we could be interested in *Teen Mom* or Oprah, maybe we'd be normal. We wouldn't need psychiatrists. But seeing the teen mom or a movie star staring up at me every week from some magazine on the coffee table, knowing that millions of people everywhere get some kind of pleasure from it, just reinforces how abnormal I am. Why don't I care? Why don't I know what TV shows people watch or what bands they listen to? I'm sixteen and should know these things. Even if I made fun of them, at least that would show some interest on my part. Really, those magazines depress the hell out of me.

"Badi?" Dr. Elliott opens the waiting room door and sticks his head out. It's a nice head as heads go. One of those bald ones.

I pick up my backpack and personal reading material, checking to make sure I've left nothing behind. One day I dropped my favorite pen here—I know I did; I know it—but when I came back to look later that night, it was gone. Some-one had swiped it. Everyone got in a twist because I broke into the building (no alarm, simple pin-and-tumbler locks, which are easy to open with a pick and a tension wrench).I know it was illegal, but there was no malice. I needed my pen and forgot about the surveillance cameras. That won't happen again. Anyway, there's nothing left behind today. No, wait, there's a thread. It obviously came off my shirt. I try to pick it up, but it seems to be stuck to the chair.

"Badi?" Dr. Elliott says again. He has one of those really calming voices that serves him well in his profession. "Just leave it."

"There's a thread," I say.

"That's okay. I'll take care of it later."

"But it's from my shirt."

"I think it's just a loose thread from the chair cushion. See? It's part of the fabric."

I tug on the thread. And he's right; it is part of the chair. And I still can't leave it alone. And this pisses me off even more.

"What are you doing?" he asks. "Really, just leave it—"

I wrap the thread around my finger and yank as hard as I can. It hurts. I mean, it's practically cutting off my circula-tion now; the tip of my finger has gone bone white above the thread. I keep pulling. The thread is cutting into me, and above it my fingertip is bloodless: an empty, dead thing.

Dr. Elliott puts his hand on my shoulder and doesn't say anything. He has a mild expression on his face that tells me he sees this kind of thing all the time.

"I can't let go," I say.

He pats my shoulder. "You can."

But I can't, or I won't, and he has to help unravel me.

The actual office, where we do all our psychiatristing, is much different from the waiting room. The lights are low, and there's a potted bonsai tree—really the tiniest thing you ever saw—and one of those tabletop fountain things with relaxing water sounds. The chairs are comfy. It's a decent room. It looks like Dr. Elliott uses the decorating tips from his Oprah magazine.

"So, how's your summer going?" he asks as we settle into our chairs. This is how we start off each session, like we are two normal people having a normal conversation. We chat about the weather and things like that. I have to hand it to him—he really knows what he's doing. Five minutes of me talking about the weather and my bus ride here, and I almost feel like a regular person. I hate when those five minutes end.

He asks what's going on with my family. It's such a casual-sounding question but so impossible to answer without my head exploding. I'm surprised he can ask it with a straight face.

"Oh, you know . . . ," I say. My voice sounds fake. It makes me sick.

He smiles but doesn't say anything. He prompts me with silence a lot, which they must learn in psychiatry school.

I try to be a good sport. It's not Dr. Elliott's fault that I have to come here. "My parents don't seem as mad at me as they did in May. My mom can look at me now without collapsing in tears all the time. But I still catch my dad doing that thing where he stares at me in confusion, like he doesn't know what I'm doing there in his house. But at least he's not screaming that I've ruined everyone's lives anymore."

"That sounds good."

I know it sounds good. But it's not true. My dad does still shout in my face that I'm ruining his life. I try to put a positive spin on things because I think if Dr. Elliott really knew the truth about me—the escalating panic, the pills I won't take, the lies I tell, the things I steal—he would need a psychiatrist himself.

I gather up my resolve here. I rarely disclose anything meaningful (or honest) during these sessions, so today I latch on to the one authentic piece of news I have. "They've decided to withdraw me from school."

He glances at my file. "I see. But you weren't expelled. Your parents don't *have* to enroll you in a new school." He has to check his notes on me. My life isn't interesting enough for him to memorize all the pertinent facts.

"I could not go back to that school after . . . everything."

"Everything?"

"Don't make me say it." My voice is flat.

"You know I wouldn't."

I go on. "Anyway, my parents think that with everything that happened and how the principal and teachers and the students feel about me now, it's better to start me off somewhere new."

"Hmm," he says. "Maybe."

See, at this point I get kind of irritated, because I just want him to say something definitive, like "Oh, they're so wrong!" or "Absolutely the right thing to do." Saying "maybe" leaves me feeling very wobbly, if you know what I mean, like there are no right or wrong choices, that more bad things can happen no matter what I—or my parents—choose to do.

"Look," I say, "I know I wasn't a model student."

Suddenly, Dr. Elliott doesn't even have to consult his notes. He recites from memory: "Badi, aside from the danger you pose to yourself, you damaged school property. You threatened a student. Your teachers found your notebook with that 'Enemies to be eliminated' list of classmates. You tampered with the school water supply. You blew up a toilet."

"I don't want to get into this again," I say. I look away because I feel the hate boiling up in me, and I don't want to spew it at Dr. Elliott. If I let it out, it's a tsunami that will drown innocent people in its wake.

He waits, but I don't give in. I'm not talking about it. I've been through all this with him before, and with the principal and my parents and the police, too, and I'm tired of everybody misinterpreting my act of self-defense as a murderous urge. I've *had* murderous urges. I know the difference.

"My parents have arranged for me to go to Magnificat Academy in August. It's a private school, Catholic. They think the discipline will be better for me."

"Hmm," he says. "Maybe."

Then he asks what I think about that. That's his way of asking about my feelings. He thinks boys don't respond well to talking about their feelings, so he uses the word *think* all the time. It's so obvious.

"I don't think it matters one way or the other," I say, and I can feel that dull deadness creep into my voice.

Dr. Elliott jots down something in my file. His eyes linger on the page. "I didn't know your family was Catholic."

"My dad calls himself a lapsed Muslim. My uncle's an Assyrian Christian. My mom was a Buddhist for about ten minutes when she was into yoga, but she's currently into Catholicism. We go to mass once in a while."

"Do you like that? Going to mass?"

"I like the long periods of standing."

"How do you think you'll adjust to such a different school environment?"

I cross my arms. "I don't believe in God, if that's what you're getting at."

"Oh?" he says. I know that tone. It's so mild and neutral that he thinks it will compel me to open up.

"I mean, I guess I'm Christian and we go to church, but if there is a God, I don't think he's interested in me."

We talk more, I say things, I don't even know what. Sometimes I just say anything to pass the time there. Or I make up stuff. I look at his bald head a lot. It's impossible to ignore. It's actually very well shaped; maybe that's why he shaves it. But the moment the light hits it there's a big glare, and his head looks so shiny that I just about can't stand it.

I take the Western Avenue bus back home. Dr. Elliott's office is only six blocks from our apartment, and I could walk it, but our session is over at 7 p.m., and I read in the police blotter that more murders took place at 7 p.m. in Rogers Park last year than at any other time of day. People even get killed for their transit cards. I'm not the most imposing guy. My weight is up to 130 now, which is better, but I'm only 5'8". That is actually average for a guy. Not tall, not short. But the combination of the average height with the skinny build, orthodontia, acne, out-of-control hair, and Middle Eastern features make me a walking target.

The bus drops me off less than a block from home, and I run the rest of the way. Lamely, I am out of breath by the time I push open our front gate. My older brother, Dariush, is kneeling in front of the apartment buzzers with a bottle of glue and little pieces of paper littered around him.

"Did you have fun?" he asks without turning around.

"Loads."

"Sorry, man. Just teasing. It's rotten luck you have to go there." I shrug. He says, "But I suppose it's better than juvie hall."

Juvenile hall. A detention home. It's hard to know how to respond. On the one hand, incarceration would ruin my chances of getting a botany scholarship. On the other, the idea that anyone could actually imagine me in juvie hall without falling to the floor in hysterics is really gratifying.

"What are you doing?" I ask, peering closer at the buzzers.

"Replacing the nameplates."

"Why?" After all, our dad owns this building, and everyone who lives in the three apartments is related to each other. Nobody would ever move out.

Dariush just laughs. It's a low, mirthless sound.

I can smell dinner before I reach the third floor. Tonight it's orange chicken *koresh*, and when I open the door to our apartment, it's all around me: orange, lime, cinnamon, cardamom. Mom knows it's pretty much my favorite food of all time. But then it is a therapy night, so I'm not surprised. The psychiatry journals would say my mother is "compensating" or has a "guilt complex" because I have to go to therapy. So there are perks to seeing a shrink.

7

My sister is hunched over the desk by the front window, her college textbooks spread out in front of her. My younger sister and brother are killing each other on the Xbox. Nobody says anything.

The windows are open, and I can hear kids playing outside in the alley, a dog barking somewhere, Mexican pop music from the neighbors across the street. I like the mix of noises. It really sounds like people are out there living. Once in a while we hear gunfire, which adds a subtle nuance to the urban soundscape.

Dad is sitting in his recliner in the living room, reading the paper. With his round glasses and round head, he reminds me of Gandhi. He glances up at me with that wary expression I've grown used to. It says: *What have you done now?* But I haven't done anything. I say hi and he says hi, and then it's time for dinner.

We're halfway through when Dad clears his throat, puts down his fork, and turns to me. "Son, I have some news for you."

My eyes tighten—I can feel them—and my heart rate triples.

Dad lifts his palms in a gesture of surrender. "Now, now, do not derange yourself." My father emigrated to this country—right here to Chicago, in fact—from Iran thirty years ago, and while he has only the slightest accent and is completely fluent in English (and Farsi and French), he's retained some dialectical oddities.

I agree not to derange myself, and he says, "I have made a little change for us. It is practically nothing, a mere formality. But I wanted to make you aware."

Dariush snorts and continues eating, propped up on one elbow, his arm protecting his plate. My mother frowns at him. The rest of my siblings are all looking at me, so it's obvious that everyone but me has heard whatever this news is.

"When you enter Magnificat Academy, it will be under a new name. Our family name will be shorter. Easier to pronounce and spell. You know how Americans are."

"Well?" I ask, waiting.

"Hess," he says.

"Hess? That'll be our last name? Isn't that, like, German?"

He dismisses this with a wave of his hand. "Melting pot. Everything in America is jumbled."

Dariush mimes setting off a bomb, screws his eyes shut, plugs his ears, whispers "*Kaboom.*" He sniggers as Dad clucks his tongue in irritation.

"Well, yes," says Dad, "there *is* the unfortunate stereotype. Middle Eastern people are not all bombers." He levels his gaze at me. "Not all of us."

There's no point in arguing. If you think there is, then you don't know my dad. I realize our last name is—was—ridiculous and unpronounceable, but do we really have to change it? I don't have a clue what to say. How often do you find yourself in this situation? You sit down to dinner after a session with your shrink, and your dad tells you he's changed your name.

"I think Hess is a fine name," says Mom. You can tell she's lying, because she opens her eyes too wide and nods about a thousand times.

"It fits really easily on the buzzer plate," says Dariush.

"See?" Dad smiles. It looks fake, and nobody is fooled. "Everyone wins."

"Well . . . I guess it's okay," I say, like I have any choice in the matter.

"You'll see," Dad says. "It'll be fine. Also," he adds, "your first name is now Bud."

Almost midnight. I can't sleep. Every so often I turn on the light and look at the new Social Security card my dad presented me with after dinner. "Bud Hess," it proclaims, along with my number, tangible proof that I'm American and harmless. No militant Muslim am I! I am Bud Hess. I say it to myself over and over: Bud Hess. You can't do much with two syllables. No matter how I try to change my inflection, I sound like a white kid from the fifties.

You should have seen the way my dad handed me the card, like it was an award. The card isn't just proof of my new name; it's my father's way of telling me this is irreversible. He went to court and down to the Social Security office and did all the paperwork and whatever for all of us kids. Can you even do that? Is that legal? It must be. I'm only sixteen and a child in the eyes of the government. In the eyes of my parents, too.

So now I've got a new school *and* a new name. I was never particularly attached to Badi. It's a Muslim name that means "marvelous." But now I feel like I can't live without it. Worst of all, my siblings all get to keep *their* first names. Apparently Arman and Dorri sound American enough, and Dad said with them being only eleven and twelve, it would be too hard for them to change.

"What about Azita?" I had asked.

"It's different for girls" had been his answer. "And Azita is nineteen." Pretty flimsy explanation, if you ask me. But no one did ask me, which is a recurring theme in this household.

"And Dariush?"

"Hmm . . . yes, him. He also is an adult, though one would never know it."

"The first floor isn't changing their name," I had grumbled, referring to my aunt Rana, uncle Nouri, and cousins.

"Of course not. Khaleh Rana is your mother's sister," he had replied, using the Farsi word for *aunt.* "She has her husband's last name. This is not their affair. It is ours alone." He held my gaze until I looked away.

There's a knock at my door, and I quickly shut off the light and put the card on my nightstand.

"I know you're awake, Badi," Dariush whispers.

I sigh. "Come in."

He sits at the foot of my bed, picking threads off my old quilt. I wonder if he can stop himself from doing it without a psychiatrist there to guide him.

"I can't believe you didn't warn me outside," I tell him.

"It wasn't for me to say."

"And I can't believe you're going along with this. You're a grown man. Why are you letting dad change your last name?"

Dariush looks at me. Even with just the hall light on, I can see his expression. You could only call it defeated.

"Dad's done a lot for me: tuition, bail. I haven't exactly lived up to his expectations, so I guess this is the least I can do for him. It's not a big deal. Lots of people change their names when they live in a different country."

"Not after living there thirty years! He's just doing this to punish me."

"He wants things to be easier for you."

"How is this easier? Now I have to go to a new school with a new name. Harder. Not easier."

"You know he did it *because* you are starting a new school, dork." Dariush grins as he says it. He's eight years older than me and completely different. Long hair, tattooed, unemployed. He is trying to follow his own path in life instead of being a good Persian son and doing whatever Dad says. So he's not the pride of the family, but he's the closest thing I have to a hero right now.

"They can call me whatever they want, but I will still be the same dork."

"That's the spirit." He takes something out of his back pocket and presses it into my hand. "Good night, Badi," he says, heading for the hallway.

"Bud," I correct him. He stifles a laugh as he shuts the door.

I flick on the nightstand lamp. In my hand is a slip of white paper from the mailbox buzzers, thirty years old, the edges worn: HESSAMIZADEH. It's my dad's handwriting, I'd know it anywhere: those cramped, careful, faded letters.

At first I want to crumple it up and toss it in the waste-basket, but then I change my mind. I put it in the drawer of my nightstand, and it's immediately lost amid the candy bar wrappers, beat-up journal, zit cream, back issues of *Young Botanist*, and all the other reminders of who I really am.

August

There's a uniform at Magnificat. This appeals to me. White polo shirt with a crest in blue and gold, the school colors—it looks like a badge with a shepherd's crook and a football, but that can't be right—and the motto *Vox populi vox dei* underneath. "The voice of the people is the voice of God," it means. Latin is kind of a hobby of mine. Maybe I will fit in there after all.

The pants are blue Dockers, the shoes are optional. I mean, you have to wear shoes, that's not optional, but the style is optional as long as they're not sneakers. My mother took me to Payless and chose the shoes for me: black wing tips in a leatherlike material.

"You look smart," she said as I tried on the shoes in front of those mini-floor-level mirrors. I thought I looked elderly, but I don't suppose anyone will notice my shoes much.

The regular school bus service for Magnificat does not include my district, so I'm stuck taking the city bus. I'm used to taking it since my parents don't like to lend out the car. I can catch the number 49 Western Avenue north, then transfer to the eastbound 290 Touhy Avenue bus. It should take forty to forty-two minutes, I calculated, including walking the two blocks from Sheridan to the school, which should be ample time for the antianxiety meditations that Dr. Elliott wants me to use. I'm supposed to breathe normally, whatever that means. And repeat things like "I am open to happiness" and "I am getting through this" in my brain. I'm serious; he really said I should do this.

Mom had made me scrambled eggs this morning. I ate them, even though my stomach was heaving. Protein amino acids can calm hyper nerves like mine. I packed up everything, all my school supplies and whatnot, in the briefcase I used at my old school. It's the only old thing on me today, the only thing from my old life. It felt weird when I picked it up this morning. My parents had stared at my briefcase. I knew they were wishing they'd bought me a new one so that I would not remember or repeat my mistakes.

Mom had kissed me a bunch of times at the door. It was, like, enough already, but I didn't want to make her cry by asking for a little personal space. Dad shook my hand. I felt like an enlisted man shipping off for service.

"Try to enjoy school, *Bud*," Mom said carefully. "Everything will be fine, I just know it." She smiled so brightly that a giant medicine ball of dread descended in my gut.

"Do well," said Dad. "You shall do well because this is your last chance. I have no other chances for you."

Yeah, thanks for that. I ran down the three flights of steps and out the front doorway, pausing only to throw up at the corner by the mailbox. A truck honked at me as it passed.

So here I am, forty-two minutes and maybe eighty meditations later, at the front walk that leads up to Magnificat Academy. I stare up at the imposing sprawl of brick and limestone, this building that will be my new institution. The architecture looks both natural, with its boulder arrangements and wildflower garden, and sleekly modern, with its metal detectors and overt bigness.

At the top of the school is a bell tower with a clock. I watch the sweep of the second hand across the pale clock face. Drifts of stone rise like gun turrets and guard towers on either side.

Then I walk in.

The chaos of activity before the tardy bell reminds me of public school, except for the uniforms and lack of gang affiliation. But there are always gangs, right? Just different kinds with different weapons. I check in with the school secretary, a grandmotherly type named Mrs. Kobunski. She is wearing a choker necklace made of beige velvet; it looks just like a broccoli rubber band, and I can't stop staring at it. This is the kind of thing Dr. Elliott always tells me to acknowledge and then move on from, these obsessions with crazy things that should not affect me—but always do. The secretary goes to my file and hands me a copy of my schedule, a map of the school, and a temporary ID. In my head I say, *I acknowledge that her choker looks just like a broccoli rubber band and that's fine and now I am letting that thought go*, but of course it doesn't go. The broccoli rubber band is a little tight, and it bites into her neck so that a roll of flesh protrudes from the top and underneath. It can't be comfortable, it just can't. There's no earthly way. My neck starts to hurt just looking at it, and my pulse starts to race the way it does when these things hit, and I swear I can feel that broccoli rubber band closing around my own throat, I mean it, I really can. What technique can I use, what tools has Dr. Elliott taught me? *Come on, think!* I picture myself loosening the broccoli rubber band from her neck, and that helps me feel better, but in my mind, somehow I am then *tearing* off the broccoli rubber band, and with it comes her head, which rolls away into the copy room amid the FedEx boxes and mailing tubes.

I feel like I'm going to throw up again except, thank God, there is nothing left in my stomach, and I hang on to the counter to keep myself from crashing to the floor. I'm dizzy, and there's black and blue spots in my vision, and the secretary is staring at me and murmuring something kind, but she sounds a million miles away and looks like she is standing at the wrong end of a telescope.

This passes. It always does. The secretary tries to make me go to the clinic—what could be worse? It would be all over school by lunch: *Did you hear? That new kid fainted when he walked in the building!* I say I'm fine, I'm just lightheaded because I didn't eat breakfast, and she admonishes me gently for that, and it's all over, and this is everything that happens before the tardy bell rings at 8:10 in the morning.

By homeroom I'm almost normal, or normal for me. Nobody in the classroom is openly hostile. So already this is an improvement over my old school.

There was some momentary curiosity during roll when the homeroom teacher, an old nun called Sister Timothy, introduced me as the new guy. I sat perfectly still with a pleasant but not psychotic smile on my face, so the interest faded. As a new student, I have been assigned a "Homeroom Buddy," a classmate who's supposed to help me fit in.

"So, *Bud*, I guess I'm your *buddy*," he says. "Hilarious, huh?" At least he's trying.

His name is Dylan, and what I have noticed is this: he

has that easy popularity that comes from years of no effort, from every little thing just falling into your lap. You know what I mean. People seem to like him, and he's nice in a nonpartisan way to everyone. There's probably more to him than meets the eye, but really, do you *need* more than that?

He asks, "What school did you used to go to?"

"Sullivan," I say.

"Whoa. Wasn't some kid just shot there?"

Kids are always getting shot there. And some kids just get beaten with a golf club underneath the Safe School Zone sign outside the building. But I don't say any of that.

Dylan goes over my schedule with me and points out the worst teachers. As he's doing this, Sister Tim hands out boxes of chocolate bars—we're supposed to sell them by Thanksgiving for the school fund-raiser. I look down at a box doubtfully. I can't see myself going door-to-door trying to unload these things.

Dylan asks, "Were you in any clubs at Sullivan? I can get you a list of the different extracurricular activities and clubs we have. The first meetings are next week."

"I tried to start a Stephen Hawking Fan Club, but nobody joined." Dylan looks at me blankly. I continue, "He's a theoretical physicist. But very accessible for people who aren't used to thinking about things like alternate dimensions."

"Oh. Well, I know Computer Club is always looking for new blood."

I should have seen that one coming. I look like I would be into Computer Club, and I have some of the right requirements (D&D experience, a collection of pewter miniatures, hair like a mushroom cloud, and a chip on my shoulder), but

I wouldn't fit in there either since I am by all accounts an academic bust.

He tries again. "Sports?"

I eye him warily, but he doesn't seem to be screwing with me. "Yeah, I used to play baseball." An outright lie. Why did I say it? I don't know. Then I try a little truth. "Do they have a fencing team here?" I ask.

"Like . . . with swords?"

"Foils," I say. "They're called foils."

He shakes his head, and a fog passes over his features. Is it *that* weird, fencing? You think the things you like are just ordinary things, just part of your personality—fencing, croquet, explosives—but maybe they are a little weird, and when you're sixteen, small weirdnesses build a case for people not wanting to be around you.

"Well, I'll get you that list by tomorrow," Dylan says, rising as the bell rings. He walks me to my locker and asks if I know where I'm going next.

"Yes, first period is Chemistry, room 107. First floor, north wing."

"Me, too. See ya there, but I gotta take a leak first. Good luck, Bud." He raises his hand, palm outward, waiting.

I try to high-five him but miss.

I make it through the morning. It's not like in the movies, where everyone is staring at the new kid and laughing at all his mistakes. I'm just a leaf floating in the current. I push through the crowded hallways; I sit unnoticed in classrooms.

A small vestige of a panic attack grips me as I wade through the throngs of kids; after all, there are fifteen hundred of them and hardly one of me. I breathe like I'm supposed to and it goes away, and nobody notices that it happened. Actually, I haven't gone *completely* unnoticed; there have been more than a few glances at my shoes. So I was wrong, people *do* notice shoes. And they've noticed that mine are from Payless.

Another thing the movies have wrong is the idea of the new kid, or the unpopular kid, eating alone. There is no room to eat alone. You couldn't eat by yourself if your life depended on it. I'm scouting for an empty chair, stumbling about with my tray, my apple rolling around precariously, when I spy what I'm looking for: a table of people who are all trying to act as if they are eating alone. Some are reading, some are texting, some are staring off into the fluorescent murk of the cafeteria, and some are tunneling into their chili mac with pornographic zeal.

"Is anyone sitting here?" I ask, indicating an empty chair.

They shrug and barely look at me. I sit down and try to eat. My mother has instilled in me the importance of a well-balanced meal: milk and fruit and whole grains and all the rest, but after a few bites I find I can't eat any more. I just can't. I'm afraid I'll throw up all over the loner table, and then I'll really be up the creek.

I arrange the food into a color wheel around my plate. There's nothing to stand in for blue except for one corner of my tuna salad sandwich. The girl next to me has shaggy blonde hair that hides her face, and she is hunched over a notebook, doodling a figure with a mustache and an ax buried in its brain. She draws droplets of blood that look extremely realistic. She's not a goth girl, but she wears a dragon-claw ring (clearly nonregulation uniform) that could double as finger armor. She has a sticker on the cover of her three-ring binder that says KILL YOUR TELEVISION.

She glances over at me. I lower my gaze immediately to my color wheel.

"Are you new?" she asks.

"Not really," I say. "I've been at this school for over four hours." I try to smile and feel a clump of tuna salad in my retainer.

She goes on as if I haven't said anything. "Because the tuna salad sits out all morning. It's common knowledge."

"Thank you," I say. "Where is the nearest bathroom?"

She directs me down the south corridor, and I make it just in time before my stomach gives a mighty heave.

By sixth period I am not exactly a mess, but I'm pretty close. I want this day to be over. I can't take any more episodes of random vomit. I would kill for a swig of Listerine.

I'm at my locker. I can't remember the combination, and I'm going to be late for sixth if I don't get this thing open. I must have spun the tumblers a million times when this custodian miraculously appears at my side. His shirt has a patch with his name: MR. SANTOS. He says, "Don't worry," and then he consults a little device like a BlackBerry and opens the locker for me.

I thank him and he smiles, then he disappears down the hall as the late bell sounds.

My Modern Lit teacher, Ms. Viola, glares at me as I slip into class. Instead of teaching us anything on the first day, she talks about her favorite books, none of which are on the syllabus. When anyone has a question, she flaps her hand in a "shut up" gesture.

Someone asks, "Are we going to be tested on this?"

"Are you serious?" Ms. Viola barks. She has hair like the Bride of Frankenstein, wears a sweater vest, and snaps the chalk in her hand. She is the only teacher I have who refuses to use the whiteboard. On my class schedule, Dylan wrote next to Viola's name: *Cra-zee!* So I feel a kinship with her.

Coincidentally, the girl from my lunch table is in this class. Her name is Nikki Vrdolyak, and when she pushes aside the tangle of hair, you can see she has black-framed glasses and a pair of shrewd green eyes that miss nothing. She kind of waved at me when I first walked into the room. She has a face full of character. She *must* have character since she seemed unperturbed when I ran ninety miles an hour out the cafeteria door with my hand clamped over my mouth.

I approach her after class. "I never properly introduced myself. Bud Hess," I say. I stick out my hand. She stares at it and then shakes it. Her fingernails are bitten down, the cuticles raw; she wears a cheap digital watch; the dragon-claw ring dwarfs her knuckle. I like this hand with its vulnerabilities. This is a hand that has seen things.

After eighth period and many wrong turns, I find my locker. I get out my nylon windbreaker, my folders, my briefcase, my everything. I've looked around enough today to see that my everything is all wrong here. No one wears windbreakers or pleather wing tips, no one uses folders without storing them in a three-ring binder. But I don't like three-ring binders because they don't fit well in my briefcase, which nobody carries either. I know all this; I knew all this. Still, I've had to give up a lot this summer, and I couldn't stomach giving up these other things, too.

Dylan surprises me as I shut my locker. "How'd every-thing go today, Bud?"

My face gives it away.

He laughs. "Happens to everyone." He jerks his thumb over his shoulder at a girl behind him. She wears the stunned look of livestock. "My sister. Freshman. Got lost on the way to every single class today."

It's nice of him to check in with me. I don't want him to think he's a bad Homeroom Buddy just because of my panic attacks and vomiting. I begin to ask him about dress code violations and the demerit system when I can feel him distancing himself from me. Gazing over my shoulder and calling out to someone else down the hall.

"Oh, never mind," I say. "I'll figure it out."

"You sure? Okay, cool," he says, his relief obvious. "Catch ya later."

"Yeah, see you tomorrow!" Oh God, I sound so bright and cheerful, I want to rip out my tongue. I can't even drawl out the "ya" the way everyone else does. No, I have to say "you."

After he walks away, I must look lost, because a passing teacher asks, "Bus or car?"

"Car," I lie, and he directs me to the cafeteria.

I walk through the cafeteria to the parking lot, even though I'll have to angle back toward the front to catch the 290 Touhy bus. Why'd I lie about having a car? I don't know. I just want to walk out of here with the kids who drive, the kids who have somewhere to be and some way to get there.

CHAPTER THREE

September

Well, it's your funeral," says Azita, laughing.

I position my mallet. I don't let her get to me. Her only defense during our more brutal croquet matches is to try to batter me emotionally. I use a wild stop-shot and whack her ball clear out of the yard and behind the garbage cans, where it bounces against the alley gate.

"Nice," says Dariush. He offers his fist to me, knuckles down. I inspect it but see nothing amiss.

"You're supposed to bump it with your fist, dumbass," says Azita.

It's Dariush's turn, and I pretend to concentrate on his shot—we're a competitive croquet family—but inside I'm beginning to worry that my sister is right: I am a dumbass. Not because of the fist bump, but because, as I just explained to her and Dariush, I'm petitioning to start a fencing team at Magnificat, which is going to kill any chance I have of being seminormal and accepted.

After his shot (a standard drive), my brother says, "I think it's a great idea, Badi. Getting involved in something you like will help you be less of a total misfit at school."

Azita stops in midswing and gawps at him. "Are you

nuts? He wants to start a *fencing* team! He's going to embarrass himself."

They go on for a bit like that as if I'm not standing right there listening.

My parents have been hounding me about how school is going for the last three days. There is nothing to report. I haven't learned anything yet as far as I can tell. I haven't had any more panic attacks and haven't thrown up, so that's good, but I don't have any friends. Even at the loner lunch table, which I've come to think of as a real clique even though all of the participants eat there unwillingly, I haven't talked to anyone much. Nikki Vrdolyak is polite but prefers drawing violent cartoons to conversation.

My dad has been eavesdropping on our croquet chat, and I can tell he's about to bust a gasket now. He roquets my mother's ball into the remains of her vegetable garden and motions for me to come over there.

I consider not walking over. He always expects us to go to him. Even when I was a kid, he'd say, "Come here to me so that I may spank you." But I cave and walk over, just like always.

"What is this about fencing, Bud?" he asks. I still cringe at the sound of my new name, especially the way he pronounces it: *bod*.

I shrug like it is no big deal. "I might want to start a fencing team, that's all. Their sports curriculum lacks one, and I feel—"

"Why not join a sport they already have? What is so special about fencing? Yes, I know you took those fencing classes last year, but that was for fun. Not a life pursuit. This

I never understand with you, why you make everything harder."

I try again. "It interests me. I'm good at it."

"We gave you tennis lessons for two years. Now, *that* you can do for life."

"I don't like tennis. In fact, I suck at tennis."

I know he's upset, because he ignores my slang. "What of academic clubs? They have no engineering, no science, no computers?"

For real? Engineering Club? It's like he has no idea who he's talking to. Again I try to explain my theories on extra-curricular involvement—those clubs are for overachievers, which clearly I am *not*—but he tosses aside his mallet and waves his hands around in front of his face like my words are a bad odor he needs to fan away.

"I will tell you what I think, Bud. I think you need to con-centrate on your studies. You never get good grades You are not dumb, but you are unfocused. Ever since all the trouble . . ." His voice trails off here. He can't bring himself to say it. He's half right, you know: I'm not dumb. But I *am* clinically depressed and have an anxiety disorder, which interferes with things like studying and learning and breathing and living. He thinks it's something I can just turn off and on with willpower.

Dad switches gears. "You should not be wasting time with sports. I want you involved, yes, but not with something silly, something that will not carry weight on transcripts. Join a club at Magnificat, by all means; join French Club, yes? Or something else ordinary that will not take up time. You do that, yes, and all will be fine. You shall be happy in this place. Not like the other school."

He's manic now, stumbling over his words like an English 101 flunky.

My mother says, "You could start a Botany Club. That is more academic."

"Maman, I would love nothing more than to share my enthusiasm for botany with other people, but nobody would be into it. Fencing is a better bet. I'm more likely to find kids who'd be willing to stab each other with pointed sticks."

Now everybody in the family is listening, and everybody's offering their lousy opinions. My aunt and uncle and bratty cousins from the first floor, my little sister and brother, pretty much every Persian in the county is in our backyard waving a croquet mallet and discussing the merits of private school and tennis and Calculus Club. Everybody except for Dariush, who's lighting a smoke and watching me and not saying anything. Finally, he walks over and claps his hand on my back.

He says, "You'll be okay, Badi-jan, whatever you join. Fencing sounds pretty awesome, actually, with those straitjackets they wear."

Dad hears this. You know it's bad when he storms over instead of just summoning you to appear at his feet. "And you just shut with that right now, Dariush. Putting stupid ideas in his head, you who have no children or responsibilities. You think it is funny to encourage him to act like an idiot. You think it does not rub off from you, you and your stupid, horrible cigarettes."

Then *they* start going at it: the cigarettes, the chronic unemployment, the tattoos and weird friends—all the stuff that makes my brother so much cooler than the rest of the family. My mom yells, too, because she can't stand to be left out. The hippie neighbors come to watch the show. The hippies, the ones who fed their dog marijuana brownies, look concerned. You know your family's got problems when the hippies with the stoned dog are worried about you.

Everybody's so involved and fired up, they don't notice when I go back inside the building. I nuke a plate of Wheat Thins with American cheese and eat it in my bed, even though eating in bed is strictly forbidden by my mother. My cat comes and sits next to me. He doesn't want any food, just a little scratching under his chin. I know he has bitten other people in my family, but never me. He often pees in Azita's closet.

By the time everyone comes in, it's after eight. I turn off my light, get back in bed, and ignore the knocks at my door because there are some nights when I can't take any more drama. But eventually, Dariush busts in without asking.

"I'm sleeping," I say.

He throws himself into my desk chair. "I have to tell you this one thing."

"Sleeping."

He leans back in my chair, and it creaks. "This morning I passed a woman driving a car with two baby seats in the front and scrap metal in the back. God, I love Chicago."

I raise myself up on one elbow and squint into the semi-darkness. "That's what you had to wake me up for?"

"It was an excuse. But you weren't asleep. It's only eight thirty."

"It's been a rough day, and tomorrow will be, too. And you know what? Here's my prediction for junior year: it's going to suck, just like the rest of my life."

"Dude," he says. I wait for more, but that's it.

My eyes grow accustomed to the dark, and I can make out little things in my room, but that's only because I already know they're there. The pewter miniatures (I have an undead army that's been half painted for a month; I can't seem to get into it again), my Godzillas, a poster of Albert Einstein sticking out his tongue, irregular underwear my mother bought at Walmart, bookshelves (every edition of the *Player's Handbook* and *Dungeon Master's Guide,* Stephen Hawking's *A Brief History of Time,* the *MIT Guide to Lock Picking*, assorted sci-fi, botany guides, and a Thomas Jefferson biography), the cat's basket that he never sleeps in, expensive Saucony tennis shoes worn a total of nine times.

Dariush says, "Look, I just wanted to tell you that you'll get through this. High school, I mean. And life. I know you can do it."

"It's a cliché to say that it feels like everyone else knows something you don't, but really, I feel that way. That everybody my age knows how to have fun, knows what's expected of them, knows how to get through life. But I don't have a clue."

"I feel like that a lot. I wonder how people can hold down jobs and tolerate it and have families and be responsible. Life would be so much easier if I felt like they do."

"Great. So things will never get better for me either?"

"It's not that. Most people are a certain way: they fit in— or want to—and follow the rules. But others, you and me, we're different. What we want out of life is intangible—you know what that means?"

"Something indefinable, something you can't touch."

He stretches and gets up. "The thing you have to understand about people," he says, "is that most of them suck, and you don't want to be like them anyway. Just get through high school. I won't lie: people suck after high school, too. But you'll be older then and will have given up, so it won't be as devastating."

"I just want to understand why my brain misfires."

Dariush looks so sad. I wish I never said that. He says, "I know, Badi, but listen to me: if you ever try to harm yourself again, I will pound the hell out of you."

Harm yourself . . . such a mild way to describe a failed suicide attempt.

I lie there for a good hour after he leaves. I make some sorry attempts at writing in my journal the way Dr. Elliott says to, getting my aggression and depression onto paper so they don't fester in my brain. But I give up. Aggression and depression really need to be channeled at *people*.

I try not to think about what Dariush said, or about anything really. But I never brushed my teeth. I can feel all the crumbs stuck in there, and I lie still, telling myself one night without brushing is not going to kill me. But what if it *can* kill you, what if there is one bacterial germ that wedges itself under my gums and shoots straight for my blood vessels? Also cavities? Breathe, man. *I am getting through this . . . I am not going to die from tooth decay.*

I have to get up and brush. I'll never be able to get this out of my mind.

On my way back from the bathroom, I hear it. I stand frozen in the hallway, rooted to the darkness covering our Persian rugs, and listen. There it goes again—an animal's cry: a deep, mournful howl. A wolf, a dog. I slip into my bedroom. Wow, I can feel my heart pounding like a panic attack. I look out my window, the one on the south side toward the back-yard. Oh, it's just the hippies' dog. I feel relieved but stupid.

He starts up again, this time low and rumbling then ascending in volume, full of joy and grief all at once. An amazing, fearsome sound. I can't believe this is the same dumb dog who barks at clouds.

You know when they talk about the hair standing up on the back of your neck? That's a total lie. What happens when you get creeped out is you feel something like icy Jell-O ooze down through your spine, and then it leaks into your stomach, and you feel like you're going to empty the contents of your gut one way or the other. I shake my head, trying to shake out the sound. Then it stops. I slide back down in bed as silence takes over me and the room gradually darkens in my sight, and maybe another hour goes by until eventually sleep comes.

CHAPTER FOUR

enied?" asks Nikki.

"Denied," I affirm.

My request to start a fencing team or even a fencing club was shot down by the principal, Mr. McNeill. I guess it doesn't matter, knowing my dad would go ballistic if I went ahead with my plan.

"Mr. McNeill said, 'Well, son, I can't have kids poking each other with those swords.' They're foils, not that I corrected him. He said there were no teachers available to coach a new team or moderate a club."

Nikki shrugs and goes back to drawing. I thought we had bonded over my fencing-team idea—she was all for any type of athletic event where people could get stabbed. I don't want to lose her interest. Without her I wouldn't have a single human being to speak to all day.

"I was thinking about joining the Engineering Club," I say.

She looks up. "Oh no. You don't want to do that."

"Why not?"

She tilts her head at the table behind us. There are six boys and two girls sitting there—the Engineering Club—arguing about differential equations and picking spitballs out of their hair.

"I have to join something," I say. "My dad wants me to get involved, but not *too* involved. Nothing that will get me thrown out of school."

She taps her special doodling pencil against her teeth. I notice she has a little overbite. I've always had a thing for girls with overbites. Finally she says, "What about the school newspaper? I did it last year when *my* dad told me to beef up my extracurriculars. I was one of the staff photographers, but you don't need any special skills. Anybody can join."

"Hmm," I say. Is this an invitation? Is she joining with me? Or am I on my own here? If I'm on my own, I might as well throw in the towel now and join the Religious Activities Committee instead; they don't do anything but pray and clean up after the annual Chicken Barbecue fund-raiser.

"The first meeting's today after school," she says. "I'm going. Come on, it's not too painful. Crazy Ms. Viola from Modern Lit is the faculty adviser."

I pretend to think it over as if I have other options to consider. Then I say, "It's just the kind of thing my dad would approve of."

Nikki's bright-green eyes regard me thoughtfully from behind her glasses. "You said you wanted to get involved with something that wouldn't get you thrown out of school. What does that mean? Why would you get thrown out of school?"

I look away. "A joke."

The student newspaper staff room smells of photo developer and nicotine. Nikki says Ms. Viola sneaks in here to smoke. It's at the far end of the second floor in the south wing, an area of the school where I don't have any other classes. The carpeting is different up here, mustardy, and the hallway is painted a calming shade of prison green. Nikki says this used to be the student lounge years ago, back when students still had free time. My old school had a sort of lounge; it was an unofficial lounge, I guess you would say, as it was in the boiler room. I tried to conduct my Dungeons & Dragons campaigns there, but the burnouts didn't like me horning in on their toke-up territory. They pantsed me and set fire to my hall pass.

Nikki is already here, seated toward the back. I sit next to her and take out a notebook and pen so that I look like I know what I'm doing. There's a tall guy I recognize from both our cafeteria table and Chemistry next to her, but they're not talking, and nobody's talking to me, so it feels a lot like lunch so far.

Ms. Viola passes out past issues of the school newspaper, the *Vox Populi*, which comes out twice a month in print and online. She describes the kinds of articles we'll be working on: recaps of Prom and various sporting events, essays on study habits and nutrition, tips for the college-bound, that sort of stuff. At first I think this is an easy way to boost my extracurricular profile and please my dad. But then it hits me: I have never been good at this sort of writing. I can't even type. I am wasting precious time trying to be a journalist, and then I am going to waste more time trying to justify my time here on the newspaper, until the only thing left to do will be to declare the whole thing a failure and move on to community college.

I look around. The student editor-in-chief, a guy with combed hair and a bright future sparkling in his eyes, is talking now. He's so enthusiastic and well-adjusted that I can't even understand what he's saying. Everyone says they are psyched to write about the annual Chicken Barbecue fund-raiser; someone volunteers to conduct a school-wide poll about whether Phys Ed should be an elective in junior year. Only Nikki, me, and the tall guy from our lunch table are just sitting here, not saying anything—us, and Ms. Viola, who fled to a table in the back and thinks no one can see she is reading a book.

So. It's not a full-blown panic attack, but I feel this strangling kind of pressure in my chest. Panic attacks often hit you out of the blue for no reason whatsoever, that's what Dr. Elliott says, but I know *one* reason the anxiety is creeping up my bones right now: this newspaper thing is all wrong for me, and I don't want to do it, but I have to do something, and why can't it be fencing? Why, why? It's not like I'm suggesting we start a fight club. Though maybe . . . no, that would never work, I'm no good at hand-to-hand combat.

Nikki says, "Are you all right, Bud?"

"Yeah." My voice sounds about an octave too high.

She points to a drip of sweat that clings to the tip of my nose. I feel more following, lemmings ready to take that big dive off the cliff.

"Oh, that. It's nothing." But even as I say it, spots appear in my vision, and the periphery gets all dark. How can I faint? I'm sitting down! Please, God, if you are there—and I'm not saying you are, because in desperate times we all clutch at the crazy ideals of our youth—please do not let me faint at the newspaper meeting. Do not let me faint in front of Nikki Vrdolyak.

Suddenly I'm burning up. I lower my forehead into my

hand, but it feels clammy. "Need fresh air," I say. My heart is hammering, and now this is it, this is an authentic anxiety attack, and it's so, so lame because I don't actually feel all that anxious, only tired and worried and depressed and disappointed as hell.

I stand up and say I'm going to take a little stroll, all casual-like, which fools no one. My knees buckle, and I'm about to crash. Next thing I know, Nikki is on one side of me and the lunch table kid is on the other. And they're walking me out the door. Ms. Viola seems irritated at this interruption to her book. She blows a blast of air through her nostrils and snaps, "Would you get him to the clinic already?"

"Not the clinic," I mumble once we're in the hall. My pulse is still hammering.

"What do you take me for?" Nikki says.

They walk me to the drinking fountain, and I pretty much drown my face for a while. It feels good. I gulp some of the water, and that feels good, too.

"Sit down or walk? Are you sick?" Nikki asks. The lunch table guy stands there with his hands out, as if I'm going to fall.

This is extra-embarrassing, and I'm halfway between humiliated and nauseous. I'm not sick, and that sounds so wimpy anyway. It seems cooler to admit "It's a panic attack. I get loads of 'em."

They exchange glances, looking worried. I understand. It all sounds so . . . adult.

The tall guy, still nameless, asks, "Do you have medication?"

Instead of saying yes or no, because that would be way

too easy, I launch into an explanation *as if anyone cares.* I can't help it. That's how I roll. "My shrink prescribed a low dose of a kind of drug called a 'selective serotonin reuptake inhibitor' to help me cope with depression and anxiety, and he thinks I take it because that's what I tell him—so do my parents—but I stopped in July because it made me feel dizzy and gave me the dead eyes. Like I've been watching reality TV all day and eating Fritos. I know you're not supposed to just stop, but it wasn't really helping anyway. So the nutshell answer is No, but the expanded answer is No, but maybe I should be because I can't seem to shake these attacks like I could this summer, but I'll be all right if I can just walk it off and breathe and repeat calming mantras to myself.'"

"Okay," Nikki says like it's no big thing. Even the dude relaxes his arms and nods like what I've said sounds reasonable. And you know, they make me feel like it *is* reasonable, and I start breathing and walking and slowing it all down.

They follow me at a distance until we end up in the gym lobby at the end of the first floor. Inside you can hear the squeak of gym shoes and some team practicing. Maybe volleyball.

"I think I'm okay now," I say. The reason I think I'm okay is because I now feel that my embarrassment outweighs my crazy.

They're looking at me. I shrug. They shrug back. That's all. None of that fright I see in my parents' eyes whenever they witness a minor freak-out. And with that, with those kind of curious but nonjudgmental shrugs, I feel something sort of like acceptance.

"Thanks, Nikki," I say. "Thanks . . ." I look at the lunch table kid.

He sticks out his hand to shake mine. "Reggie Thigpen. Chess team president."

"Bud Hess. I think we're in the same Chemistry."

Nikki points at a plaque hanging among others on the wall of the lobby, right next to the trophy case. The plaque has a chess piece—the black king—engraved at the top, and its uppermost gold plate, the one with last year's date, bears the inscription STATE CHESS CHAMPION REGGIE THIGPEN and underneath that in smaller letters MAGNIFICAT'S FIRST AFRICAN AMERICAN CHESS CHAMP.

I say, "Congratulations."

Reggie says, "Yes, I'm a trailblazer. And it looks good on the school brochures to have pictures of nonthreatening black people playing chess."

Nikki snorts, then Reggie does, and for the first time in forever, I feel like laughing. So I do.

The squeaking of the gym shoes gets louder, along with calls of encouragement from one teammate to another. Instinctively, I want to move away from this sound.

Nikki glances into the gym and says, "I think it's programmed into my DNA to avoid team sports," and walks out of the lobby.

Reggie and I follow. I am staring in awe at the back of Nikki Vrdolyak's head. It's like we are soul mates.

Nikki turns to us. "I don't really want to sit through the rest of that meeting, do you?"

Reggie says, "Come on. I've got an idea."

• • •

We are riding in Reggie's car. It's a nice car, an SUV, and I'm in the back and they're in the front, and I'm not even wearing my seat belt. This is almost as I've imagined it to be, being normal, being in a car with people who are not members of my family or officers from the Chicago Police Department.

"Anybody hungry?" Reggie asks.

"Sure," says Nikki, "but I only have a couple dollars."

I tell them, "My parents don't like to give me pocket money. Maybe they think I will blow it on extra visits to my shrink."

Nikki looks at me, which gives me a funny feeling in my gut, so I stare out the window.

Reggie heads north on Western, and I think I know where we're going. In Rogers Park there is a restaurant known as the IHOP at the End of the Universe. If you drive at night north on Western, past Lunt and Estes and the park, you will reach the northernmost border of Chicago, and suddenly all the streetlights disappear. You can see the world's edge before you, dark and boundless, but before you plunge off into the shadows of suburbia, the blue-lit sign of IHOP appears. You feel saved somehow.

I say, "The IHOP at the End of the Universe."

"You know it," says Reggie.

We get there, and Nikki and Reggie both order coffee. So I do, too.

"I don't usually drink coffee. My mother says it will stunt my growth."

"Trust me," says Reggie, "you don't want to be too tall. Brings you nothing but grief."

I don't want to say anything because it seems so obvious and maybe even racist, but he beats me to it. "Basketball, right? You were going to say why don't I play basketball." I shrug.

He glances at Nikki. "Remember what you said about team sports? That's how I feel. Except for the chess team, and that's only because it's individual competition with group results tabulated from the specific matches. My dad wishes I played real sports instead of, as he calls it, 'fag stuff.'"

We pool our money. We've got enough for one order of Rooty Tooty Fresh 'N Fruity pancakes. The waitress gives us a cold stare and collects the menus.

I glance around at the flags decorating the walls. "There's no Iran," I point out. They look at the flags, too. "No Iranian flag," I clarify.

Reggie says, "You're new, aren't you? Where'd you go to school before?"

"Sullivan." Here we go. I don't want to get into it, but I know it's coming, and all at once, I don't know—I feel like *I sorta want to get into it.* I'm totally baffled by this.

They ask what Sullivan was like, and I lie and say it was good. Inside I'm fighting against what I'm saying, because something about Nikki and Reggie makes me want to tell the truth. They seem outcast, but cool outcast. Not oddball outcast. Still, it's too soon to be the real me.

"Why'd you leave?" Nikki asks.

I reach for something close to the truth. "It was my dad's idea. He thought the Magnificat experience would be better for me. I mean, a better education."

The food comes, and we all dig in. I'm weirded out by repeatedly sticking the forks that have been in our mouths into our communal pancakes, but Reggie and Nikki seem all right with it, and maybe that's just how normal people do things. All I know is my mother would have a heart attack if she saw this.

Reggie says, "So what's it like?"

"What?" I ask.

He gestures at me, as if that answers the question, then adds, "The panic attacks."

"Oh." I set down my coffee. How to explain the unnatural awfulness that has begun to feel awfully natural? "It began a year ago. Out of nowhere, there's intense fear. Fear that something terrible is happening. That's what happened today. Other times it's *not* out of nowhere but a reaction to what is going on around me. My brain feels jumbled, like the thoughts are coming way, way too fast for me to process. It comes at me like a freight train. It actually physically hurts to have my heartbeat, to have a pulse. Sometimes I shake. Sometimes I get dizzy, like I'm going to pass out or feel like I'm being smothered. Honest to God, smothered like somebody is freaking murdering me with a blanket over my face. And the worst part—when it gets to the worst part, which it doesn't always but sometimes does—is it attacks me from the inside out, radiates like a fire spreading in my stomach up to my head, and I'm afraid that I'm about to die, or that I am losing control of my entire self, or that I am breaking into pieces and losing my mind."

They sit there. I watch their eyes. I have gotten really good at watching people's eyes over the last year. I can tell when people are repelled by me, or tuning me out, or feeling pity for me. I have seen all these things in my parents' eyes. But I don't see any of that in Reggie's or Nikki's. I see what looks like openness. I don't know any other way to describe it.

"Actually," Nikki says, "that sounds pretty cool."

Then, like completely normal people, we start to talk. And not just me talking about being mental. We're all juniors We complain about school, we talk about the newspaper—this will be Reggie's third year on staff—regular stuff. They convince me to stick with the *Vox Populi* for a while, that it's not as bad as it seems. I get this little twinge. No, that's not right; in reality it's an absence of twinge: a sense of calmness, of quiet. And I think, *I can do this*. School, extracurricular, friends even. I can do this.

Then Nikki says, "Come on, Bud. Tell us why you left Sullivan. Nobody waits till junior year to transfer for a better education."

And that's when I let down the gates, let them—my new friends—in and let the truth out. Goddamn my dad. I *want* to get into it, and I do, and I start by saying, "There was an incident."

CHAPTER FIVE

istakes were made," I continue. "I have some problems. But I was *not* kicked out. I was asked to leave.
If I refused, they wouldn't have expelled me, because in
the end I wasn't charged with anything and nobody was
harmed. The toilet that exploded was unoccupied."

I pause, wanting to say this right. I don't want to give the
impression that *Boo-hoo, I feel sorry for myself, nobody liked
me, my life was a series of humiliations, and I was the target
of relentless bullying.* But my life at Sullivan *was* a series of
humiliations, and I *was* the target of relentless bullying. And
eventually I stood up for myself.

I go on. "With the exception of fencing and croquet, I'm
not athletic. This would not be a problem if I got good grades,
which I don't. I mean, I'm smart enough but not in any way
that matters at school. I know every poisonous plant native
to the Midwest, and I can rig up a toilet to explode remotely,
but you can't put that on your transcripts.

"Anyway, it went down like this: you know what swirlies
are? When the jocks give your head a ride in a flushing
toilet, right? I got those regularly. Atomic wedgies, people
slamming my locker shut on my fingers, gum in the hair,
Kick Me signs, all that cutesy-violent stuff. And I didn't even

get the *worst* of it. Everyone knew that the seniors on the football team violated the freshmen JV with, um, well . . ." I glance at Nikki. "I don't want to be offensive here—"

"No, please," she says, "be offensive."

I trip over the words quickly. "Violate them with duct tape applied to certain areas. Also, let me see, what else . . . the varsity volleyball girls initiated new players with some kind of secret ritual involving blindfolds and dog feces. The fat kids, of course, were constantly ridiculed and chased into the parking lot—forced to run so that everyone could laugh at the way their body parts flopped around. And I don't even want to get into the things done to the special ed kids. But it's everywhere, right? And I'm not even talking about the gangbangers. It's so much worse than I'm telling you.

"But you can only take so much. You can only witness so much depravity before you start trying to chew off your own arm. So first I made a—a list. A list of the worst offenders in school."

"A shit list," says Reggie.

"It was pure poetry. 'Enemies to Be Eliminated.' As if I had the power to decide who would live and die. I wasn't going to *do* anything about it! I'm not crazy. I'm like a minor threat at best. Even my shrink is always telling me it's healthy to *cathart*—I'm not sure that's a real word, but whatever—to find a release for some of my frustrations, and writing that list *was* cathartic. Tell me the world wouldn't be a better place with one less football player taping up some poor kid's junk for laughs. Wouldn't life be happier without feral gangs of cheerleaders randomly ostracizing unpopular girls each week purely for sport? Wouldn't life be better if freshmen weren't recruited for gangs directly under the No

Gang Activity Tolerated Here sign? Oh, but hell, I wrote it down! I shouldn't have taped it up in my locker, I guess, but jeez, it's not like I was dumb enough to post it on Facebook. I was naive to think my locker was actually mine and off-limits to other people, though."

"A shit list doesn't sound so bad. . . . ," says Nikki.

"I'm not done," I say. "My friends and I played D&D in the school boiler room, where these burnouts used to hang. The burnouts decided that they didn't want to share the space with us, so they pantsed me and burned my hall pass. Hall passes were hard to come by, even forged ones. So I tried to retaliate by rerouting the emissions from the radiators backward through the pipes, hoping to steam them out. Accidentally, I shut off the hot water, and the water pipes froze—this was in February. What they call 'damage to school property' and 'tampering with the water supply' *I* call a plumbing mishap. I was wrong to confide in my fellow D&D'ers about this, because those guys buckled under the first line of inquisition. If it were me, I'd never narc on a friend, no matter what."

Reggie says, "The burnouts brought it on themselves. I think you were justified."

I'm shocked to be understood, but I plow on. "In spring I planted seeds from a few medicinal plants—monkshood, pennyroyal, foxglove—in some pots at home under grow lights. I wanted to see how they'd do in our climate, but my mother won't let me plant anything in her vegetable garden or our backyard croquet lawn, so I had to turn to the school grounds. Everyone knows that medicinal plants can also be poisonous, but it was just an experiment! No one was in danger at all. Some teachers saw me transplanting the seedlings and acted like they made some big discovery, like I was trying to keep it secret or something. Believe me, if I were trying to keep anything a secret, it would remain a secret."

I take a breather here because I'm getting all worked up again. Nikki and Reggie are utterly silent, staring at me. I'm not sure what this means—have I traumatized them? Have I revealed too much? Do they think I'm nuts, a future Unabomber, a Columbine time-bomb? But I've gone this far. I might as well wrap this puppy up.

"There's more," I say, "if you care."

Nikki says, "I care so much I should probably remain two hundred yards away from this story at all times."

"Okay: the beginning of May I'd received my bimonthly swirlie from some wrestler. You'd think by then I'd have been used to it, but I guess filth and I will never be friends. I struggled against him, but since he outweighed me by about a seventh of a ton, it was useless. And something cracked in me then . . ." I hesitate. It's hard to explain. Even to Dr. Elliott it was hard to explain. What had been the old me cracked in half and peeled away, like a rubber mask. I couldn't take being tortured anymore. It's like they tortured the old me into oblivion, and a new, pathological person took his place. The current me.

I go on. "That wrestler guy, I admit, I did threaten. It was just a note I slipped into his locker. But he told on me! Can you believe it? After what he did, *he* actually told on *me*. Of course, when it all came out and I was forced to defend myself to the SWAT team who'd been called to school, I explained how I had been provoked. But the wrestler *lied* and said I made it all up, that there had been no swirlie, and because there were no witnesses, the administration didn't know what to do with me. They're standing there—the principal, trustees from the school board, a police officer—all with Xeroxed copies of my note, and they're mumbling that they have no proof he gave me a swirlie."

Reggie asks, "What did your note say?"

"I will get you in the crosshairs, and I will take you down."

"Oh," he says.

"It's just a line from this movie *Rushmore*. My older brother's always quoting it. I don't even have crosshairs! I don't have a gun and wouldn't know how to shoot one if I did. It was a threat of words, because words are all I have. I stood up for myself with the only weapons I possessed: notebook paper and a Sharpie. Then the principal tells me that even if the kid *had* provoked me, it was inappropriate to retaliate. They have a zero-tolerance policy at Sullivan. Apparently not a zero-swirlie policy. People who give swirlies get suspended, while those of us who retaliate are asked to leave. I mean, I'm glad I wasn't expelled or ultimately charged with anything, otherwise Magnificat would have learned about my past and probably wouldn't have accepted me. But I was still punished for defending myself."

"What did your parents do about all this?" Reggie says.

"In the beginning I told them about being picked on, and my dad said, 'Keep your head down and your eyes on the prize.' Like you can keep your eyes on the prize when you're blinded by flushing toilet water. And what prize? Good grades, I guess. I stopped telling them because they never did anything."

"You had to take matters into your own hands," says Nikki.

"Exactly." But it was more than that, and less than that, too. I don't know what else I can tell Nikki and Reggie. I can't tell them about all the pills I took that night last spring . . . ending up in the hospital, the psych ward, feeling my parents were more concerned about damage to my permanent record than damage to me.

It's not that my parents didn't care about the bullying, but they thought I should be strong and ignore it. Since 9/11, plenty of people made problems for us. One time a drunk guy outside a White Hen Pantry chased Dad down the street with a tire iron. Another time our building was egged, although that could have been random vandalism. At Sullivan I was a walking target: someone wrote "Camel Jockey" on a sticker and slapped it to my jacket; guys threw firecrackers at me while I waited for the bus; kids pushed me off the trampoline in gym, calling me "Dune Coon," and the gym teacher saw, then asked what *I* did to provoke *them*. Anyway, my parents have been and still are afraid.

I don't say this part to my new friends. Dad wants to keep it secret, and the part of me that is an obedient Iranian son must comply.

Reggie nudges me. "But what about the exploding toilet? I've been sitting here for half an hour waiting to hear about the exploding toilet."

"Well, I had to take my frustrations out on something. I couldn't punish the wrestler, right? So I made the toilet, scene of all my misery, pay."

"You punished the toilet," he says.

"Put that way, I sound mental. But, yes: I punished the toilet."

"How? I need more information."

"I used a tremendous amount of fireworks."

The explosion took place one Friday after the school emptied out for the weekend (I had the pass code and the keys, stolen from the janitor, but that's another story).

"It was a really satisfying detonation. M-80s, M-100s, and a quarter stick of dynamite," I say. "That is one toilet that will never live to see another swirlie."

Nikki says, "I was hoping the story would end with the wrestler getting blown up while sitting on the toilet."

This is another instance where movies do not imitate real life. In a movie, the wrestler would get blown up on the toilet, suffering injuries and humiliation, and we'd rejoice for the nerd who fought back. But in real life, wrestlers rarely are seated on exploding toilets at the right time. In reality, they get suspended from school for two measly days while the nerd waits in a holding cell at Twenty-Sixth and California, talking to the Bomb-and-Arson Squad for three hours without an attorney.

Reggie swings back down Western to drive us home. It's starting to rain softly. I don't think I've told the truth about myself to another human being for years, except Dr. Elliott, and even then I lied so many other times it canceled out the truth-telling moments. So it feels good now, but also scary. Being yourself can be such a bad idea sometimes. Reggie and Nikki know a lot about me now, and I still don't know much about them. I want to know about them, but it's hard to ask without sounding insincere, like I'm making small talk: So, tell me about yourselves. So lame. I look out the window.

We head east, toward the lake. I'm not sure what I expected, but Nikki's house blows me away. She's down-to-earth—she wears a beat-up hunting jacket, her hair's a mess, and her glasses don't seem in style—but it turns out she lives in one of those really nice houses off Sheridan.

She says to me, "There's a lot more to you than meets the eye."

I say thanks, because I've looked in the mirror a lot and know exactly what meets the eye.

The front of her house has a huge window, and you can see everything in the living room. If we had one of those on our building, my mother would slap some burglar bars on it so fast. I can see two little girls jumping on the couch. A lady passes by them with a wineglass in her hand, swaying, like she's dancing to music. A man follows her into the room, gently squeezing her shoulder. Nikki watches this, too.

I say, "This is a nice house."

She stares out the window and asks, "Can you make our toilets explode?"

Of course I can, but I don't want to brag.

Nikki gets out and waves goodbye to us. Despite the rain, she doesn't bother to pick up the pace, just ambles down her front walk, getting soaked.

I move to the front seat and give Reggie directions to my apartment. "Corner of King Sargon and Lunt."

"King what? There's no such street."

"On the contrary, 'King Sargon Boulevard' is the honorary name they give to four blocks of Western Avenue around where I live. Sargon was an Assyrian king, and there's a lot of Assyrians in my neighborhood, so—"

"So it's the corner of Western and Lunt."

"Technically."

When Reggie pulls up in front of my building, it's his

turn to be surprised. He says, "Wow. You're the first place on the street to have your Christmas decorations up."

I don't explain that my dad put up twinkle lights as a joke last month to celebrate Ramadan. I guess we'll end up as one of those stereotypes: the people neighbors complain about who leave their Ramadan decorations up all year.

"Which one's yours?" he asks.

"The top floor." Suddenly I feel self-conscious about our minimal front lawn, Ramadan lights, and hippie neighbors wandering the alley in search of their pothead dog. Old red curtains hang in our front windows; they look faded and ragged even from down here. Dariush's windows on the second floor are open—held open by bricks, that is—and he's blasting New Wave music from the eighties. The first floor, where my aunt and uncle and their kids live, has the curtains closed for once, shielding the depressing view into their dingy and fluorescent-lit apartment.

"See ya tomorrow," Reggie says, and I say it back, even the "ya" part. It doesn't sound too unnatural, but then the muffler on his car is loud.

My family is sitting down to dinner. Mom asks, "Where have you been, Bud? You should have called."

I remind her that I don't have a cell phone. My parents feel they encourage time-wasting chitchat. She says, "You have quarters, I'm sure. Next time, call from a public pay phone and tell me you'll be late."

I don't even know if they *make* public pay phones anymore.

"I'm not hungry," I say. "I had pancakes for dinner. And coffee."

She stares at me. "The kind with caffeine?" I nod, and she shakes her head in disappointment.

Dad asks where I've been. He has this condescending smile on his face as I talk about the newspaper and my new friends. *Enjoy this little diversion,* his smile says, *but remember that's all it is. Keep your head down and your eyes on the prize.*

So I shut up abruptly, and you know what? He doesn't notice that I've stopped talking. Nobody does, except Dariush. He stares at me. He still looks young with his emo glasses and tattoos. But old, too. Our dad treated him this same way, and now he has to watch it the second time around with me.

After dinner I clear the table so my mom can do her bird-watching homework. Seriously, there are assignments for her adult education class. She opens the window and murmurs, "A murder of crows. Curious at this hour, no? And in the rain, too."

Nobody else says anything, so I ask, "Are they eating out of the Dumpster again?" Mom is the only one who asks about botany or anything else I'm interested in.

"Yes," she says, and makes a notation in the margin of her book. "They will eat anything. Roadkill. Poison ivy. Frogs. I have personally observed a crow flying overhead with an entire pizza in its beak." A car speeds by, and the throbbing subwoofers cause the birds to take flight. Their wings sound like hoofbeats.

I go to my room and don't do my homework. I stare out my window at Western (that is, King Sargon Boulevard), watching the cars zoom by in the rain's gray half-light.

I can hear the hippies' dog barking to be let in. This happens every night. I have heard him, Rex, howling for years. Mom keeps a record for the day she finally airs her grievances to their landlord. I don't know what is wrong with the hippies. If that were my dog, I wouldn't be able to stand it. I would be attuned to his moods, and he would never need to bark for more than two seconds.

My cat curls around my legs. He wants to jump up on my lap, but he can't. I scratch him under his chin, jangling the tag that reads KING SARGON. He's not an old cat but moves stiffly and slowly. He can't see well because there is something wrong inside his head. There is something wrong inside his head because Azita kicked him when he was a kitten and thinks I don't know, but I do, and I saw, and I didn't say anything because I am still, after all these years, a complete coward.

October

I'm kind of at the point where I can't stand Chemistry any more, which is a bad sign, because it's only six weeks into the semester.

It's not the subject matter (as you might have guessed, I like learning about the chemical properties of compounds that explode when combined), it's the teacher. He's one of those guys who went into teaching so he'd never have to leave high school. That means Mr. Ryndak acts like the ringleader of all the sixteen-year-olds and pits us against each other. Bullies like to maintain friction among their followers so that they're too confused and scared to stand up for themselves.

"You know that a compound," Mr. Ryndak tells us, "is composed of two or more elements. So that means they can be decomposed into simpler substances. Examples are methane, methanol, aluminum."

Did he really say that? I look around. His statement is met with indifference, except for the kids who are nodding to mask their ignorance. My hand raises itself. I swear I had nothing to do with it.

I say, "Aluminum isn't a compound. It's an element."

He blinks. "I didn't say aluminum."

It occurs to me that this is the first time I've ever volunteered information in Chemistry, the only time I've ever raised my hand, and then it occurs to me that this is probably not the best debut I could have made. "Um, I think, actually, yes, you did. Didn't you? I mean, by accident."

He rises from the corner of his desk, where all the casual teachers perch. "Well. I meant ammonia." Then he stares at me for a second, and I know I have made a mistake. And not about aluminum. You're not supposed to correct teachers, certain ones anyway. You let them make factual errors, and you keep your mouth shut.

He turns to the other side of the room, and I can't see his face, but he does something, because everyone over there laughs.

Chief among Mr. Ryndak's followers are Dylan, my Homeroom Buddy, and some other guys who are good at life. They're all football players, but they're also smart, so they've cornered those two markets. Life just isn't fair, you know?

When the bell rings, they look at me with a new expression on their faces, different than the normal one where they're trying to see past me to something interesting. This expression says, *Who do you think you are?* When they pass by my desk, one of them jabs another as if he were holding a fencing foil, and they all hoot.

Dylan doesn't wave goodbye to me like he used to at the beginning of the year. Reggie watches this.

"Don't worry," he says as we walk out into the hallway of rushing students. "Those guys are asses. So's Ryndak."

"I'm not worried," I say.

At lunch I eat only Tater Tots. I'd been in line trying to

choose between chicken à la king and something brown. The sign said Salisbury steak, but no way could it have been that. It looked like maybe Swedish meatballs. This is *food* I'm about to *eat*; I just want to know what I'm getting myself into. So I asked the food service worker, who insisted it was Salisbury steak, and I asked if she was sure since I'm not crazy about chicken à la king. Then this guy, Jason, behind me groaned, "Jesus Christ, come *on*. Just pick one."

The girl with him muttered, "Seriously," and rolled her eyes in that way that girls do. It's not my imagination, okay, they looked at me for like two seconds too long, and it was really aggressive. Like they were so *pissed* they had to wait in line behind me for chicken à la king. My dad says I make too much out of everything, and maybe that's true, but listen: I would never do that to someone. I'd let someone stand in line for ten hours if that's what he needed.

I gestured to them to go on ahead, and when Jason moved past me, his arm brushed against mine. And dry little flakes of skin from his arm—his arm dandruff—were suddenly on me, and it was all I could do not to chuck the tray and run for the antibacterial soap. In my head I used Dr. Elliott's mantra: *I am getting through this. It's just skin, not anthrax.* God, it was all I could see, those dead white flakes: shed skin, like from a snake, but worse, from a human.

Anyway, so, Tater Tots. And now I'm here at the table, and Nikki and Reggie are hunched over a Watchmen collection, and though they've invited me to scootch over and read, too, I beg off. Comics should appeal to me, given my other interests, but they don't. They seem kind of cool, so of course that means they're beyond my grasp. Plus there's an undercurrent of third-wheel-ness about the invitation.

"Did you write that article on the chocolate bar fund-raiser?" Nikki asks. I nod, and she says, "That must have been a joy."

True, the subject matter is boring. But I think it turned out okay. We have a *Vox Populi* meeting after school today, and I want to get Ms. Viola's opinion on my writing. Maybe she will read it over and suggest that I have my own column.

Nikki says, "I had to take pictures of the football team in their new uniforms. One of the seniors tried to get me to photograph him in his new jockstrap."

"What a pig," I say, outraged on her behalf.

She shrugs. "They think I'm a lesbian, which really aggravates them. Yes, I hate boys, but that doesn't make me a lesbian. I hate girls, too. Sometimes I think these extracurricular activities just aren't worth it."

Reggie turns the page of the comic book and says, "Oh, wow. Carnage." Nikki leans closer to get a better look. Her shoulder is touching his. I look down at my arm and it's impossible, but I know I see that guy's dead skin flakes on me, and then it seems like they're alive: the flakes move; they're bugs, lice, worms, burrowing into me. No, stop it, brain. *I am getting through this.* Oh hell, Dr. Elliott, give me something I can *use* here.

"Can you die from contact dermatitis?" I ask no one in particular. I scratch my arm with my fork. Nobody answers.

I arrange my Tater Tots in a starburst pattern around my plate. I eat some, but they're not very good, and I leave the rest.

Everyone is busy in the newspaper staff room by the time I get there. Ms. Viola is sitting at one of the computer terminals, pretending to help the graphics department with the preliminary layout. She keeps yawning and rolling her eyes. Nikki's at another computer, uploading photos. She waves at me. I was hoping for a smile, but she doesn't just dole them out without thinking. I smile at her, though, because, trust me, when I think about every single thing that I already know about Nikki—not that I've plumbed the depths by any means; there is far, far more to plumb with her—I can't help feeling happy.

"So," Ms. Viola says, sidling next to me at the table, "you finished your article."

"Yes, I e-mailed it to Trevor last night." I have a hard time even saying the student editor-in-chief's name. He seems so secure and shiny, he nauseates me. I guess that's pretty mean. It's not his fault that he's well-adjusted.

She says, "I know. He sent me a message suggesting I take a look."

"Really? Wow," I say. I wasn't expecting his support. "I hope you like what I've done, juxtaposing the traditional roles of student and teacher on a hot-button issue."

"This is the one on the chocolate bar sales?"

"Correct."

We move over to the computers, and she pulls up my document. She hunches over and begins to read silently. She either has a twitch in her jaw or she grinds her teeth.

Annual Chocolate Bar Sell-a-Thon— Harmless Fund-raiser or Forced Labor?

By Bud Hess

Watch them as they trudge the streets in uniform,

bent to the will of the administration, loaded up like pack mules. Yes, I'm talking about us and the yearly chocolate bar fund-raising sale thrust upon us. It sounds harmless enough: sell chocolate door-to-door to raise money for the school. But is it? Are we too robotic to see where this leads?

Recall the school-wide assembly when Principal McNeill shouted into the microphone and commanded us to get out there and beat each other. The upperclassmen vowed to crush the freshmen's efforts. The basic human drive to compete manifests itself in these all-out campaigns to hawk gross candy.

Fund-raising should be done in the normal way: badger our parents to fork over more cash. That's what they signed on for when they enrolled us here, isn't it? Plus, adults have already given up, so they're likely just to cave in more and pay higher tuition. Why pester us, the innocent children? We'll learn about mob rule and conformity soon enough.

Ms. Viola has a tiny blue vein that throbs in her forehead, right between her eyebrows. She should see a pulmonary specialist about that.

I ask, "Is it too much? The part about us being 'innocent children'? I can kill that in the second draft."

She's staring at the screen and her vein is throbbing and she continues to grind her teeth. I'm sure it *is* teeth grinding and not just a twitch, now that I can hear the creak coming from her jaw.

She says, "Uh, yeah, actually it is too much. The whole thing. It's utterly absurd."

I'm not a complete moron; I expected some resistance. I say what I've rehearsed in my head. "I understand, but I feel passionately about this, and what else is a newspaper for but to lay down the ugly truth?"

"I'm not saying you don't have a point or that, off the record, I don't agree with you. But, Bud, come on, don't be an idiot! This is a school newspaper, for God's sake. You know we can't print this. Principal McNeill would eviscerate me. And you, too."

Other staff members have stopped what they're doing to listen to us, but I'm too fired up to quit. "I'm willing to sacrifice a little in order to be true to myself."

She laughs bitterly. "Maybe you are, but I'm not. Not anymore. We could never let this go through. Not in a million years."

"Maybe I could rewrite it as an opinion piece," I suggest. "Like a firsthand account of someone who. . . who refuses to sell the candy bars."

Ms. Viola looks up at me sharply. "Are you refusing to sell them?"

"I . . . think . . . so. Yes." How in the world did that come out of my mouth?

Nikki leans back in her chair, arms crossed, grinning. Reggie quietly leaves his table on the other side of the room and sits at the neighboring computer station.

I notice that Trevor is whispering with some other guy by the layout table, and now they're both staring at me. At first they look puzzled, but the reality sets in as I return their gaze. Trevor does *not* support me. In fact, he looks downright hateful.

"I told you," he says loudly, turning toward Ms. Viola.

She waits a beat and then rubs her hands together briskly, rising from her chair. "Yes, well, let's not get into a tizzy over this. He screwed up. Big deal. Everyone in this room has turned in slop that needed revising. Okay? Bud, I don't want a first-person account of anything. Stop with the feelings and pious outrage. I just want a puff piece on the stupid fund-raiser."

She practically runs back to her desk.

Everyone is still looking at me. I don't know what to do. My vision collapses into a narrow tunnel amid a dark, surrounding sea. I feel hot as hell and clammy at the same time. Then I feel Reggie clap me lightly on the back.

"I thought it was pretty cool," he says with a wide smile.

"I know, right?" says Nikki.

Ms. Viola assigns some girl to help me rewrite the article to "administration standards." It is now a boring, prosaic heap of oatmeal. Just what everyone wants.

The meeting goes late, and by a quarter to six I have to leave. Reggie offers me a ride home since he's driving Nikki, but I decline. Tonight is my shrink appointment.

I head toward the front door instead of going my usual route through the cafeteria. It's desolate at this hour by the school office. No broccoli-rubber-band-wearing secretary merrily waving to me, no freshmen trying to wheedle their way out of Phys Ed with the nurse. The hall is dark, the sky outside darker.

"Yo, wait up," someone calls from behind me. I turn but only see a silhouette backlit by the few fluorescent lights left on at night.

I don't answer. This scenario feels familiar. You're better off saying nothing.

But it's only Trevor, not a menacing gang. He keeps on walking toward me, in no hurry. When he finally reaches me, he says, "I didn't know you were new. I can't keep track of all the underclassmen."

I'm *not* an underclassman. But I don't say that. I say, "Oh. That's all right."

"So where'd you go to school before?"

"Sullivan."

"Why'd you switch?"

"For the education." It sounds so prissily uptight, but I don't function well under pressure. And in my experience, conversations with people in dark hallways after hours most definitely qualify as pressure.

"You know Brad Bates?"

"Who?"

"At Sullivan. Brad Bates. He's a friend of mine."

"Uh, no. No. It's a pretty big school. I didn't know everyone. So, no."

He holds out his hand to shut me up now that I am spazzing in front of his very eyes. "Okay, okay. I know you're new and everything, and maybe you're getting used to the school, but some of us take writing for the newspaper really seriously. It's not extracurricular brownie points for us. Acting psycho is a sure way to get yourself kicked off the staff. We've had a lot of jokers who think writing crazy stuff is funny, but they don't last long. I'm just saying."

Trevor turns around then and walks back down the hallway, waving lazily over his shoulder with a "Later," and then he's gone.

CHAPTER SEVEN

I'm fourteen minutes late for my appointment, which might not seem like much, but the sessions are only fifty minutes—thirty-six now—and I try to get there a little early so I can sit and relax in the waiting room with the crappy magazines and try to rearrange my thoughts. I've noticed that when I get there late, I feel guilty about the money my parents have wasted on the lost minutes, and then I get freaked out and tense and tend to say stuff to Dr. Elliott that I wish I hadn't.

I sit on the couch for a change.

He settles into his usual chair, smiles at me. He bypasses our preliminary chitchat about the weather because we have less than thirty-six minutes to conquer this week's demons. "We haven't discussed how you've adapted to your name change. You're sure you're okay with my calling you Bud? I can go back to Badi."

"Why bother? My parents made the switch pretty damn easily. And Hess is shorter, so that's good."

His mild smile doesn't change. He waits.

"It doesn't bother me as much as you would think," I say.

"Why not?"

"If you had to repeat your name every time you were introduced to people and then hear them mangle it anyway for sixteen years, you'd be happy for the break, too."

"People usually identify with their names."

"Not me," I say. I'm not Badi, I'm not Bud—I don't know who I am. I don't say that. We just blew two minutes.

"You haven't been here in a couple of weeks. Tell me how school's going."

"Okay, I guess."

There's silence, and then I crumble. He's too good. He knows I can't handle sitting there in silent scrutiny.

"Actually," I say, "I think it's going really well. I'm not sure. But I think so. I'd say it's seventy-five or eighty percent likely that it's going really well. And I have these two friends who are awesome. And they're real friends, not just people to play D&D with in the boiler room, you know? I've told them a lot about myself, and they accept me and like me. It's kind of hard to believe."

"What are their names?"

Sometimes I think he asks me detailed questions like this because he knows I make up stuff. It irks me, but then I realize I bring it on myself. "Reggie Thigpen and Nikki Vrdolyak." Who could make up those names? "Reggie's a nationally ranked chess champ, and Nikki draws cartoons of the principal with an ax buried in his head. She convinced me to join the newspaper staff, and I really think this is going to be my opportunity to show people what I can do. I like it a lot. The three of us went out and had pancakes at IHOP, and I noticed that IHOP did not have an Iranian flag. In fact, they only had flags from the NATO countries. They should call it the NATO House of Pancakes."

"You seem pretty excited."

"I am! It's great having friends and sort of a career, if you want to call it that. I mean my being on the newspaper."

"Good, good. How are your classes?"

See, why's he gotta do this? I'm all happy, talking about the newspaper and my friends, and he immediately has to dig for something depressing. If I wanted to be grilled, I'd have stayed home and let my parents do it for free.

"Oh, okay," I say. "They're okay. I'm doing okay." C-average is okay, isn't it? I mean, it's the very definition of *okay*: not great, not horrific. Ask anybody.

He stares at me with the same nonexpression.

"I could be doing better," I admit. "AP Biology: A. Catholic Doctrine—that's religion class—C. AP Chemistry: B, but he hates me, so count on that dropping to a C. Modern Lit—I don't know; the teacher has odd grading methods. Phys Ed: D probably—don't ask about the rope climb. US History: B. Precalculus: C. But it's only midsemester. I have time to bring those up."

"Those are not as high as your grades were at Sullivan, are they?"

"No, but Magnificat is harder. Eleventh grade is harder. Plus, I'm taking seven classes—lots of juniors take only six—two of which are *science*, and two of which are AP. Well, okay, Phys Ed is only three times a week with a study hall the other two days, but it still counts. So in a sense I'm ahead of the game. And at Magnificat, some people actually seem to be interested in learning. You could get an A at Sullivan for not shooting anyone in the middle of class. No one there cared about learning, or teaching." Each class was basically a staring match between disinterested idiots, relieved only by sporadic violence.

"You know," he says, "you often tell me that you're a mediocre student, but look at you: you're in two AP classes. You must have some brains to be in those, even if your grades are not up to par right now."

"I'm a brilliant underachiever."

"How's your family?" God, first he says nothing, then he jumps from topic to topic, not giving me time to rehearse my answers. Is it because we have only twenty-four minutes left?

"I don't know. My parents hover around me, pummeling me with questions. Dariush is always fighting with them. My cat seems depressed. Azita gets whatever she wants just because she's at Loyola. My dad bought her a brand-new laptop, while I have this hunk of junk I have to boot up by rubbing two sticks together."

We talk more—that is, I talk because he goads me into giving answers—and mostly I'm pissed we can't return to the one topic that made me happy.

Finally I say, "I'm sick of talking about my mom's stupid bird-watching class, all right? No, I don't think she's abandoning me for adult education! And I don't care about getting a D in gym. Even if LeBron James were in my gym class, he would get a D. It is impossible to do that rope climb—yesterday I fell off the rope and actually landed on someone. Why can't we go back to talking about my friends? Nobody ever wants to talk about the things that I want to talk about." I sound like a huge baby, but time is running out—we have only twelve minutes left—and if I don't leave on a good note, talking about things that make me happy, I will 1) be too keyed up to do homework, 2) have to listen to my mother's endless questions about why I'm always in such a bad mood, and 3) spiral downward, which will just prolong these sessions until I end up either dead or in jail.

Dr. Elliott doesn't look bothered. He must have people like me yelling at him all day long. But really, I cannot *believe* he is just sitting there saying nothing again!

"I'm paying you, or at least my parents are, which amounts to the same thing, and I don't want to talk about this depressing shit anymore. You're always saying I'm more than my 'pathology.' Well, here: I want to talk about more than my depressions and compulsions. I want to talk about my friends, the only good thing I've got in my life."

He shifts in his chair, and the light from the floor lamp next to him glints off his bald head. I never noticed before that he has stubble on the sides, the remnants of a fringe of last-hurrah hair. It hits me then that Dr. Elliott shaves his head not because it's cool, but because he is losing his hair, and then I feel kind of awful for him.

"Okay, Bud," he says pleasantly. "Let's go back to your friends. Reggie and Nikki, right? Are they boyfriend and girlfriend?"

"What? No! Why would you say that?"

"My mistake. You mentioned their names together, and I made that assumption."

Now I'm all discombobulated. "Well, they're not. They're just friends. We're all just friends."

"Have you told them what happened at your old school?"

"More or less."

"Not everything?"

I say quickly, "Everything that matters."

"Do they know about your suicide attempt?"

"No."

"You don't think your suicide attempt matters?"

How can I possibly answer that? He looks at me, still waiting for an answer. I feel that wound open up in my mind. I have to close it before it swallows me whole.

I say, "It's not the kind of thing that comes up in casual conversation."

"You like to use humor to defuse tense situations or uncomfortable topics." He announces this like it's some great revelation.

That old, remembered pain fades. I can close it up if they don't make me *talk* about it. "Stop trying to mess around with me and turn this back to what happened last year. I'm done with that topic, okay? My friends don't need to know that about me. I want to talk about *now*. Me and them."

"All right. Go on: about Nikki."

He knows when to quit, I'll give him that. "If you want me to be honest, I have kind of a crush on her. She's really cool. It's like she just doesn't care what anyone thinks, not the popular cliques or adults, and she has her own style, and . . . and I really like her."

"That's wonderful. It's wonderful to have those good feelings about someone."

"Yeah. I just wish she could feel that way about me."

"Maybe she does."

"Why would she, though? What about me is attractive? My retainer, my 'fro? My panic attacks? Maybe it's the muscles I have from spending all my summers playing D&D in people's basements."

"You run yourself down a lot," Dr. Elliott says. "Why do you think you do that?"

Four minutes left. There could be 444 minutes left, and it wouldn't be enough time to answer that one.

When I get home, my mom, dad, and Dariush are all sitting in the living room, glaring at each other. I feel like I've walked into a war tribunal.

"What's going on?" I ask. I set my briefcase down on the floor and brace myself.

My mother flies into one of her rages. "Haven't I told you a million times not to throw your things all over this apartment? Always I am picking up that stupid thing, that stupid briefcase, and your books, and your miniatures, and your Godzillas, and your coat and hat! I ask only that you would pick up after yourself, Bud."

Dariush says, "Don't take it out on him just 'cause you're mad at me."

"We will speak to him as we wish," my dad says. His voice is flinty, and he stares down my brother. "When you have sons of your own—unlikely as that prospect is—*you* can do as you wish."

Dariush leaps up off the couch and storms by them. He says to me, "Don't worry, Badi, everything's fine. I'll talk to you tomorrow when you swing by for your morning doobie." He claps me on the back as he passes, and my mother propels herself about seventeen feet out of the chair, like she's been sitting on a rocket launcher.

She shrieks, "How dare you make jokes! If nothing else, at least Bud is not addicted to the pot like you are. *Two* good-for-nothing druggy sons, I would die."

The pot . . . good-for-nothing druggy . . . Dariush smirks as if he's trying not to laugh. But I'm not fooled. Emotions flood and sink beneath his features: embarrassment, anger, defeat.

"What?" I swivel my head from Mom to Dad to Dariush. "What is going on?"

My brother walks out the doorway. His quiet footsteps fade as he goes downstairs.

"He has deranged us for the last time," my dad says, looking at my mother. She nods violently.

He continues, looking at me now. "One must be firm with sons, Bud. Your brother is wasting his life, he has not paid in three months the rent, and I am tired of the scent of marijuana through the heating vents. He must move out and get his life together. That means he must find a job, and that is why he is mad at me."

"You're kicking him out?" I sputter. "You can't! He's family. Where will he go?"

Dad takes off his glasses, rubs his hand over his eyes, and pinches the bridge of his nose. "I cannot be in charge of everything. Please go to your room. Maman will warm up some dinner for you."

Don't have to tell me twice. Except when I get there, I find Azita at my desk, sitting in my chair, working on her laptop.

Before I can even ask what the hell she is doing in my room, she says, "Don't have a fit. This is the only quiet room in the house. I can hear everything in the living room when I'm in mine."

"Doesn't Loyola have a library you can use?"

"Shut up, shit-for-brains. I'm going now that the screaming match is over."

"Is Dad really kicking Dariush out?" I'm afraid of the answer because Azita always gives it to me straight.

She snorts. "Are you a complete moron?"

"Yes, but that doesn't answer my question."

"Mom and Dad are both sick of him, and I can't blame them. He mooches off them, he won't work, he doesn't pay rent, he has all those weirdo friends."

"I like his weirdo friends," I say, thinking of the times they let me play Trivial Pursuit with them.

"Whatever. Mom and Dad think Dariush is an embarrassment to the community."

"He's not an embarrassment. He just marches to the beat of a different drummer."

She cackles so hard that spit—actual *saliva*—shoots forth from her mouth and lands on various surfaces around my room. "You are the most clueless individual I have ever known."

"What community are you talking about?" I think of our neighbors—the hippies with the brain-addled dog, the people who like the Mexican pop music, the skateboarding slackers in the flophouse on the next block. I can't see that any of them would have great interest in my family's personal business.

Azita sighs, closes her laptop. "The Muslim community, ass. Everyone's credo is 'Work hard in school, work hard in life.' Science, med school, something. Dariush couldn't even hold that job at the car wash."

"Well, who would want to work at a car wash? Anyway, we're not Muslim—I go to Catholic school now, or did you forget? Nobody in this building even believes in God except for Mom, and then it's only for the bad things."

"I'm talking culturally."

"That's a piss-poor reason to kick your own family out of the house."

She gets up and heads for the door. "He'll be gone in a month. We'll probably only see him on Christmas and for the croquet tournaments."

She's baiting me, practically licking her chops, so pleased to bear such terrible news. She wants me to yell and lash out at her so she can laugh in my face like always. But I've learned a thing or two from Dr. Elliott over the last five months. I sit and stare at her, knowing silence will speak for me.

Disappointed, she simply turns around and leaves.

How could Dad do this to his own son? And to me, too, if you really want to get down to it. I try to imagine life in this building without my brother, my only friend, my only ally, but it's too painful.

Blood roars in my ears. I feel an invisible blanket closing around my mouth, and I swear it is a hundred degrees in here. My heart hammers my puny rib cage. I envision my ribs, thin as chicken bones, snapping in half one by one, my torso exploding in a gory mess all over my pewter miniatures. I'm aware of all this, that the panic is about to detonate, and I try to talk myself down.

I am surviving this. I am getting through this. I am more than my pathology, more than some deviation from the healthy and good.

Then I hear it, that sound. Not a wolf. In the cold, hard light of reality, I remember it's just Rex, the half-baked stoner Lab.

My skin prickles with heat, but I can breathe again. I go

to the window. I can't see anything out there except dark-ness. *Breathe.* Heart still pounds, but it's not going to kill me. *I am getting through this.* Watch the blackness swallow up the sky, watch the gloom creep in through the sides of my window. Hear that mournful howl.

A sad, strange, lonely sound. Growing louder. I know it can't be, but it sounds like it's getting closer, coming for me.

CHAPTER EIGHT

Our first issue of *Vox Populi* comes out this morning. I'd be more excited if they'd let me keep my original article, but I'm glad to see my work in print. I was going to say "my name in print," but I'll never get the same thrill from seeing "Bud Hess" in a byline.

In homeroom, nobody says hi to me when I walk in. For the first few weeks, Dylan would greet me or wave, but he stopped doing that a while ago. I don't mind. It's easier to fly under the radar when no one's aware you're alive.

Though *Vox Populi* has been placed on the desks, almost nobody is reading it, except other people who are on staff, and we're all just trolling it for our own pieces.

I can't tell you how much this disappoints me. The bell sounds for first period, and I trudge into the hallway. My collar won't stay down, and there's a stain on my pants from breakfast (*sarshir* cream with honey on Iranian flat bread), but I no longer care about my appearance. Nobody will be reading my masterpiece; nobody will read *Vox Populi*.

By the end of Chemistry that is no longer true. As we leave

Ryndak's class, Reggie points out something to me in the Letters to the Editor section.

The first two letters are the typical complaints about senior-year course load—but then I see the third.

To Whom It May Concern:

I would like to voice my complaint. The football team has new uniforms, but the Computer Lab has machines that are at least five years old. Also, half the Computer Lab serves as the Remedial Reading classroom, so the computer workstations have been squashed together. Why is this? So that the room accurately simulates the cubicles we will one day occupy in the offices of corporate America? I suppose that doesn't matter, as long as the new football uniforms look sweet.

This leads to my second point: the football team itself, and next month's barbaric ritual, Homecoming. Why are we honoring these savage jackasses? Why do they get so much? Computer Club only gets one measly camping weekend, and they have to raise the money for it themselves. But football? They get pep rallies, Bonfire Night, the Homecoming game and dance. That's kind of a lot for a bunch of violent jocks who terrorize other students. Oh, you didn't know about that? You didn't know they haze the freshmen on JV? And you know they sneak onto Loyola Beach every year after the Homecoming dance for a party to crown a "Gridiron Queen," right? They slather her with Jell-O shots, a beer shower, and acts of perversion.

Some adult MUST know about all this, right? After

all these years? It's easy to turn a blind eye when the football team is championed by so many parents and is the only extracurricular activity that actually brings in money to the school.

But I'm not worried. Stupid rituals like this fade away, one way or another. People who participate in these rituals fade away, too. Know what I mean?

Sincerely,

Anonymous

"When did this show up?" I ask. "It wasn't there when I left the meeting."

Reggie says, "I don't know. I worked on the layout till six thirty that night, and it wasn't there then either."

I scan the letter again. "I kind of agree with it."

"For real. Plus signing it 'Anonymous'? Genius. Nobody's allowed to submit letters anonymously to the paper. Nobody's allowed to do *anything* anonymously here."

"Except pray and donate money."

"Oh no," says Reggie, "they don't want you praying anonymously, man. They want you down on your knees in front of everyone."

Reggie grins at me and I grin back.

I sit next to Nikki in Modern Lit. She's reading the newspaper and chuckling to herself. Ms. Viola taught for half the period and then abruptly told us to read quietly. Now she has her head down on her desk. People who sit in the front of the room turn around every now and then as if they are looking at me. They watch me as I sort my collection of Bic pens and orange highlighters.

Nikki stretches, eases back in her seat, and says, "This is the best thing that's happened all year." She lays the newspaper in front of her, opened to the Letters page.

"Reggie and I were just talking about that."

"Lots of people are talking about that. It's the first time anyone has ever discussed anything that was in the newspaper."

When the bell rings, Ms. Viola gestures for Nikki and me to come over. "I'm calling an impromptu meeting of the newspaper today after school," she says. "There'll be an announcement after eighth period, but I just wanted to let you know."

"What's it about?" Nikki asks innocently.

"What do you think?" says Ms. Viola wearily. "Don't worry, it'll be brief. I've got to coach archery after."

Nikki and I walk out into the hallway together. We pass my Homeroom Buddy, Dylan, and some other guys loitering by the boys' restroom on the first floor, and they stop talking to stare at me. I hear Dylan say in a low voice, "That's him."

At the *Vox Populi* meeting, Ms. Viola claps her hands to get our attention. "This will only take a few minutes. You'll still be able to catch your rides if you quiet down and listen."

Everybody shuts up immediately, because no one wants to be stuck on public transportation like me.

"Principal McNeill has asked me to talk to you about something. I know you've seen the anonymous letter in the paper. At any rate, take a look at page two if you don't know what I mean," she says. But nobody opens the paper. We all know what she's talking about.

She continues. "The last night of production, we finished the layout around six thirty. The letter was not in at that time." She looks to the graphics team, Reggie among them, and they nod in agreement. "The next morning Trevor e-mailed the final file to the printer. I just checked the time stamp on the document, and it was modified at seven. And there in the layout is the anonymous letter. That means someone came into the staff room here and inserted the letter between six thirty and seven. It's not a big deal, so if you're afraid to speak up, please let me put your mind at rest," she says in a completely unconvincing way. "All I want to know is, Who was it?"

Crickets chirp. A lone tumbleweed blows by. Nobody says a word. The silence roars like ocean waves at high tide. We're all craning our heads, trying to catch the guilt in someone's eye, like playing Murder after curfew in the park.

Trevor clears his throat. "Ms. Viola, isn't it possible that it was someone *not* on staff? The rooms aren't locked; the building isn't even locked until seven o'clock most nights. I checked and, besides us, the following groups had practice or meetings that night: football, archery, poms, Computer Club, and Student Council. Could have been anyone."

"Anyone with a grudge against the newspaper," Ms. Viola says, "or against *me*."

"I think it has to be someone who has experience with graphic design," offers one of the production people. "Or else the whole rest of the layout would've been messed up with the addition of new text. They would have to know the software."

"Oh, anyone could figure it out," says Ms. Viola. "After all, *you* guys can do it. We're getting off track here. I can't have random screeds inserted into the newspaper without my knowledge. Everyone in the faculty lunchroom was haranguing me about this. For the last time, if anybody knows anything, just tell me and we'll sort it out."

But again nobody says a word. In my opinion, Ms. Viola approached it all wrong—she came from that teacher angle, putting everyone on guard with false promises not to punish the culprit. Nobody believes that shit *ever*. All teachers ever really want is for us to narc on each other, and then they leave us hanging.

She lets us go, and everybody is amped up about it now, knowing that it's causing a teacher some anguish.

Reggie's got a chess team meeting, so Nikki and I walk out together. We stop at the crossroads where the corridors meet. A mirror hangs on the wall of the intersection, the glass dark with splotches where the reflections disappear. I'm told it's been there since the charter of the school and is worshipped as some kind of relic. Beneath it hangs a plaque that reads: YOU CAN MAKE A DIFFERENCE. I glimpse my face in the mirror and then look away.

"That letter's got everyone all worked up," I say to Nikki. She looks thoughtful, her green eyes fastened on the announcement board hanging across from the mirror.

"Ye-es." It comes out weird, like two syllables, like she has something else to say.

"What? It's funny, isn't it?"

"I'm worried about something," she says. "During eighth period, I heard some kids talking about it. One of them was that dickwad Dylan. The thing about that letter is, some people think you wrote it."

"Me?" My voice squeaks, but I don't care because this is the coolest thing anybody has ever thought or said about me in my life. "That's awesome!"

She blinks. "They weren't saying it in a good way. They were saying it in that way guys do before they dog-pile on you in the locker room and beat the crap out of you for fun. You have a little experience with that, don't you?"

"Well . . . but, I mean, why would they think that? It's absurd."

"I don't know. Were you ever, you know, being yourself around them?"

"What's that supposed to mean?"

She sighs. "You know what it means. I think you rock. But you know the dickwads can't tolerate anyone unusual or cool. You're different, and their DNA is programmed to beat up people who are different. They almost can't help themselves."

I'm torn here between feeling ecstatic because Nikki thinks I rock and worrying that I'm already on somebody's shit list.

I say, "I don't see how this is my problem. I can't help what they think. What do you want me to do?"

"I don't know," she says, biting her cuticles. "I agree trying to announce that you're innocent is a waste of time. But I don't want them to come after you, Bud, and I don't want them spreading lies about you that'll get you thrown out of school. Considering what happened at your last school, we can't take that chance."

We. She's using *we.* This can only be a good sign.

"It's just one letter," I say. "I'm not going to get thrown out of school because someone wrote one anonymous letter."

She says, "I hope not."

At that moment Trevor catches up with us. I knew it was him when I heard the "Yo, yo" from down the hall and saw the black girls roll their eyes.

"Yo, Bud," he says when he reaches me. "You're welcome."

"I am?"

"Yeah. For my putting that idea into Ms. Viola's head about it possibly being someone not on staff. The anonymous letter writer, I mean."

"Why should I thank you for that?"

"Oh, right." He snorts. "You didn't have anything to do with it."

"Of course he didn't," Nikki snaps. He barely glances at her.

I shake my head. "Why would you even think that?"

"It had the stamp of 'lone gunman' all over it, so naturally I thought of you."

Nikki says, "Maybe that's just what someone *wants* you to think."

Trevor stares me down for a minute, but I stare right back. I have nothing to hide.

He says, "I hate the jocks, too, but who gives a shit? This is my senior year. I'm applying for a scholarship to Northwestern—the Medill School of Journalism—and I don't want some half-wit screwing up my newspaper and making me look like a fool. So consider this your warning."

He pushes past us, and Nikki looks at me like *See? I told you so.* But what can I do? If I protest and stand up for myself, that puts me on the defense, which is never a good place for someone like me.

Trevor stops right before he gets to the cafeteria. He turns back to me, issuing his coup de grâce: "Oh, I checked with my friend Brad Bates. He never heard of you."

Pointless to remind him that I never heard of that guy either. He lifts an eyebrow at me then, like this explains everything. Oh, brother, if you only knew.

"What's all that about?" Nikki hisses as Trevor leaves for real this time. "Who's Brad Bates?"

"I don't know," I say, and then I shut my mouth. I cannot get into the whole name change/Middle Eastern bomber thing right now. "Let's just talk about it tomorrow, okay?" I turn away.

Nikki tugs at my sleeve. "Wait, are you really not going to sell the chocolate bars? We've had them for weeks and you never told me you were going to do that, and then you announced it to Viola at that meeting. I thought you were just winding her up. Was that true?"

"I don't know."

"Because people are talking about that, too," she says.

I leave, not because I want to, but because I don't know what I've gotten myself into here with the chocolate bars and now this letter. I'm confused, and my head is vibrating.

Just beyond the parking lot are the playing fields: the football field and the track that runs around it, the baseball diamond, and an overgrown meadow used by the Archery Club. There's not a lot of land for urban schools, even private ones. The head janitor, Mr. Santos, is barking orders at some burnout pushing a lawn mower through the meadow.

I wave to him—Mr. Santos, not the burnout—and he waves back. He's a nice guy, and I'll be honest here: it's been to my advantage in the past to cultivate relationships with the custodial staff. I'm telling you, they hold all the secrets to a school. People hardly notice them, so they don't watch what they say when the janitors are around. Students constantly drop notes; leave papers and books behind in classrooms; sneak off to dark and empty corridors to perform evil, illegal, or private acts they think no one knows about. The janitors always know, and they're only human; they like to share the dirt. And while they don't always resent the students the way I would like them to, they're objective in a way the teachers never are. Teachers are always them vs. us or they try too hard to be one of the crowd, which they never are. Janitors observe from the outside without getting involved.

At Sullivan, the first time the janitor rescued me from the locker that the golf team had stuffed me into—the *golf* team—he felt sorry for me, and I milked it. I'd shoot the breeze with him whenever I saw him, and it got to the point where he'd look the other way when I conducted my D&D campaigns in the boiler room. Then one time when I was setting up for a game, I found the Sullivan keys and pass code in a lockbox down there (laughably easy to pick, especially if you carry paper clips and an Allen wrench on you at all times). It was nothing to steal the keys, copy them, memorize the codes, and have it all back nice and tight by the next morning. No one ever knew how I got back in the school to rig up the exploding toilet, although I bet the janitor suspected. But he never ratted me out. There's honor among the invisible.

The archery team has set up their equipment in the meadow. The tall grass brushes against their shins. Ms. Viola yells at them to ignore the mower—"Practice time is practice time"—and she leads the team in drills. She is wearing a padded suit and running in front of the targets while students shoot stray arrows at her. Her face looks funny, even from here. Kind of pulled up on the sides. Then I realize what it is: she's smiling.

When I get home, I see that Mom has put out some chrysanthemums in pots and tied some sad cornstalks to the front gate in homage to fall. A pumpkin sits there, too. Why does she bother? It will be stolen, smashed, or otherwise defiled by dawn.

I pass Dariush's door by the landing and hear strains of music from his stereo. I know that song, "Kiss Off" by the Violent Femmes. I knock. He doesn't answer, so I knock louder. A shadow passes behind the peephole. In our building, the peepholes let us know which family member is standing outside the door so that we can choose to open up or not.

He opens. "Badi-jan," he says, a smile breaking across his face. He has a can of Red Bull and a cigarette in his hand, which he sweeps toward the living room in a gesture of welcome. I throw myself on the folded-up futon and toss my briefcase on the floor. He follows me, singing along with the music.

I can always drop by his apartment without any advance notice. Without any real reason, too, and he never questions why. It's as if he enjoys talking to me.

"Want something to drink?" he asks, going into the kitchen.

"Do you have any caffeine-free Red Bull?"

"What would be the point of that?"

"I don't want to stunt my growth. I've already had coffee this year."

Dariush brings me a can of Red Bull. "Live a little."

We don't really *talk* talk. We hang out and say whatever. It's comfortable, normal. He doesn't treat me like a kid and I don't think of him as a grown-up, so we meet in between.

The only mention he makes of the other night is when he says, "I guess you've heard I'll be moving out."

"I hate them for this," I say. The sudden venom grips me.

"Don't," he says. "It'll be okay. But I'll miss seeing you and making fun of Mom and Dad behind their backs. And the food. God, I'll miss the food. Mom is a great cook."

"Everything's going to seem so much harder, so much worse, without you around." I'm whining, but I don't feel embarrassed really. After all, he is Dariush, the only person who accepts me completely as I am.

"How are you getting on with school?"

"It's basically intolerable, but that's to be expected."

He laughs. "Been there. Of course, you're so much smarter than I was. You really could do anything. I mean, what do you *want* to do? What do you want out of school? To graduate with honors?"

"To graduate with friends," I say. "All I want is a normal high school experience, but it seems so out of my reach that I get angry. And then I just want everyone to either leave me the hell alone or else . . ."

"Or else?" Dariush *knows* me. I can let the worst of me come out.

"Suffer," I say.

He nods, tapping his cigarette ash into his empty Red Bull can.

"I guess I don't really want *everyone* to suffer," I amend.

"Everyone does suffer in his own way. Look at Dad: he's got us for sons. You know it kills him that we're not going into engineering or medicine. Remember when he got me an interview for that research job in his department?"

"Yeah, you didn't show up."

"Man, was he pissed at me. Never saw him so mad."

"You and Dad working together at Abbott Labs . . . God, what was he thinking?"

"He was thinking I could have been a miserable chemist like him. We could have carpooled. We could have eaten lunch together every day."

"Just promise you won't go back to the car wash."

"Oh God, the car wash." He stretches in his chair and locks his hands behind his head. "How I love being unemployed. I'm gonna have to get some kind of job, I guess. My life sucks so bad right now they should name a vacuum cleaner after me."

I don't want to laugh, but I can see that he wants me to, so I do. The good thing about laughing is that you can fake it till you make it. Sometimes you can force yourself to smile and laugh, and after a while you sort of feel naturally happy. At least, that's what I've heard.

CHAPTER NINE

On Saturdays I like to get up early before everyone else and eat breakfast and look out the front window and pretend I live alone. It feels very adult. It would feel more adult if I was not eating Cocoa Krispies and drinking chocolate milk.

King Sargon Boulevard is quiet this early on a Saturday. There are only a few trucks and stumbling drunks moseying home. A movement halfway down the block catches my eye. That swishing tail, that uneven lope, veering from curb to front stoop, occasionally bashing his head against some unsuspecting lamppost—it has to be Rex. Why's he out alone? Why do the hippies do that? They either forget him out in the backyard for hours or let him out the front door like they live on a farm in the middle of nowhere. I know it sucks to have to get up early to let your dog out, but please. Rex is too brain damaged to get around by himself. Plus, people in this neighborhood steal stray dogs to use as bait for dog-fighting practice. It's common knowledge.

I am half out of my chair, ready to slip out the door to bring Rex home, when the phone rings. Who would call at 7:30? I grab it before the ringing can wake anyone.

"Hello?"

"Bud? Hi, it's Nikki. Did I call too early? That's a stupid question. I know I did, I'm sorry."

"It's okay," I say. "I've been up for a while pretending I live alone."

"Alone," she says wistfully. She *breathes* it. It reminds me of the way my mother says "adult education symposium."

Before I can say anything else, she blurts out, "Look, I have to get out of this house today. I just have to or I'm going to blow up."

"What's the matter?"

"Assorted family bat shit," she says. "You in?"

"I . . . I'm not sure." I would like nothing better than to meet with her—on a *Saturday* no less, a nonschool day, a day of casual clothes and relaxed social customs—but I also wanted to hang out with my brother today.

"Come on. You don't want to be responsible for my head exploding, do you?"

Take charge, I tell myself, *stop mealymouthing.* I suggest the NATO House of Pancakes, but she vetoes it in favor of the Heartland Cafe, a restaurant my mother distrusts because they serve nine-dollar veggie burgers.

"I'm in," I say.

She says she'll pick me up in thirty minutes. I bolt for the shower, load up my hair with taming product, and then check myself out in the mirror for no reason. I sneak back into my room to dress. I don't want anyone waking up and asking me questions. It's too hard to formulate believable lies this early.

I peer into my closet. Is this a date? It could be. I've never given much thought to my clothes before, and now I'm paying for it. I love the Magnificat uniform because it removes personal responsibility from looking like a complete jackass. At Sullivan I was on my own, and I didn't do myself any favors by wearing clothes my mother picked out.

I hear stirring coming from my parents' bedroom, so I grab the first things I lay my hands on: a plaid shirt, jeans from Walmart, tennis shoes. I button up my shirt to the throat, slip into my Navy peacoat, and prepare to dart out the front doorway. I catch sight of Mom's purse hanging on the back of a kitchen chair. Silently, I take out her wallet, remove a twenty, and slide it into my own wallet.

I scrawl on a Post-it—*going to library, back in afternoon*—stick it on the front door, and then close the door softly behind me. I wait outside with time to spare. I'm stoked and realize I haven't had a panic attack in more than thirty-six hours.

A silver car turns the corner, and at that moment I see a blur of brownish fur amble out in its path. Rex. Without thinking, I dive for him and drag him back onto the sidewalk. The car probably wasn't going to flatten him, but you can't take chances.

"Bud!" shouts Nikki, the driver of the silver car.

I shrug modestly. I could not have planned this any better. I look heroic, I feel heroic, even though Rex seems unaware that Death nearly snapped him up in its jaws. He pees against our fence and then bonks his head repeatedly on the hippies' gate until I let him in their yard.

I get in Nikki's car and say offhandedly, "It was nothing."

"I almost ran you over, you idiot," she says. She doesn't look that impressed, but I'm still going to chalk one up for my side.

• • •

At the Heartland, Nikki orders French toast and I get a breakfast burrito. She orders coffee and I—reaching a new level of lunacy—order a carrot, beet, and celery juice. She just stares at me, and I act like I drink this stuff all the time.

"Too bad Reggie couldn't come," I say, fishing. I need to know if this is a date or if I'm just a stand-in, because if it *is* a date, it's my first one. "Is he busy today?"

She shrugs. This gives me no information.

"It's the twins' birthday," she says, answering my unspoken question about why she wanted to get out of her house. "There was an excruciatingly special breakfast at the ass-crack of dawn, which I declined, and then later they're going to the Children's Museum with twenty of their closest friends."

"Your mom likes to go all out for birthdays, huh?"

"My stepmother. When my mother was alive, we'd just have cake and presents and sit around. Which was fine." She drums her fingertips on the table. "Which was actually *great*. But my stepmother likes *events*."

"I'm sorry about your mom. I didn't know."

"I was nine." She pushes her glasses up the bridge of her nose, and I notice her eyes look red. "Then my dad met his *current* wife when I was ten, they got married the next year, and the year after that the twins were born."

I nod, waiting for her to go on.

"I don't hate her, but she makes me nuts," she says after a moment. "Brenda. She's, like, reasonable and sort of nice. She tries to connect with me, know what I mean? Like shopping and stupid shit like that. Cookies after school. Katy Perry posters, even though nothing could be further from my musical taste. She tries. But I don't want her to try. Our whole house is different since she moved in. There's fancy shit everywhere that you're afraid of ruining. We're always doing things and going places, and there's always people over, playdates for the twins, Brenda's moms group from church, book clubs. When my mom was alive, we had furniture you could sit on, and we ate Cheetos and watched movies and life was just happy and simple, you know?"

She's gathered steam by now. I sit there and pretend to sip my beet juice.

"And then my sisters. My God. It's not enough that they're cute and into ponies and ballet, things my mom and I would have totally made fun of. *No*, they've got to be twins. What could be cuter than twins? Twin girls who love pink and ponies and *pink ponies* and who shower love on everyone, including me, and oh, I just want to puke."

"What did your mom die of?" I ask. The loss of her mother, the impending loss of my brother. Okay, they are way different losses, but still you can't ignore the parallels.

She gives me a look, and I think I've just put my foot in it, but then she says, "Nobody ever asks about my mom anymore. They're afraid to mention her or something. Anyway, cancer."

"My grandfather died of colon cancer," I tell her. I remember his last days, how he spoke only in Farsi, yet I was able to understand phrases that meant *What is wrong with that kid?* and *Can't you send him to camp?* "It was quick," I say.

"Breast cancer," Nikki says. "It wasn't."

We sit for a while, quiet. Not the bad kind. Some white guy with dreadlocks walks by us and announces to nobody that he is going to "tickle the ivories," and he sits down at a piano in the corner and murders out some of the worst blues I've ever heard.

It's not even 10 a.m., but I ask if she wants some dessert. That always seems to help girls feel better. I look down at the menu. "Want a vegan gluten-free mousse?"

"I'd rather eat my own head," she says. We just stare at each other, and then we both snort a little. And then—who knows why? It wasn't even that funny—we both burst out laughing. It totally takes us over, makes our shoulders shake and my stomach hurt in the best way possible.

We split the check (that's a black mark against this being a date), and when we leave, I toss an extra dollar on the table, bringing up the tip to twenty-one percent. It's easy to be generous with stolen money.

The rest of the day we are free to do exactly what we want, except for having to drop the car back at her house.

"I'm not allowed to drive downtown," she says.

"So you follow rules," I say.

We take the Red Line downtown to the Jazz Record Mart, and we both hunt through the used-record bins like we know what we are looking for, even though 1) we don't, and 2) neither of us has a turntable. She buys an album by a spacey-looking old African man called Sun Ra, and I buy an album by a trumpeter, Chet Baker. Even though I don't know anything about jazz, I know that I will have a lot in common with Chet Baker, that this will possibly be the record that defines me, and I know this just from the titles of the songs: "Just Friends," "You Don't Know What Love Is," "I've Never Been in Love Before," and "Let's Get Lost."

"I think I'll like this." Nikki examines her Sun Ra album as we leave the store.

"Maybe jazz on vinyl will be my new thing," I say. "Most of my MP3s are songs my brother gave me or turned me on to. He's into old-fashioned music, like New Wave. The Smiths, The Cure, The English Beat, that kind of stuff."

"So what's your favorite song of all time?"

I don't even have to think about it. I sing the first line, *"I walk through the valley of the car wash of death . . ."*

"Is that an old song? I don't know that one," she says.

"It's called 'Car Wash of Death.'"

"Who's the band?"

"Um . . . they're also called Car Wash of Death. It was actually my brother's band until they broke up last year."

"Sounds cool. I like it."

We have a lot in common. She must see that.

We go to the gigantic Salvation Army on Grand. We separate: I look for a Halloween costume; Nikki disappears to find nonschool clothes. My mom would *kill* me if she knew I was shopping here. She says you don't want shoes that already have someone else's footprints in them and that used shorts can give you crotch rot.

After all that, we don't have enough money to eat lunch and take the train back up to Rogers Park, so we skip the food. I would have been willing to forego the train and walk the fourteen miles home if it meant we could hang out a little more.

On the L ride home, someone crazy but not dangerous sits next to Nikki. Just your garden-variety crazy: a man talking to himself and picking at his face. Nikki's not even bugged. You know how many girls would freak out by the proximity of crazy on the L? *Many.* Being that I ride public transportation every day, I see my fair share of crazy, and sometimes it's not pretty. Like the lady who brings the baby carriage on the Western Avenue bus, but it's holding Duraflame logs and bottles of orange pop, not a baby. And there's always a guy peeing on himself. Always. It's like a rule. Homeless people who yell at the bus driver; homeless people who are nice and not yelling but still don't have bus fare; homeless people who are trying really hard not to seem like homeless people, but they are dragging kids with them and taking suitcases onto the bus and their money is always carried in some complicated contraption tied to their belts. That's how I know Nikki is a decent human and not just a rich girl who lives in a nice house in the city: she takes crazy in stride. You *could* just get up and move away from the crazy people, but she stays put.

One more stop and then our station comes up, Morse. Then for her it's just a short ride on the eastbound 96 Lunt bus to Sheridan. For me, it's the westbound 96, all the way to Western. Opposite sides of the tracks and all that.

The L has left the Loyola station, and I feel like this is it—the end of the date or whatever you call this outing—and all I know is, whatever this is, I don't want it to end. But I don't know what to say, nothing comes to mind, and I want to just take out my Chet Baker album and point to various song titles and hope they convey my meaning. I would point to "I Fall in Love Too Easily."

Instead, I say, "That was a nice BMW you were driving this morning," because I roll like a spaz.

"It's my dad's."

"I just saw one like it in a commercial. It was silver, too, and kind of sliding through a big puddle." Oh my God. What? They're what, and they slide through what? On TV, they're *all* silver, and they *all* slide through big puddles.

She's peeling what's left of some green nail polish off her pinkie. She says, "Bud, I'm still worried. You know, about the letter. That douche bag Dylan was telling his idiot friends that you were a weirdo—I heard him in History. And what about Trevor? He was whispering with his little pack of panting dogs that he thinks you wrote it, and you're trying to mess with the paper because you're jealous of him."

"You don't think I really wrote it, do you?" I ask.

"You know I don't, but listen: you don't want these guys on your bad side. They can make life really unpleasant for people they don't like."

"Unpleasant?" I laugh. It's a harsh, barking sound. "*Unpleasant?* Don't forget who you're talking to, Nikki."

"I know it was bad at Sullivan, but these guys can be ruthless."

Then it comes.

Not the panic attack. It's the rage, and it's on slow burn.

"Ruthless," I say, "is being cracked in the face with a cafeteria tray, and the teachers on patrol don't notice because they're busy calling the riot police to break up a gang fight. Ruthless is being beaten with a golf club on a public sidewalk underneath the Safe School Zone sign. Ruthless is seeing *towelhead* and *sand nigger* Sharpied on your locker. Ruthless is watching an ambulance cart away a dead fourteen-year-old as you wait for the bus." I tell her, "I can handle Magnificat's brand of ruthless."

She watches me. Those eyes are an astounding shade of green, and I have to turn away.

"All that?" she asks. "All that happened . . . to you?"

"To me."

She takes her camera out of her bag and scootches close to me, her arm slung around my shoulders, and holds it out in front of us. *Click*. Was I smiling? I hope my teeth aren't stained from the juice.

"Morse," the conductor calls out over the loudspeaker. We get up and fall in with the line of passengers waiting to exit through the sliding doors.

I walk Nikki to the eastbound 96 bus stop. I'll wait with her for her bus, then cross the street to catch mine.

She says, "Why 'sand nigger'?"

"I'm Iranian. My name is not Bud Hess; it's Badi Hessam-izadeh—or it was. No one's supposed to know. I mean, Magnificat knows because they have my old records, but they're probably relieved my dad changed it so they don't have to provide each teacher with a pronunciation guide." Ever had that feeling when you're half asleep, half in a dream, and you think you're suffocating, but then you realize the air is there and it's just a matter of pulling the blankets off your face? Yeah. It's like that. Whoosh.

Nikki's bus is coming. She says, "I want to know it all. One day. When you want to tell me everything."

She's looking right at me; I almost can't stand it. "They spelled it *nigga*," I admit.

She blinks. "Sand nigga?"

"Yeah."

She shrugs. "It's practically a compliment."

The driver opens the door. Nikki gets on and waves goodbye. I love that sound when the bus doors open and the compressed air thing slides back. Like it's sighing.

Nighttime, in my room. I thought my parents would go

ballistic that I'd been out all day without calling, but they didn't seem to notice. They were carving pumpkins with Dorri and Arman, and my mom was busy making this amazing pumpkin soup. It was so good, creamy with cinnamon and cloves. Sometimes I think she puts all the nice words she wants to say (but can't) into her food.

I told them it was too early to carve pumpkins, that Halloween was still weeks away and the jack-o'-lanterns would rot.

"Then I'll carve more," Mom had said, not looking at me. I almost said that was stupid and a waste of time, but I changed my mind and went to my room instead.

She hasn't said anything about the missing money. Maybe she hasn't noticed yet. I don't have any left to put back in her wallet, and I feel bad about that, but it's not the first time, and one thing I've learned about myself over the past year is that the more I lie and steal, the easier it is.

I should do homework, but it's Saturday night and I don't want to. I lie on my bed and read a biography of Carl Linnaeus, best botanist ever. I turn up the radio and prop the Chet Baker album against it. Maybe I should have just caved and bought the CD, but the LP looked forlorn there in the bin, like it needed somebody to buy it. Why not me? My brother has a turntable, and I know he'll let me listen to it in his apartment. Hearing it in my room would probably ruin the experience, with Azita screeching in the hallway and Dorri and Arman fighting for control of the Xbox in the living room.

Mom knocks on the door and pushes it open before I can respond.

"Hi, Bud." Her eyes dart all over the room. Is she trying to catch me at something? Uncover clues that will help explain me? She does this all the time.

"Hi, Mom."

"Want dessert? Pumpkin bread."

"Yeah, that sounds good." I start to swing my legs over the side of the bed, but she sits down, so I swing them back and wait for whatever it is she wants to say.

"How was the library?" Her eyes come to rest on the Linnaeus bio, and I know she assumes I picked it up today.

"Great. You know me. I love the library."

Then her eyes fall on the Salvation Army bags I had to sneak in when I came home. I just threw them next to my dresser without anticipating that I'd be interrogated about them later.

"Oh," I say. "I also stopped at the thrift store on the way home. For my Halloween costume."

She shakes her head. "You did not buy shoes, did you?"

"No, I know: other people's footprints."

"It's true. You look inside someone else's old shoes sometime. You'll see their footprints. It's unsanitary." She cocks her head. There's that look. She's trying to read my expression to see if I'm lying or hiding something. It feels really invasive, and I just *hate* it. But I keep my eyes wide and innocent the whole time.

"So what did you buy?"

I pull the clothes out of the bag. "First I was going to be a ghost for Halloween, but then I got this great idea in the store: a cat burglar. Black turtleneck, black pants, black cap. I can get a plain black mask at the Dollar Store."

Mom gawps at the clothes. "Pants? You'll get crotch rot!"

"I'll wash them."

"Even so. They're probably full of bugs."

"Seriously? Just because they came from the thrift store, they're full of bugs?"

"Why else would someone get rid of a pair of perfectly good pants?" she says, fingering the fabric. "Maybe someone died in them."

"Maybe someone *famous* died in them," I say.

"I will clean all of this." She gathers up my clothes. "Or soak them overnight in lye if I have to."

I see her looking at my Chet Baker record.

"Where did you get that?" she asks. Her voice, I know it so well, is loaded with suspicion. Why doesn't she just come out and say it? *Where did you get the money for this?* But she doesn't say it. So why should I?

"The library. They lend out records."

"But we don't have a record player."

"Dariush does. I'll listen to it at his place."

"*His* place." She sniffs. "For *now*."

Which way are we going with this? Will she rip on Dariush and make me defend him? We watch each other. If we were dogs, we'd be circling right now.

"How much were the clothes?" she asks.

"Six dollars."

She keeps looking at me, and I keep looking right back.

"Let me give you the money," she says, one last-ditch effort to call my bluff. "I'm happy to buy your Halloween costume for you."

"No, it's fine."

"Please, it's the least I can do." Mom has a pleading look on her face I can't fathom, and suddenly I am weary of this dance.

"Fine, Mom," I snap. "Go get the money."

She narrows her eyes at me, and I swear for one second there I think she hates me. She rises from the bed and stalks out of the room, returning a few moments later with her purse. She unzips it with unnecessary force, whips out the wallet, and tears out some bills. She tosses them at me, and they sail in frantic arcs across my bedspread. I snatch up each one, even the dollar that drifts to the floor, and stuff them into my jeans pocket. Slowly, she makes a show of opening her wallet wide, turning it upside down, and shaking it to prove there is nothing else. At that moment I know she knows I took the twenty, and this is how she tells me. But I don't say a word and neither does she, because that is our way. She whirls around, and then she is gone.

The dog barks outside. Poor Rex. He's too dumb to realize he's in his own backyard. I pick up my Chet Baker record and turn off my radio. That mournful wail goes right to my bones. But nobody else seems to care.

I look out my bedroom window. I don't see Rex. But that doesn't mean he can't see me. In the windowpane, I see myself reflected back. I'm still holding my Chet Baker LP. The black night revolves like an endless record out there. I look down and run my finger under the song titles. How can Nikki be so right for me and not even know it?

"Let's Get Lost," I say when I reach the right one, as if she can hear me, as if anyone can.

CHAPTER TEN

To Whom It May Concern:

I haven't forgotten about the football team, people, but I have other fish to fry.

The administration dangles more incentives to spur us into unloading more boxes of chocolate bars for the fund-raiser. Now, the class who sells the most gets a day off from school. This enticement might work on some, but it makes no sense to me. Why don't we just skip school? You can get as many free days as you want that way.

You think my complaints are all fun and games? That I'm just a big joker? This is no joke. They think if we concentrate on silly activities like selling chocolate bars, we won't be able to concentrate on bigger issues, like why our teachers and parents encourage us to compete against each other, to exclude each other, to focus on our differences instead of our similarities. Why does the administration look the other way during football team hazing and the Gridiron Queen date-rape party? See, I haven't forgotten.

You shouldn't just take this stuff lying down. I'm not. Watch me.

Sincerely,

Anonymous

Nikki throws down the paper on the lunch table in disgust. "I knew this would happen. They're out to get you, whoever they are. They even wrote it in your style."

I pick up the paper to scan this newest Letter to the Editor. "I have a style?"

"Yes, and this is totally you," she says. "And not just your style, but the topic, too. It's so obvious. Everybody on staff knows you hate the chocolate bar fund-raiser. Someone has it in for you. Which one of those jerks did it?"

Reggie clears his throat, puts aside the book he is reading. "Maybe it's not someone trying to get Bud in trouble. Maybe it's just someone who thinks like him."

I look at Reggie. The title of his book is *The Genius and the Misery of Chess.*

"I don't know," says Nikki. "It's awfully coincidental. The first time the *Vox Populi* ever gets anonymous letters is right when Bud is pissing off the dickwads?"

Reggie says, "I don't think the dickwads are smart enough to write this."

"Trevor is," I point out.

"But Trevor wouldn't jeopardize the reputation of his precious *Vox Populi*," Nikki argues. "He's already whining that Bud is going to wreck his chances of getting a scholarship, that these letters make him look like he can't control his own newspaper."

Reggie makes a dismissive *pffftt* sound. "Bull. Until these letters started appearing, barely anybody read the stupid thing. Remember, this is my third year on staff, and I know Trevor pretty well. He's an uptight bastard, but he's determined to make his newspaper a success, and success is defined by numbers. He was bragging this morning in religion class that they had to run off an extra hundred copies and that they increased the rate of the ad on the back page."

I turn to the back of the paper. There is a half-page ad for Pickett Johnson's Funeral Home.

Reggie continues. "Trevor knows that all Northwestern will care about is that the *Vox Populi* circulation increased under his regime. They'll never hear about some little anonymous letters, and they wouldn't care."

"So you think it's him?" I ask.

Reggie looks off into the distance, thinking. "On the one hand, yes, because it boosts the profile of his paper. On the other, no, because . . ."He hesitates. "It's just that the letters seem *sincere*, you know? Like the author really believes what he's saying."

"That's not how I see it at all," Nikki says. "It's manipulative. And if there was anybody at this school who really had these feelings, we'd know about it. Wouldn't they be drawn to us and our Island of Misfit Toys? Wouldn't we know them?"

Maybe we do, I think, stealing a glance at Reggie. But I don't say it.

• • •

In Modern Lit, Ms. Viola varies from the syllabus. This causes a lot of whispering in class because everyone knows that since she started teaching at Magnificat fifteen years ago, she never 1) uses the whiteboard, 2) attends Faculty Appreciation Day, or 3) varies from the syllabus. Year after year it's the same books. Can this class really be considered modern?

"We're going to do *As I Lay Dying* instead of *A River Runs Through It*," she says, and passes out copies of the Faulkner book. They smell of mothballs and chalk dust, as if she's been keeping them in an underground bunker along with a stockpile of sweater vests and blackboard erasers.

"Actually," she adds, "I really wanted to do *The Chocolate War* by Robert Cormier, but Principal McNeill shot down my suggestion due to its profanity. It's too bad, because I love that book. Anybody here ever read it?"

I begin to raise my hand and then see that no one else has, so I lower it.

"You'll like *As I Lay Dying*," she says. "The buzzards circling the decaying corpse in her coffin are fun. Not as relatable as the story of a boy who refuses to sell his school's chocolate bars but, oh well."

Crap. More than a couple of people turn around and look at me. *Thanks, Ms. Viola, just what I need.*

We start discussing Faulkner. I'm having a hard time paying attention. I don't know about anybody else, but I cannot take my eyes off Viola's sweater vest, which has punctuation marks knitted into the pattern.

After the bell, Nikki and I pause by Ms. Viola's desk. "Are we going to have another spontaneous staff meeting after school?" Nikki asks her.

"No." Ms. Viola tosses her papers and books into a briefcase that looks like mine.

"Well, don't we have to talk about how another letter got into the paper?" Nikki demands.

Ms. Viola looks up. "We've already tried that, remember? Nobody's telling me the truth, and I'm sick of listening to baloney. I have archery practice."

Nikki falters. "But . . . but we have to find out who's behind it."

"McNeill's probably taking me to the woodshed on this one, but what am I supposed to do? Station armed guards outside the staff room? Download spyware to find out who's messing with the layout after hours? I don't know anything about technology. I don't even know how the coffee machine works."

Nikki glances at me. "Okay, but I think someone is trying to get Bud in trouble with these letters. The whole chocolate bar thing, you know. Didn't you see how everybody stared at him when you mentioned *The Chocolate War*? Somebody wants us to think it's Bud who's writing the letters." She jerks her thumb over her shoulder at me.

Ms. Viola jerks her thumb at me, too. "Him? No, I don't believe it. Why?"

They both look at me, waiting for me to say something.

"I don't really know," I say. "I guess I rub people the wrong way."

Ms. Viola eyes me for another second. "No, impossible." Then she pauses as if thinking it over and asks, "You did read that book, didn't you? *The Chocolate War*?" I nod. "I thought I saw you start to raise your hand. What did you think of it?"

I say, "It's a very realistic story of human cruelty and conformity."

A strange light comes into her eyes. Then she stands up. Wow, she is tall. You wouldn't notice it ordinarily because she has horrible posture and is usually slumped over her desk, eating Tums and violently rubbing her temples, but here, standing over us with her archery gear under her arm, she must be six-foot-one.

"You don't drink coffee, do you?" I ask.

"Decaf," she says.

I *knew* it.

"Listen," she says, looking from Nikki to me, "between moderating your staff and the archery team, I don't have time to stake out the computer terminals or organize reconnaissance missions in the south wing. And I'll be honest with you: I'm torn. I like to see a little spirit, a little rebellion in the students. It's not often anymore that I do. But at the same time, I don't understand how, after fifteen years of advising the school paper, something like this can happen to *me*. It's fine to oppose the chocolate bar fund-raiser, but why do they have to use my paper to do it? Can't they vandalize something?"

"Maybe it's not happening to *you*," I say. "Maybe somebody just needs to speak his mind."

She says, "At least when the archers on my team shoot me in the back, they do it to my face. Well, you know what I mean."

"Are we still talking about the letters?" Nikki wrinkles her nose, confused.

But Ms. Viola doesn't answer.

The late bell's about to ring, so Nikki and I head out.

"Teachers take everything so personally," I note.

"We've gotta kick this up a notch," says Nikki. "Meet me in the caf after eighth."

Reggie and I wait by the vending machines. I brown-bagged it today at lunch—one lousy PBJ—and I'm starving but as usual have no money. Reggie gets a package of Toastchee out of the machine and hands me three of the six crackers.

"Thanks," I say, wolfing them down.

"No sweat," he says. "So what do you think? Obviously Nikki and I are at odds on this. Do you think somebody here is really out to get you? It seems improbable."

"It's hard to say. I'm paranoid by nature."

"Well, I'm optimistic by nature, and I like to think that there has to be somebody else here at this school who has had it with, with . . . well, not *fund-raising* exactly, but with authority, I guess you could say. That's what the letters seem to be. Antiauthority."

I nod. Reggie is a cool guy, different from kids I was friends with at Sullivan, if you could even call them friends. We didn't have anything in common except an ongoing obsession with *The Lord of the Rings*. You can't base a whole friendship on that. Reggie is smart and he's focused, and if he's an outsider, then he seems okay with it. Which makes him admirable, as opposed to pathetic and sad like me.

I ask, "What was that book you were reading at lunch?"

He takes it out of his backpack and hands it to me. "It's about the world of competitive chess."

"Oh, like Bobby Fischer and Garry Kasparov?"

"You know Kasparov? You play chess?"

"I dabble," I tell him.

"Those are the success stories. There's some of that in there. But there's other stuff, too, like how chess has also driven people to nervous breakdowns, or insane asylums, or bankruptcy."

"A feel-good book," I say.

He says, "My dad gave it to me. He tolerated my playing chess and being the team captain of the Checkmates—despite it being 'fag stuff'—until I told him I wanted to play on the professional circuit one day. He almost had a heart attack. You'd think I said I wanted to play Texas Hold 'Em for a living."

"When I told my dad I wanted to study botany, he said, 'Why stop there? Go on to engineering or medicine.' It's like he was embarrassed of botany."

"Mine's completely embarrassed of me. He's always throwing a ball at me and shouting, 'Think fast!' and any time I get hit in the face or gut with it, he calls me Regina. That's my punishment whenever I make a mistake: he calls me a girl's name. I used to show him awesome strategies on Chess.com, but he'd just stand there saying, 'Uh-huh, great' in a bored voice. Can he even make the effort to humor me, pretend he's interested?" Reggie must see the disgust on my face, because he adds, "Yeah. My dad's a prick."

For all his shortcomings, my dad is not intentionally cruel. Embarrassed, distant, judgmental, sure—but he's not a mean-spirited guy.

"Well, in general, dads are never happy with anything," I say to cheer him up.

"I'm glad I have chess," he says. "And you have botany. *Why* botany, though? I mean, what is it that interests you about it so much?"

"Plants are good and beautiful," I say. "Unlike people." My mom was the one who got me interested in it. She'd give sunflower seeds to the birds, and the seeds they dropped grew into flowers. To a little kid, that's mysterious. And the way she'd gaze at birds struck me as important somehow. I know now that it's an escape for her, escape from the drudgery of mom life, especially Persian-mom life, especially for an educated woman like her. I mean, it's not like a law. Lots of modern Persian moms work, like Khaleh Rana, my aunt. However, my cousins are spoiled brats and dumb as a bag of hammers, and my dad chalks it up to the absence of constant mom influence. I chalk it up to inborn nastiness and idiocy. Anyway, bird-watching helps my mother escape, and botany does the same for me. Instead of escaping boredom, I escape people.

Nikki walks up. I sense something shift in our dynamic. Reggie and I were having a good old time bashing our fathers, and then Nikki appears and a barrier goes up. Reggie stands taller and shoves his hands in his pockets and watches her without blinking, and I realize he likes her, too.

Nikki says, "I've made a chart."

We sit at a table and look at the paper she draws out of her three-ring binder. It's like a Venn diagram and a flow chart and a database rolled into one.

She points to column A. "This represents individuals who we know actively dislike Bud. Column B, people who have had grievances against the school in the past. Column

C—and this is pure conjecture here—general groups of people who seem like they *would* hate Bud. And then," she says, "there is X."

"What is X?" I ask.

"X represents the unknown. Someone or something we have not yet thought of."

I say, "You've put a lot of effort into this. The Religious Activities Club? Really? Why would they have a grudge against me?"

"You went to public school," she says. "It's like you're bringing an atmosphere of pagan worship into Magnificat. You don't know how rabid those religious bitches are."

Reggie peers at the chart. "You put Jason Amato there? And Rebecca Lagore?"

I explain. "The Salisbury Steak Incident."

"Well, who's Colin McCool?" Reggie asks.

"Bud fell on him during the rope climb in Phys Ed and broke his finger. You know Colin: Bieber hair, snaggle teeth? He plays guitar for the young people's mass at St. Jerome's, and now he's out of commission for a month."

"That rope climb is impossible!" I say. "I'm telling you, if Jesus were in my gym class, he would not be able to do it."

"I had to include all possibilities," Nikki says. "I'm leaning toward Dylan and his cronies."

Reggie counters, "I'd pick Trevor. I can't stand him."

"We're getting off track here," I say. "This isn't about who we all personally dislike. It's about the overwhelming number of people who I had no idea until this very moment *hate me*."

Reggie says, "Don't forget column B, the coincidences.

People who have grievances against the school. Or against Ms. Viola."

"Everybody hates Viola," Nikki says. "If she's the one that people are out to get, I'm going to need an Excel spreadsheet."

After half an hour, the faculty patrolling the caf start kicking everyone out. For safety reasons they don't like people hanging around after school, and McNeill has bumped up security since the letters began appearing in the paper.

"Quit malingering," says Mr. Blankenship (girls' tennis coach/Phys Ed), clapping his hands at us like we're squirrels at a birdfeeder.

We gather up our stuff while Mr. Santos comes in with his industrial mop and bucket to clean the floor. He sees me and gives a little wave and a smile. I hardly wave back, but Nikki sees.

"You friends with the janitor?"

"Not really," I say.

She watches Mr. Santos slop hot, sudsy water on the floor by the vending machines. "He's cool. Once he caught me smoking in the john and didn't turn me in."

I'm appalled both by Nikki smoking and my own embarrassment at Mr. Santos's greeting. I shouldn't be embarrassed—after all, janitors are people, too—but when you're treading the tightrope between barely acceptable and completely ostracized, you have to be careful. Still, I'm ashamed of myself. Mr. Santos has been helpful to me in a lot of ways, like that time he rescued me at my locker and looked up my combination on that BlackBerry device. He's a nice man. And as you know, I've found it useful in the past to cultivate friendships with school custodians. So I shouldn't be such an elitist wuss about waving hi to the janitor. Sometimes I just make myself sick.

I say, "You shouldn't smoke."

She says, "Everyone has a vice."

The three of us go out into the parking lot, and Reggie brings up my next assignment for the *Vox Populi*: covering Bonfire Night this weekend. Nikki and I volunteered at the last meeting to document it. Even though it's not nearly as important as the Homecoming dance, Bonfire Night is kind of a big deal around here. People even bring dates.

"Guess what?" Reggie says. "I'll be seeing you two at the bonfire after all."

Nikki stops walking. "You're going? With anybody, or alone?"

"Neither," says Reggie. "McNeill just approved my band to play at it! The band that was booked, Civilian Swine, backed out yesterday. Their drummer came down with mono."

Is it my imagination or does Nikki seem incredibly relieved to hear that Reggie is not going with a date?

"Mononucleosis," I say. They both just look at me as we stand outside Reggie's car. "It's the full name," I clarify.

"Yeah, well, isn't that great? It's our first official gig, but don't tell McNeill."

So Reggie is a nationally ranked chess champ *and* he's in a band. He only plays the keyboard, but that still counts. And he's tall, don't forget that. I feel myself growing invisible, if such a thing can be felt.

"Wow, that is killer," says Nikki. "I can't believe I'm actually saying this, but I can't wait to go to the bonfire now."

Now. Now she can't wait. Before—oh no, *that* was not going to be fun when it was just me and her, but suddenly *now* it's an amazing adventure. Granted, we weren't going as a couple, more as a team, but *still.*

Maybe she senses my brain convulsing next to her because she quickly adds, "Remember, Bud, we thought we'd just go and be bored and make fun of it? Taking notes on the lameness? Now we have something cool to look forward to."

"Yep," I say.

Reggie says, "I'm stoked about this. I know we've only been together a month, but we're ready. We finalize our set list tomorrow."

"What kind of music?" Nikki asks.

"We've been having some creative differences over that, which I'm sure we can iron out by this weekend. I guess you could say we're a fusion of metal/performance art/jazz. We try to elevate the form."

"Have you named the band yet?" I ask, trying to seem interested instead of merely petulant.

"We're called Blüdphärt."

"Blood Fart?"

He says, "There are umlauts."

Nikki says, "Cool," drawing it out into a thousand *ooooooo*s.

"You've never suffered through Bonfire Night," Reggie says to me. "It's so rah-rah, you'll hurl. It sucks almost as much as Homecoming, and just wait till you witness *that.*"

I nod and smile fakely.

"What's the matter?" says Nikki.

"Nothing."

"What's that grinding noise?"

"Just my teeth," I say. "And it's called 'bruxing,' not grinding. That's the authentic dental term."

"Want a ride home?" Reggie asks. Nikki practically leaps into his SUV.

"No," I say, even though it kills me.

"Come on, Bud," Nikki calls from the passenger seat. And I see it: me in the backseat like the family pet, the whining child, the incontinent grandma.

"No, thanks. I've got like ten million errands to run." I turn and try to wave backward over my shoulder like Trevor and half the population of normal people do, but it feels stupid and wrong, like I'm doing an over-the-shoulder puppet show. I walk around the parking lot to the front of the school and the 290 Touhy bus stop two blocks away.

It's true, you know. I do have errands to run. I have work to do and things to plan. And what some of this work should be became clear to me on this walk of shame to the bus stop. As I wait there, it starts to rain, and the temperature plummets. Perfect.

CHAPTER ELEVEN

Friday. I sneak out of the pep rally in the darkened gym auditorium after five minutes. Sister Tim doesn't see me slide off the edge of the bleachers and drop to the floor. The kids who do notice just think it is one of my dork moves.

When the gridiron Sheep come pounding across the floor in their blue-and-gold uniforms and the student body erupts in cheers, standing to applaud and stomp their feet, I sidle down the aisles toward the locker room entrance. Teachers are always supposed to keep watch on the exits during assemblies, but right now most of them are too misty-eyed or hyped-up to pay attention. I cannot understand why teachers would give a damn about a pep rally and a bunch of adolescent football players and their 0–4 record. But then there's a lot of things I don't understand.

In the locker room, you can feel the vibration and hear the booming echoes of the pep rally. I stop and look at the lockers, innocent in their beige-ness. Why are gym lockers exactly the right size to stuff skinny people into? At Sullivan the janitor rescued me the first time the golf team stuffed me into a locker, but the second time, the gym teacher heard my screams and let me out. Those guys had wrapped a nasty, mildewed towel around my head with electrical tape—towelhead, get it? The tape was stuck to the hair at the nape of my neck. It hurt like a bitch when the gym teacher yanked it off. He looked irritated. Irritated with me, as if I had asked for it.

I hear footsteps behind me. There's a row of lockers blocking me from sight, so I stand perfectly still. The footsteps stop. Scenarios run through my head—all of them end in me peering through the locker slats from the inside. I'm never going back in there. I ball up my hands into fists, prepared to fight, which isn't that hilarious if you stop to think that 1) I have perfected a number of fencing strategies that use my opponents' tactics against them, and 2) I have a stockpile of rage that could give me superhuman strength.

Then the footsteps start again, and from around the end of the lockers Colin McCool appears, the boy I injured with my rope climb. I breathe a sigh of relief, then notice that he's coming for me, hands balled up. I raise my palms and say, "Whoa," like he's a charging mustang.

He stops dead in front of me. "What are you doing in here?" His voice is squeaky yet still menacing.

I parry with "What are *you* doing in here?"

"Student Council class rep, room 230," he says by way of explanation, which explains nothing. "I saw you sneak in. No one's supposed to leave during the pep rally."

"So? It's not like you're a hall monitor. As a class rep, you have no jurisdiction here."

He crosses his arms in front of his chest. I notice that he's still trying to make a fist with the hand that has the broken finger, the one in the gigantic splint. He's about my size. I could take him.

He says, "You did it on purpose. I saw you."

"Saw what?"

"The rope climb! You fell on me on purpose. I saw you look down at me, then open your hands and drop."

"That's insane. Why would I do that?"

"That's what I've been trying to figure out. At first I thought you were picking on me, not like I haven't had my fair share of *that*. Everyone laughed when I started crying. Not only did it hurt, but you ruined my chances of taking first chair for the guitar mass. Very original: pick on the band nerd."

The idea that I would pick on someone else is so absurd, I don't know whether to be flattered or insulted. Colin commands an army of geeks, the band nerds, but he's far from ostracized. Geeks with a common interest or ability are never the lowest of the low.

He goes on. "But then I heard your friend's band got the headlining gig for Bonfire Night tomorrow, and it all made sense."

I pretend to glance at my watch. "This is fascinating, but I have an appointment, so if you can just cut to the chase—"

He shoves me with his good hand. "With me on the disabled list, my band has to bow out! We were supposed to play, it was all set, then suddenly some jerk falls on me during the rope climb, and now Civilian Swine is out and Blüdphärt is in."

I pause, processing this. "You're in Civilian Swine? But I heard your drummer has mono, and that's why you're not playing."

"He does, but so what? He's only the drummer. I could

have easily replaced him with John Piche from jazz band."

I shake my head. This is too ludicrous and paranoid even for me. "You think I sabotaged your band so that Blüdphärt could get your gig? With all due respect to mentally ill people, that is *crazy*. I would never purposely hurt someone who had done nothing to me. I suck at the rope climb and most other sporting activities, so anyone could tell you that it was only a matter of time before I injured myself or someone else."

"But you didn't injure *yourself*," he says.

I try to push past him, but he shoves me again. This time I lose my footing and actually stumble back into the lockers. I reassess this situation. He's stronger than he looks, and he's got unstable anger on his side. I start to speak in that prisoner-calming voice that Dr. Elliott uses, but Colin takes a step forward and interrupts me.

"You know what I think? *You* think you're still back at your old school. Yes, I know where you went. Lots of people do, because lots of people have been talking about you lately. Everyone knows there's a huge gang problem at Sullivan. What are you anyway, Mexican?"

"I'm not Mexican," I say, anger boiling up. I spit it out: "I'm Iranian."

"Oh wow, even better," he says. "Then for sure you need to know we don't tolerate violence here at Magnificat."

"Oh, like pushing people into lockers—that kind of violence?"

"Retaliation is not violence. It's standing up for yourself."

You got that right, brother. I lower my shoulder and shove into him as I charge past. He falls, of course, but you know what? I've got other things to worry about.

"Sorry," I shout back over my shoulder, hoping he didn't break any more fingers. Nothing personal. Collateral damage.

I book down the hallway. Mrs. Kobunski must hear something, because she peeks out from the front office. Her broccoli rubber band is invisible from here, but I know it's there. I tear around the corner where the wings intersect and catch the blur of my reflection in the "You Can Make a Difference" mirror. I don't think Kobunski sees me. The lunch ladies are in the caf, but they don't see me either. Quietly, I open the door to the service stairs underneath the main staircase. Usually it's locked, but I cornered the junior janitor (the burnout who mows the archery field) as he was coming out this morning, and I told him about the rapidly overflowing toilet in the boys' second-floor bathroom.

"Wh—whut?" he drawled, his bleary eyes unable to register anything like comprehension.

"David-Earl," I said, looking at his name tag, "you'd better get up there before the toilets flood the second floor."

He bolted down the hallway before the stairway door closed behind him. I took my opportunity to slide a piece of tape over the lock. I feel kind of bad about the overflowing toilet—I'd flushed several tube socks—but it had to be done.

Now I make sure no one sees me enter the service stairs, and then I close the door behind me and head down to the boiler room. It's easy to find my way.

On assembly days, Mr. Santos is usually tending to outside tasks with the groundskeeping staff. If the weather is bad, he'll stay inside and tackle jobs that can't usually be performed while classes are in session, like vacuuming the library or anything else too noisy or unsightly for the student body to witness. That's how I know the boiler room should be empty. I pay attention to these things.

Most school boiler rooms seem to be the same: in addition to the actual boiler, plumbing pipes, tools, circuit breakers, and backup generators, there is an annex where the custodial staff can hang out and leave their personal belongings. There's a peg for the building and classroom keys. In no time at all I find the keys I want—they've been left behind by David-Earl—and swipe them. I'll make copies at lunch (I'll have to sneak out because open campus is only for seniors, but I'll cross that bridge later) and return them before the end of the day. I won't have to leave the tape over the service door lock because I can make a copy of that key later. See how well the plan is taking shape? And it's not even ten o'clock. It's like I was meant to do this.

There's a circuit breaker attached to the wall. I open the little door and find that inside are two columns of circuits with the corresponding area of the school typed on a label next to each one, along with a crude blueprint of the building with all the alarm codes written by the exterior doors. The codes are right there for anyone to see! I write down all the alarm codes.

On the worktable under the keys, I spy that BlackBerry device that holds the combination to all the school lockers. I won't lie: I'm dying to get my hands on that thing. But that's just pushing my luck. Maybe another day.

I've only been gone from the pep rally for fifteen minutes, including the confrontation with Colin in the locker room, but that might be long enough to be missed. Running into him there really fouled up my scheme. He better not narc on me to Sister Tim or anyone else. If he does, I guess I can trot out my anxiety-attack excuse. I had an attack a few days ago and took myself to the nurse after I fell and bonked my head on the drinking fountain, so it's on record that these things happen to me.

Back in the gym, Principal McNeill is at the podium onstage delivering a Bonfire Night propaganda speech, wiping the sweat out of his droopy mustache, his five strands of hair flopping into his face. It's hard to read his eyes from down here, but I'd say he's sincere; he's really into this. The faces of the students I pass look the same. Suddenly, I feel extremely alone in this room of fifteen hundred people. How can they feel so attached to school, to these traditions? How can it make them feel like they belong? Maybe if I felt that, I wouldn't be snaking my way through the crowd, a handful of stolen keys in my pocket. I'm not dogging on my fellow classmates for feeling like part of the school community. I wish I felt like that, really I do. And I think I've tried, in my own way. It's just not the path for me.

When I get near the bleachers, Sister Tim sees me, so I don't try to sneak by.

"Where were you?" she asks.

I place my hand over my stomach. "The bathroom. I wasn't feeling well."

"Even so, you need to ask permission before you just run off."

"I'm sorry, Sister. I wasn't thinking." Then I pull out the big guns. "I didn't want to have an accident," I whisper, twisting my features into a mask of embarrassment.

I don't know if she's fooled by this tactic—after all, she's been around the block a few times—but her eyes travel back to the stage. McNeill winds down by begging the coach not to let Gordon Tech humiliate us on our home turf tomorrow night.

Sister Tim says, "Next time, tell me, and I'll write you a hall pass for the nurse."

I sit beside her on the bottom bench of the bleachers. Her hands are really gnarled, with enormous knuckles on each bony finger. Classic case of arthritis. I never noticed it before. McNeill asks us to rise for the singing of the school song.

"Give me a hand, boy," Sister Tim says, and I cup her elbow and help her to her feet. Her arm feels like a wooden ball connected to a stick, a human Tinkertoy. She cannot weigh a hundred pounds. She's one of the few nuns left at Magnificat. Mostly, lay teachers have taken over. I wonder what she thinks of that. Unlike the younger nuns who wear regular clothes, she wears an old-fashioned habit. The fabric spills around her in a black pool.

She sings in a shaky vibrato, in dedication to the school and what it probably once stood for.

> *"Here's to our dear alma mater belov'd,*
>
> *Let us give thanks to her name a-bove.*
>
> *Shepherd us back from the wolf's hungry pa-a-ack—*
>
> *Keep us close, Mag-nif-i-cat."*

The other teachers look like they are mouthing the words

as they prepare for the postassembly stampede from the gym. Sister Tim's eyes shine. For a second I feel really scummy for lying to her, then the song is over and the bell rings, and I get lost in the mass exodus like everyone else.

I get the keys copied at lunch and return them to the boiler room without anyone noticing. It wasn't hard to slip out during open campus. I told the hall monitor, a friendless fat senior girl, that I needed to get something out of my car and did I need to get a hall pass from the lunchroom faculty first? She shook her head. I am not picking on her because she is friendless and fat; I am just stating a fact. Some hall monitors volunteer for the position because they are Nazis who like to boss people around; others volunteer because they have nothing else to do during lunch or free period.

When I see Nikki later on in Modern Lit, she says, "Where were you at lunch? I wanted to show you some additions I made to my chart."

I'd forgotten, in the furor of stealing things, about the growing list of people who detest me and want to see me burn. "I was in the library. Preparing some things for our Bonfire Night assignment."

"You're quite dedicated to the newspaper, aren't you?"

I tell her, "There are some issues I want to explore."

Ms. Viola comes in then, a minute before the late bell. So I have less than sixty seconds to make my speech.

"Nikki," I begin, "about Bonfire Night, I know we said we'd just meet under the bleachers tomorrow at some point during the game, but I was thinking I could come pick you up first, if you want."

"Oh, don't bother. I can just meet you."

"Well, I really want to do this thing right. Covering it for the paper, I mean. I want to be on time and all that, and not be tied to the bus schedule, so if I drive, I'll have to ask my mom for the car. Saturday nights she likes to meet her adult education classmates for coffee, but for Bonfire Night she might make an exception and let me drive. . . ." Oh *God*, stop the verbal vomit. I can't say what I really want to say: that I have stolen keys to the school and I want to break in tomorrow and I want her with me.

I swear she can see right into the corners of my brain where I hide all the bad things about myself, but she shrugs. "Okay, whatevs."

The bell rings, and Ms. Viola smacks the top of her desk to get everyone to quiet down. She holds up her copy of *As I Lay Dying* and begins to lecture. I try to pay attention but can't. The title of that book hits too close to home. Viola's in a craptastic mood. She actually screams, "Shut up!" at girls who are whispering. I zone out and think about who hates me so much that they'd want to write those letters, and before I know it I've begun a mental shit list for Magnificat without even realizing it.

On my way out I stop by Viola's desk.

"What do you want?" she mutters without raising her eyes from her papers.

I ease myself onto the corner of her desk, but her head snaps up, and she glares at me. "*Off* my desk."

I comply. "Let me ask you this, Ms. Viola. For this Bonfire Night gig, what is the preferred dress code?"

"Dress code? It doesn't matter. Wear whatever you want," she says. "I have to prepare for archery practice now. We get the field for only thirty minutes today because the football team needs extra space to run drills before the 'big game' tomorrow." You can hear the venom when she says "big game."

"You like doing that, don't you?" I say. "Being the archery coach." It surprises me that she likes anything, but it also gives me hope.

"Yes, I do. I haven't been involved with a lot of clubs here except for archery and the newspaper. When Sister Evarista's rheumatism got too bad a few years ago, they handed me the reins to the archery club. Her elbows were shot; she couldn't hold the bow. I was sorry about that, but to be honest, I'm glad her injury worked out in my favor. An archer is worthless without the elbows."

I say, "Personally, I think her walleye would have been more of a menace on the field than her elbow."

She opens her mouth, and this completely baffling sound comes out. I realize what it is. When Ms. Viola laughs, it sounds like the rusty hinge on a gate that hasn't been opened in ten years. She starts to rise.

"Wait, I just have a couple more items here to check off: Is this Bonfire Night like a big date night? Or more of a group thing? How much do the refreshments cost? Since a band is playing, do people dance?" She's staring at me like I'm certifiable. "I'm trying to be thorough. You know, because I'm writing about it for the paper."

"Wow. That is thorough. I don't really know the answers to all your questions. I'll just say, go with your gut."

"That's horrible advice."

She mutters as she glances at her watch. "You kids are so gung-ho about school. I find it very weird. When I was a kid, we rebelled against everything."

"There's nothing to rebel against. Most of us get whatever we want no matter how we act. We'll go to colleges our parents pay for, drink alcohol they buy for us, drive their cars, and cyberbully each other on the tablets and smartphones they've given us. There's nothing to fight for."

Her eyes are locked on me. "I weep for your generation."

"But *I'm* not like that. My parents flip out if I leave my Godzillas laying around. And Nikki Vrdolyak's not like that. We're unsatisfied. We're on the outside."

She shrugs with a disdainful look and rises from the desk, snapping shut her briefcase. "Your rebellion has been co-opted and sold back to you."

"Don't get me wrong, Ms. Viola. I hate authority." The bell rings, and we have one minute before we are both late for seventh period. Kids for the next class file in, barely glancing at us. I stare at them as they pass me by. I jerk my head in their direction and say, "But I hate them more."

After school, Nikki and I take the bus to Charmers Cafe, where we pool enough money to split a bagel. She offers to buy it outright, but I say no way. Not trying to be macho, but it's hard to feel like a man when you can't even cough up the change for a bagel. She shows me her chart with some new color-coded notes, but I can't concentrate on it. I can only think of going to Bonfire Night with her.

"So I'll pick you up at seven tomorrow," I say. "Wear whatever you like."

She picks a poppy seed out of her teeth. "Really? I can wear whatever I want? Thanks!" She laughs, and I do, too. Her eyes don't leave my face.

"What are you looking at?" I ask.

She blinks and shakes her head rapidly. "Nothing. I mean, your teeth . . . they're like. . . really big and white. I don't know. Just never noticed."

Instead of making my usual remark about four years of medieval-looking orthodontia, I don't say anything; and I don't look away, though it takes every ounce of self-control I have. I'm sick of being so self-conscious. Women are not attracted to the neurotic type. Have you ever tried to hold the gaze of someone who's just complimented you? It's hard as hell. At least I think it was a compliment.

Some girls come in and grab a table near us. I recognize them from school; one is in Chemistry with me.

"That girl is checking you out," says Nikki.

I don't know if that is true—having so little experience with anyone "checking me out" other than psychiatric professionals. Nikki cleans her glasses on her shirt as we leave. I hold the door open for her, and the girl from Chemistry watches us leave.

"See you tomorrow night," I say to Nikki as we part ways at the corner of Jarvis and Ashland.

"Wear whatever you like," she calls back.

I'm almost home when the skateboarding slackers from the flophouse on the next block shoot out of the alley across my path. It's nearly dark, and one of them just about runs me over. He's a skinhead with a tattooed neck. Something in his face looks familiar. I recognize him as a guy I used to go to school with at Sullivan.

He used to be clean-cut and kind of preppy. He was on the golf team. He helped stuff me in the locker.

He eyes me as he pulls up short. "Hey," he says, "I know you."

I shake my head and try to walk by, but he blocks me.

"No, I do. Oh yeah!" He snaps his fingers, laughing. "Towelhead!"

His friends don't know me, but they laugh, too.

I mean, seriously—towelhead? Still?

"You still there? At Sullivan?"

"No," I say.

"Me neither."

"Well, see you around," I say, trying to walk by. No luck there.

He stands in front of me. "You miss setting off bombs, towelhead?"

Without thinking I say, "You miss the golf team?"

His friends erupt in laughter. "*Golf* team?!"

The guy narrows his bloodshot eyes at me. Apparently he was keeping his golfing past on the down low.

I know what's about to come; there's no escaping it. I might as well throw myself full tilt into it. He's still trying to block me, and I plow right into him so I can knock him off balance and get by. Maybe my fear, panic, and sobriety will carry me fast enough on my feet to make it home.

No luck again, though. Thanks, Universe. I'm just past him when blinding pain cracks against the back of my skull and sends me flying face-first onto the pavement. He hit me on the back of my head with the deck of his skateboard. I clutch my head, and the blood is hot and sticky as it seeps into my hair and between my fingers.

"Dude! What the hell?" Even his friends are shocked.

"You don't know this guy," the skinhead says. "You don't know what a towelhead shit he is."

I can hardly see. My vision is tripled, like in those old cartoons of drunk people. But I have got to get up and out of here because I do not want to end up dead on the sidewalk. Not like this.

Less than a block to go, but even if I could see and stand well enough to run it, I don't want these guys to know where I live. If they find that out, then it is *all over*.

I hear barking and feel paws, panting, and rancid breath on my face. Rex. Oh God, this is my savior?

But then a voice: "Rex. Rex! Come back here." The hippie from next door, getting closer. "Hey, kid, are you okay? What's going on?"

The skateboarders take off. The hippie bends down and sees the blood. "Oh shit! Are you okay? What do I do? I'm sorry, I know you're my neighbor, but I don't know your name. Do you want me to get your parents? Do they speak English?"

"No, no," I say, struggling to stand. "I'm fine, really."

"You're bleeding a lot, kid," he says.

"Just . . . just help me get back home." I lean on him, and we walk slowly. I feel bad; he's got me and Rex wobbling on either side. "Those guys, they're not following us, are they?"

My neighbor says no. We get to my gate, and he wants to come in and help me upstairs, but no way. I can't explain to him that if my parents see me like this, they will somehow blame me and end up sending me to military school.

I say thanks, at least I hope I do, because at this point it's all getting pretty fuzzy.

I make it up one flight of stairs until I reach Dariush's door, and then I collapse against it.

CHAPTER TWELVE

I sleep it off on my brother's futon and don't wake up till noon the next day. You're not supposed to sleep after a head injury. Concussion and all that. Oh well.

Dariush told my parents I had a panic attack in the hallway last night. All my parents have to hear are the words *panic attack*, and they cringe and turn away, shutting me out. Maybe it's a cultural thing, maybe it's generational, but their embarrassment about my mental problems overrides any parental concern they may have.

My brother makes me some tea and toast and gives me two Tylenol when I wake up. My head throbs like a jackhammer. The lump on the back of my head is huge, but luckily I have a lot of stupid hair to cover it up. There are no visible injuries to my face, so I guess nobody has to know what happened.

"Have Mom and Dad come down yet?" I ask.

"Mom's at her birding class. Sorry, but you know nothing stands in the way of adult education. Dad called earlier to check on you, and I told him you were asleep."

"Oh. Okay."

"Don't be disappointed. You know how they are. Be glad

they're not hovering. If they saw what really happened to you, they'd never let you out of the house again."

Dariush asks who did this to me, but I tell him I don't know. If I tell him it's the skateboarders, he'll tear over there and then what? Try to attack them with his Smiths CDs and two-foot bong? I say I think it was a gangbanger, a mugger, someone rolling drunks for the evening. I'm not sure if he believes me.

I rub the bump on my head and hope I can wash off all the dried blood before the bonfire tonight. The pain is intense but not unbearable. As for the skateboarders, I'll add their block to the list of places/people/things that I need to avoid for the rest of my life—a list that keeps growing longer and more depressing.

By nighttime I manage to hobble around without excruciating pain. In my room, I throw myself together. I feel lost without the safety of my school uniform. I'm rethinking the baggy Walmart jeans. Instead of looking like a rap star, I look like a homeless man. I change into an impulse buy from the thrift store: a skinny black suit that is a lot tighter than I thought it would be. I check my reflection in the bathroom mirror. The 'fro is tamed, thanks to product. No cystic acne. So from the neck up: tolerable.

I try to hurry by the kitchen, but my mother, who is attuned to my speed like a radar detector, flies out and collars me.

"What about dinner?"

"I'm not hungry, I have to get to the bonfire, late bye seeyalater." I try to squirm out of her grasp, but it's like a zombie death grip.

"A suit? It is a big event, then?"

"No! It's just—I don't have anything else to wear."

She tugs at the shoulder seam. "But it's so tight."

"That's the style."

She appraises me for a moment more and then sighs, smiling. "Oh. Well, I suppose it is rather smart. Your shoulders are very broad for this jacket, but you do look so handsome. Let me get Baba and the camera."

"Mom, please! I gotta go."

But she trots off, holding up one finger to indicate that she'll be only a minute. When she drags Dad in, she presents me with a flourish and says, "Ta-da!"

Dad has a million questions, but when he learns the bonfire is a social event and not a banquet honoring academic triumphs, his interest flags. He asks if I have a date, but I explain that nobody dates; people simply go out in groups. He asks who my group is, and I say it's just me and this one girl.

"And that is not a date?" he asks.

"Not really." But then I think better of this because I want to take the car. "Well, sort of."

"You must drive then," Mom insists. "Khaleh Rana can drive me to my class's coffee outing tonight. And you have to eat something. Let me wrap you up falafel." We have falafel around the house like other people have hot dogs. Arman and Dorri are eating their falafel at the kitchen table, and they giggle at my suit, but I know they are laughing only because it is something different. They are not mean little kids. Mom made pita today, and it's warm and soft around the falafel, which is sizzling hot right out of the pan; the veggies and tahini are cool. It's like the perfect food.

"Don't drip tahini on your suit," Mom warns.

I head to the door, but Dad calls for me to wait, and then appears with the potted orchid he keeps in the bathroom. "For your lapel," he says, and before I can protest, he snips off a white blossom and jams it into my buttonhole. Mom runs for her sewing kit to find a pin to keep the orchid fastened to my jacket. Then they snip off some more blossoms for my "date," and Mom binds them up with *dental floss* and puts them in a clear plastic take-out box that she had cleaned and saved.

"It's all I've got," she says. Dad snaps my picture without warning, and they wave goodbye at the door like I am leaving the Old Country on a frigate, bound for America.

I park Dad's old Subaru station wagon down the block from Nikki's, noticing that here on the nice streets, there are still bums and crazies loitering in the alleys. As I walk along, I whistle a song from my Chet Baker album, "Let's Get Lost." Dariush and I play it on his turntable every Tuesday night while I do Ryndak's impossible Chemistry homework and he plays poker with his other unemployed friends. Dariush has started boxing up his stuff for the move. I hope the turntable is the last thing he'll pack. A homeless guy rooting through a Dumpster yells, "Shut up!" I annoy even the schizos.

I check my breath as I head up Nikki's sidewalk. Minty. Then I see my full reflection in the glass front door. Oh, this freaking *suit*. I thought it would be kind of retro cool, but I look like a dork from the 1960s—Bud Hess, insurance salesman.

I shift the take-out box to my other hand and ring the doorbell. Nikki answers after a minute, drinking a Coke and eating a sandwich. She is wearing jeans, a green vintage-y sweater, and black Converse low-tops.

"Why are you dressed like that?" we both say at the same time.

"I thought this Bonfire Night was a big deal," I say.

She motions for me to come in and shuts the door behind me. "Maybe for the herd, but, I mean, we're just covering it for the newspaper and hanging out and making fun of people." A moment passes, and then she adds, "But that is a cool suit. You look like you should be laid out at Pickett Johnson's Funeral Home."

"You can put on a dress if you want," I say. "I'll wait. We're not in a rush."

"A dress? A full-on dress? For the bonfire? Dude, please."

"I guess that wouldn't be practical," I admit. "Sorry. I'm out of my depth here."

"No way, for reals?" She smirks.

I follow her into the kitchen. I don't want to be *el disgusto* here, but I'm just saying: her jeans look pretty good from this angle. I'm torn because I want her to think of this as a real date where you dress up, but at the same time, I think she looks amazing already.

"I have something for you," she says. She picks up a photo by the laptop that's in an alcove in the kitchen, and she hands it to me. It's the one she took of us on the train on our first nonsexual date. In it her arm is around me, and neither of us is smiling. I slip the photo into my inner pocket. I can feel it there.

"And I have something for you." I hand her the take-out box with the orchids in it. "You don't have to wear it, though. It's just . . . I mean, my mom thought . . ."

She stares at it. "No, it's nice. I'll put it in a vase."

"Or I can pin it on you."

"Uh-uh. I don't let anyone hold a pin near my boobs. Sorry."

This is all my mother's damn fault. "If you don't like it, please don't feel—"

"I *said* I liked it already."

"Yeah, I saw your face when I handed you the box. You looked like I was offering you a severed head."

"Now that," she sighed, "would be cool." She puts the stupid corsage in a crystal vase and sets it on the windowsill.

"Aren't your parents here? I thought they might want to meet me. And take a commemorative photo."

"Look, I told them I was covering the bonfire for the paper, Bud. I didn't know it was going to be this *big thing* with you. They like to take the twins out for wholesome family fun on Saturday nights. I think they're at the shooting range."

She takes her bike messenger bag off the table, roots around in it, and then puts on lip gloss, which makes me look at and think of her mouth in a whole new light.

"Whoa," I say.

"Don't be stupid," she tells me. "You want a Coke?"

I say, "Okay," because at this point I will take whatever I can get.

The lavender haze of dusk surrounds the school and the grounds. There's supposed to be a light rain, and we've heard distant booms of thunder, but the game goes on no matter what. The football field is all lit up: the towering stadium lights glow against the clouds like orange halos on gray angels.

Nikki takes out her camera. "What should we hit first? The bonehead jocks or the pitiful alumni reminiscing and weeping by the bonfire?"

"What about the tweekers smoking underneath the bleachers?" I suggest.

We cut through the field that leads up to the stands. You can see the telltale blaze from the joints every so often. Nikki snaps a few photos with her telephoto lens. She explains, "Ammunition. They may come in handy someday."

Under the bleachers we see it's not tweekers, just the few deadhead kids at Magnificat, the ones who play Hacky Sack on the quad and always have leaves in their hair. They're pretty harmless, so we stop taking photos and talk to them. I turn down many spliffs. I will say this about deadheads: they love to share.

One deadhead jumps at a noise nearby and says, "It's the five-oh!" His friends don't know whether to freak or to collapse in hysterics, so they do a little of both. It turns out it's not the "five-oh" or the "po-po" but only Ms. Viola on patrol. Nikki and I head right for her, giving the deadheads a chance to escape.

"What's going on here?" She looks over our shoulders at the departing kids. The scent of pot lingers in the air, but I am so tightly wound, no one in their right mind would accuse me of getting high.

"Taking pictures and writing up notes for our article," says Nikki.

Ms. Viola tells us, "Most of the teachers have been summoned to police the bonfire." So she *is* the po-po. I stifle a laugh. Maybe I've gotten a contact buzz.

We walk with her out from under the bleachers, which

are filled up now that the game has begun. I say, "Ms. Viola, I've never seen you wear jeans before." Teachers always look bizarre when you see them in casual clothes.

She looks down at her legs. "I'm going to try and be hip this year. Is it too late for me to buy those boots with the fur on them?"

"I think we better get over to the bonfire so we can take pictures," says Nikki.

Ms. Viola gazes at the darkness behind the south bleachers, where the archery field lies. She says, "You're not going to watch the game?"

We shrug.

"Inwardly, I rejoice when the football team loses," she admits. "I love to see the disappointment on the players' faces." She turns her gaze back to us. "They are taking the archery field away from me, and the archers, too."

Nikki and I exchange glances.

Viola continues. "Principal McNeill just told me the Finance Council has voted to use my field to expand the football stadium. There won't be an Archery Club next year."

"They're getting rid of archery? Can't you practice on the baseball diamond or something?" I ask her.

Actual tears glimmer in her eyes. "Archery doesn't make any money. We're just a club and have no financial backing like the sports teams do. So they're disbanding us."

"Wow. That's horrible," Nikki says.

"I remember when the team finally stopped shooting me in the back. I knew they had accepted me. It was the best I've ever felt. And by next year it'll all be over."

She wipes her nose on the sleeve of her corduroy jacket,

leaving a shiny trail. The fabric is worn thin there, as if she's used her sleeve for lots of nose wiping over the years.

"Please don't tell the archery team," she says. "They don't know yet."

I expect to see rage in Ms. Viola's eyes, but all I see is defeat. Like Dariush said, this is what happens when you get old: you lie down and take it. But I am not old.

A roar goes up from the stands. "We better go," says Nikki, pulling my sleeve.

"I'm sorry," I say to Ms. Viola. "I just want you to know that . . . that . . ."

I can't even finish it. The look on Viola's face kills me. I wish I could tell her that I won't let the school, the administration, whoever, get away with doing this to her, to us; but what can I do? I'm just Bud Hess, transfer student, underachiever, nobody.

CHAPTER THIRTEEN

Once Ms. Viola leaves, Nikki and I stare at each other. "That poor old bag," she says. "I feel sorry for her." The wind is picking up, and she shivers even though she's wearing her red plaid hunting jacket, a hundred-foot-long red scarf, and a winter hat.

I have no desire to watch the bonfire. My head is pounding again. From my back pocket, I withdraw the set of keys I copied. Having them close makes me feel safe and important. I jingle them at Nikki and glance back at the school. "Do you want to go on an adventure?"

She doesn't hesitate. A huge grin breaks across her face, and the next thing I know, we have disappeared down the dark footpath that leads away from the track.

We reach the east-wing door. I'm poised with the key above the lock when Nikki places her hand on my shoulder and asks, "What about the alarm?" Despite my clothes, I can practically feel her skin on mine.

"No problem," I say.

I've already memorized all the codes and once we are inside, I unlock the alarm box and punch in the code on the keypad to disarm the system. Inside the school it's totally quiet and murky, though not pitch-black. There's enough light to see the admiration gleaming in Nikki's eyes.

"How in the world . . .?" She just shakes her head while I shrug modestly. I have dreamed of moments like this.

We head down the hall toward the cafeteria. For the first time, I feel as if I belong here. Instead of choking fear and anxiety, a sense of calm confidence overtakes me. Maybe this is what it's like for good students and popular people. I feel more at home here right now than I ever have in my own apartment. I run my hands over the cinder block walls, their bumps and grooves familiar to me in a new way.

I dig around in my pockets until I find enough change to buy us a candy bar from the vending machines to split.

Nikki says, "If we rock the machine, the candy will just fall down."

"But that would be stealing," I say.

She looks at me. "You're weird."

What can I say? I do have a moral code, warped as it may be. For a second, memories of taking money out of my mom's wallet flash in my mind, but that is different. Technically it's stealing, I know, but it doesn't feel that way. It feels like restoring some sort of justice.

We go back to the east wing toward the gym. In the lobby, we pause by the trophy case. Inside are mounted black-and-white photos of athletes from long ago. I get a creepy feeling gazing into their dead faces.

"Check it out." Nikki points to a picture. It's the archery team; the photo is from five years ago. Ms. Viola stands off to the side towering above everyone else, eyes already sunken, hair already like the Bride of Frankenstein, sweater vest already violating our Eighth Amendment rights. She's wearing a skirt for once yet somehow manages to look masculine.

Nikki says, "If they take archery away from her, she'll go truly bonkers and probably mow down people in David-Earl's ride-on tractor."

"They'll take that field over my dead body," I say. I don't know where that comes from, but it makes me feel powerful to say it.

Nikki steps away from the trophy case. "So now what should we do?"

I lead by example. We tear off down the hallway full speed. We slam doors and turn things upside down. Not vandalism, just leaving our mark on the world. We throw away campaign flyers for Homecoming Court. We jump down a half flight of steps in the north-wing stairwell and write our names in permanent ink under the stairs.

We laugh because we thought we'd be the first to come down here and do that, but there are tons of names scribbled here.

"There's barely any room for ours." Nikki leans against me as she scrawls hers in the farthest corner. Her shoulder presses against my chest.

"Good thing my dad changed my name, because there'd never be room for the old me here."

"What was it again? Hussein?"

"Hessamizadeh. It means 'he who goes from conquest to conquest spreading fire in his wake.'"

She laughs so hard, shaking against me. Because I am high on this break-in and this wave of happiness, I reach over to her and grab her hand. I put my other hand behind her head and pull her close to me, like in the movies, and I can't keep my eyes from traveling all over her face. I don't kiss her, even though I'm desperate for it, because I know she won't want to, and I am not that guy.

Her laughter slows down. She squeezes my hand. Then she gently pushes away. Why can't she feel the electricity that passes between us? Or maybe it's not electricity, just the shock of opposites coming together. Her hand is warm and dry, and mine's wet and clammy. I try to gauge her reaction, but she gives nothing away.

I pull her up and we leave the stairwell, and in the natural way of these things, we eventually drop hands and walk on.

We're about to head back to the east-wing entrance when I stop. "Wait a second," I say. "What am I thinking? We forgot to hit the front office." Which is the main reason I wanted to bust in here tonight.

I turn, and she trails behind me. "Why are we going there?" Her voice is uncertain. "Maybe we should leave, Bud. We've been in here awhile."

"You afraid?" I call back.

"No." There's defiance in her voice now. I knew there would be.

When she catches up with me at the office, I am already at work.

She asks what I'm doing, and I say, "I don't know. Looking for stuff." And that's the thing: sometimes I get hyped up and make these wild plans—like breaking into school—just because I *can*. But if you corner me, I can't really tell you why. Maybe I want some power because so much has been ripped from me.

I'm behind the counter, rooting around in the In and Out boxes. I riffle through the teachers' cubbyhole mailboxes. I take a cursory glance into McNeill's office but don't go in. That seems, I don't know, more illegal somehow.

I pocket some peppermint candies. Stamps, a small Maglite flashlight, a ministapler—I always wanted one of those. Totems. Then I try the keys on the locked bottom drawer of Mrs. Kobunski's desk until it opens, and there I discover the real windfall.

Here it is in my hand: the BlackBerry device that holds all the locker combos at Magnificat. And who knows what else it holds? Passwords for faculty e-mail? The possibilities are endless. It's not the same one I saw in the custodial annex; this one has FRONT OFFICE stamped on it.

Nikki has not come around the counter. She can't see what I'm doing. She keeps poking her head into the hallway, worried someone may be coming. I understand. I used to feel nervous, too, the first few times I broke into places.

"Almost done here," I call out. My fingers close around the BlackBerry thing, but I change my mind and put it back. It's one thing to sneak into school with Nikki and run around like fools, but stealing this—not that *I* have anything against it—is a whole other game. I don't want her implicated if something goes wrong with our little adventure.

"Okay, let's go," I say as I emerge from behind the counter.

"What were you doing in there? Did you take anything?"

"A ministapler."

"Those *are* kind of awesome," she says.

I open and close the ministapler a bunch of times. It chatters like teeth. When you have stuff taken from you routinely—your name, your physical safety, your last scrap of self-esteem—even the smallest things feel like restitution. For a while anyway.

I reset the alarm and lock the doors behind us. Out now in the cold, wide-open air, I try to take her hand again, but the moment is awkward. She's still nervous from being in the front office, and she wants to get away from the school and back to the stadium. I slip my hand into my pocket instead. The surfaces of the stolen items are cool and varied; some smooth and rounded, some with sharp edges. But I can tell by feel what they all are, and each fits perfectly in my palm, as if they were created for me.

CHAPTER FOURTEEN

The Gordon Tech Rams annihilate the Sheep, 21–0. Nikki and I lose ourselves in the crowd that leaves the field, trundling off to the bonfire. Little kids run toward the cider-and-doughnuts kiosk; parents lag behind. I see people from my homeroom, Dylan included, hiding behind a stand of birch trees, pouring something from flasks into their hot cider.

Finally we reach the bonfire right at the edge of the archery field and see a group of students arguing; it's hard to hear about what, but as I look closer, I see Reggie in the middle. We move toward them.

"If you don't believe me, look it up yourself," Reggie is saying. "The four-move checkmate is a very effective strategy that, because of its mind-boggling speed, beginners will not anticipate."

Reggie sees us and waves. Nikki is looking at him with a goofy smile. Nikki Vrdolyak—who has said "smiling is for idiots" and "happiness is an illusion"—is smiling, and it's obvious she has a thing for him. A tidal wave of darkness washes over me. She will never look at me like that. I watch all of them: Reggie, Nikki, the chess players, the laughing children running around, the silly sophomore girls, the wide-eyed freshmen overwhelmed by the drama of their first Bonfire Night. The smell of the burning wood envelops everything. I think my nostril hairs are singed.

Nikki moves into the circle of chess team members and stands next to Reggie. I trail behind her, nothing at all like the movie hero I pretended to be for about two seconds back there. More like the dark horse. Or maybe like X from Nikki's chart, the unknown factor.

There's a stage set up beyond the bonfire, and Reggie's band is due to go on soon. Ms. Viola is off to the side by the hot-cider kiosk, speaking to Mr. Downie (AP Biology). The way their heads are bent toward each other, with Downie sort of cupping her elbow, makes it seems as if they like each other, which is gross. But I suppose teachers are entitled to sex, too.

Nikki is going to get a cup of cider for herself and asks if I want one. I say no. It looks too bright and thick to be drinkable. Reggie waves from the side of the stage, and I walk over while Nikki waits in line.

He's changed into some kind of rock-god outfit: red-sequined turban and black suit embroidered with skulls and crossbones. I wait for the jibe about my thrift store suit, but all he says is "You clean up nice."

"Thanks," I say, giving a formal bow. And then, with an awful *rrriiip*, my goddamn piece-of-crap funeral pants tear right up the rear seam.

I curse like I have never cursed before. It is sort of a freeing sensation. Then I hear laughter behind me—it's a couple of guys from the Engineering Club. I mean it: the Engineering Club is laughing at me. Do you know how low you have to be on the totem pole for the *Engineering Club* to feel confident about mocking you? It's unheard of.

"Duuude," says Reggie, investing weight in that one syllable.

I say, "Not a big deal. I was once chased across a grocery store parking lot by the Latin Kings. I think I can handle a pair of ripped pants."

He looks at me with new respect. I wasn't actually chased across a parking lot by gang members, but I've got to salvage what few shreds of dignity I have.

"I've got to fix this," I tell him, backing away from the bonfire, but I'm kind of stuck. Where else am I going to go? Any direction I turn will open up the view of my SpongeBob boxers to everyone. The suit coat is no help; it's so tight and short that it doesn't even cover my ass completely. Awesome.

A whiff of marijuana hits me. Then I hear snorting and giggling coming from behind me. It's those deadhead kids from under the bleachers. Our eyes meet, and in their hazy reflection I can almost see my ripped pants and underwear on full display.

They point at my pants and double over with laughter. And before I even know what's happening, one of them is filming me with his cell phone, while a girl, breathless from giggling, moans, "Oh, don't be mean! Leave him alone."

I can't understand it. I thought the deadheads were the nice druggies and the tweekers were the nasty ones. When I hear them gasp "YouTube," my heart and brain start racing, and without another thought, I race off, too.

I hide behind a tree and tell myself *Breathe*, because I'm

afraid my lungs won't do it on their own and I'll be discovered here dead in my boxers. I'll be forever remembered as that kid who died during Bonfire Night, but nobody will be able to mention it with a straight face because of SpongeBob. Fuck that. I'm not going down like a chump in my underwear.

Those deadheads—I want to kill them. Filming me. Laughing. Posting it to YouTube. I was so wrong about them.

I calm down, breathe, and then my brain starts to work again.

I reach in my coat pocket and find the ministapler.

Pants off, shivering like hell in my boxers, I sit down, switch on the Maglite, and use the ministapler to staple shut the seam of my trousers. You'd think I'd feel mortified sitting there in my underwear outdoors on school property, but it feels eerily normal.

It's time for Blüdphärt to take the stage. I walk over with the longest stride possible for a guy of average height wearing abnormally tight, stapled pants.

"Hey, where did you disappear to?" Nikki materializes at my shoulder as I push my way through the crowd gathering around the stage. She looks irritated.

I almost make up some excuse, but I want her to be in my confidence about all things. Okay, not *all* things, but more things. I haven't told her the 100 percent truth about me, and you can't build a relationship exclusively on lies. So I explain about the pants but not the video, which no doubt will make its worldwide debut before midnight.

She lifts up the tail of my coat and examines the back of my pants. "Well, they make your ass look great."

"Really?"

"Yeah. You should alter all your pants with the ministapler."

Definitely a compliment. You *know* that's only like two steps away from lust, right?

Blüdphärt starts playing, and they sound good. I think I like jazz/death metal fusion. In front of the stage, couples are juking, and isolated groups of girls hump each other's legs and butts while their dates hoot from the sidelines. The teachers look disgusted and afraid. They keep tapping kids on the shoulders and motioning for them to separate.

Nikki focuses her telephoto lens on Reggie.

"There are other things we can take pictures of," I say.

I step back, but Nikki doesn't notice. Her camera is trained on Blüdphärt, the girls around us, the boys feasting their eyes on them, the incompetent teachers. Each click of the camera sounds hungry to me, like a dog licking its chops at a sandwich out of reach. The image of that BlackBerry locker gadget appears in my mind. Imagine what I could accomplish with that thing. So many ideas run through my brain that it makes my head throb more. Everyone around me is in full chaos mode. Nikki is fixated on Reggie. Like two hundred pictures' worth.

As much as I would love to have that BlackBerry, I've already been in the school once tonight; it would be crazy to go back a second time. I don't want to go back in. *I want to go back in.* Nikki is lost in the crowd. Or I'm the one who's lost. I'm not bad, like a bad person. I don't do bad things to people. Okay, maybe I'm a bad student and a bad son, but it's not like you can kill anyone by being a bad son. I'm not a thief, not in the real sense. Nothing I take is missed. I don't steal from people. I only steal from soulless organizations, like school and my parents. I want to escape from my weird compulsions and anxiety and rage, but I can't. I grasp the keys to the school tightly in my pocket, an amulet against the darkness closing in on me.

Blüdphärt's on break. Girls who normally make fun of the Checkmates are following Reggie around. It starts to drizzle slightly. Just misting really, but the thunder echoes. I take cover by the cider kiosk. Ms. Viola is ladling out cups from a gigantic stainless steel bowl to all the people in line.

Mr. Downie asks if I want anything, but I shake my head mutely. Depression descends on me. I hate when it hits me like this out of the blue. Or maybe it's not out of the blue. Maybe it's a natural result of beatings, humiliating videos, and the parade of panic attacks.

Nikki catches up with me now that the band's on break. "You missed it. Perry, the singer, held up a lighter and lit his sleeve on fire. He's okay, just his sleeve got singed. The dumbass."

The pain in my head is blinding me, and I close my eyes. "What's the matter?"

"Nothing, except I got jumped by a skinhead last night and beaten up with a skateboard and my head's about to explode, and tonight some kids filmed me in my torn pants and they're probably uploading the video to YouTube as we speak."

Gently, she rubs the back of my head until she touches the lump.

I tell her, "It was one of my old pals from Sullivan."

She asks which kids filmed me, but I say I don't know. I mean, we have photos of the deadheads smoking weed under the bleachers. We could blackmail them. But, you know, why bother? What difference would it ultimately make? Someone new would just step in to harass me.

She looks so sorry for me, I can't stand it. "Come on, Bud. Blüdphärt's break is almost over. Let's go back."

"I don't want to," I say, and I go off in the opposite direction. I love her anger, but I won't take her pity. By the archery field, the bare branches from the buckthorn and black locust trees sway, resisting the wind. Most people don't know that those trees are poisonous. Most people probably don't even know the *names* of those trees, much less what they can do.

This train of thought comforts me. It takes my mind off things. I start singing "Let's Get Lost."

Behind me someone says, "You have a good voice."

I turn around to confront whoever it is that's obviously screwing with me, but all I see is this short girl from AP Bio looking at me as earnestly as a puppy. She's sitting on the ground with a small notebook on her lap, writing with a light-up pen.

"Really?" I ask.

She bobs her head, and her hair swings in dark, glossy waves on either side of her face. I can't remember her name. All I can think of is that in her outfit—black pants, red sweater, black shoes—she looks like a bridge commander from *Star Trek*.

"Mila," she says, reading my mind. "From Downie's Bio. Second period."

"Right, I know. Bud Hess," I say.

She gestures to the spot next to her and moves over, making room for me.

"What are you doing?" I ask.

She looks down at her notebook. "Just writing. My friends are dancing, or they were before the singer lit himself on fire. It kinda gave me a good idea, so I came over here to get away from the noise and take notes."

"That pen is cool." A good idea?

"It's for writing in the dark. Movie reviewers use them all the time so they can take notes in the theater."

At the top of the page she's written: *Idea for a new screenplay—A teenage boy is burned beyond recognition* . . .

"You write screenplays?"

"I write a lot of things." She picks up a twig and flicks it around her fingers.

I say, "Be careful. This tree is a black locust. It can be toxic. I read about children who have suffered nausea, weakness, and depression after chewing on the bark."

"I wasn't going to chew on the bark, but thanks for the warning." Then she adds, "Actually, that's not a bad idea," and she scribbles: *Idea for a new screenplay—A child falls into a deep depression after eating the bark of a black locust tree* . . .

I hear a rustle, and Nikki approaches us. "Would you quit ditching me?" she says, but stops abruptly when she sees I'm not alone.

I introduce the two of them, even though they probably know each other already; and at that moment, Reggie announces from the stage, "This next song is an original tune of ours, inspired by all you athletic types. It's called

'Jesus Is in My Gym Class,' and it goes out to my friend Bud."

Nikki looks at me, and both our jaws drop. This we've got to hear.

"Come on," I say to Mila, offering her my hand. She lets me pull her up, and the three of us reach the stage during the first keyboard solo.

"Want to dance?" I ask both Nikki and Mila, just like that, just like I've been successfully hitting on girls all my life.

Nikki shudders and backs away. "Something you should probably know about me is that I'm the kind of person who'd rather be shot down in cold blood underneath the Safe School Zone sign than *dance*."

"I will," says Mila.

Nikki snaps photos of us and the band and the people around us. Mila is as bad a dancer as I am, which is really rare when you consider that most girls have at least a little rhythm and can fake it on the dance floor.

Reggie sings:

> *"He can do the rope climb without chafing!*
>
> *He can run a four-minute mile!*
>
> *Jesus is in my gym class! Jesus is in my gym class!"*

"I love this song," Mila shouts over the din.

I try to keep up with her dance moves. I whirl around on my heels, then run in place while shrugging, bite my lip, punch the air overhead.

Nikki elbows me in the ribs. "You dance like you were raised in the wilderness."

"Thanks," I say, panting.

Mila yells, "Anyone ever tell you that you look like Shia LaBeouf? He'd be perfect for my screenplay."

> *"He scores from the three-point line!*
>
> *He can do a cartwheel on the balance beam!*
>
> *Jesus is in my gym class!*
>
> *Jesus is in my gym class!"*

I'm all caught up in Reggie's awesome song and the fact that a girl is willingly dancing with, or in the vicinity of, me.

Nearby, a goth girl in a black sort of Spider-Man getup hunches over and clutches her stomach.

> *"He always gets picked first for dodgeball!*
>
> *Jesus is in my gym class!"*

A guy by the cider bowl looks like he's about to heave, too. I move closer to get a better look. I don't mean to leave the girls behind, but I do it anyway.

Nikki follows me. "What's going on?" she calls out, but I keep on walking.

Then the goth girl throws up all over the front of her webbed bodysuit. One of the football players stumbles by, and then he throws up, too. I laugh when I see the jock lose it, but for a second I feel bad for the goth girl. Just for a second.

"Jesus is in my gym class!"

The song ends. I applaud wildly. I am the only one. The teachers and chaperones are watching the pukers in bewilderment. Crowds of nonpuking kids charge toward the cider and doughnuts.

Nikki says, "Ew, gross. I'm getting my camera out. I've gotta document this. Hey, where are you going? Bud!"

I keep walking. I can't help it. Maybe I'm having an out-of-body experience. My head's throbbing, people are horking their guts out around me, and I just can't believe everything I've been through in the last twenty-four hours. It's no panic attack. It's more like my brain has shut off entirely, and I'm no longer in charge of my feet.

She calls after me, "What the hell are you doing? And you totally ditched that Mila girl, by the way."

I feel the keys in my pocket beckoning me back into the school. I try to ignore them and stalk off in search of Mila.

Someone poisoned the student body. That's overstating things a bit, but that's what I heard someone say. It was like ten kids at most. Nikki's mad that I left her on the field. She's sitting on the steps that lead up to the stage, talking with Reggie. He's leaning into her. She picks up her head and spots me, locks her gaze on me. I don't know what to feel.

Mila's sitting on the bottom row of the bleachers with some other girls.

"Ugh," she groans when she sees me. "This is so embarrassing."

I sit down and slide close to her. "You got sick, too? Are you okay now?"

"I guess so, except for the extreme mortification. I heard it was food poisoning from the cider or doughnuts. I bet someone spiked the cider." An image flashes before me: Dylan and his friends, behind the trees, pouring something from flasks into their cider. They probably were just spiking their own drinks with alcohol. Weren't they?

"Did you get sick?" she asks. I shake my head. "What about your friend Nikki?"

"No, she's okay." I glance across the field at Nikki and Reggie. Nikki is watching me with Mila.

Mila follows my gaze. "Is she your girlfriend?"

"I guess not."

Silence. Then she says, "I respect your stance on not selling the chocolate bars."

"My what? How do you know about that?"

"Nikki told me after you ditched us. I wanted to tell you I think that's cool."

"Well, thanks. I think."

"So are you really not going to sell them? Won't you get in trouble?"

I can't believe this is what we're talking about. "I don't know. I haven't thought that far in advance."

She says, "You're a conscientious objector. You know, like in a war."

"Well, I did get inspired by the book *The Chocolate War*. Although now I'm not sure that was such a great idea, because someone gets his ass beat at the end."

We talk about Bonfire Night—not the vomiting part, just the dancing and the music and who was drunk.

She says, "Ooh, this gives me a great idea for a movie. A high school is quarantined after a food-poisoning incident, except it really isn't food poisoning. It's a serial killer poisoning all the students one by one."

"It's kind of a coincidence," I laugh, "me telling you about those toxic black locust trees, and next thing you know, people are hurling all over the place."

But she doesn't laugh in response. "I could say the same thing about you, Mr. Poison-Know-It-All. Besides, I got sick. You didn't."

"That's the ultimate cover-up."

More silence. That awkward moment when two people suspect each other of poisoning the student body . . .

Now we don't know what to say, and I can't regain my focus. I keep thinking of that locker device in the front office. I want to try to get our conversation back where it was. I don't want to have stolen shit in my pockets and obsess about other stuff I want to steal. I want to be a regular person, not a crazy thief.

I say I have to go. She looks down and nods. I want to tell her I'm not some idiot guy ditching her, but maybe I am.

CHAPTER FIFTEEN

I do it again, this time alone. I could disable this alarm system with my eyes closed. I book down the hallway to the front office. I'm going to grab the BlackBerry thing and leave. It'll be like I was never here at all.

I find it right where I left it in Mrs. Kobunski's locked drawer. How many secrets does it hold? I see a few other choice items in the drawer: a USB drive, some money, a cell phone. For a second, something dark and dominant grips me. *I am not stealing*. It's only like three dollars. And I am not going to do anything bad with these other things. Another person might use them to perpetrate random acts of cruelty and violence, but not me. I slip all of it into my jacket's inner pocket as I hear a door slam.

The east-wing entrance. I never locked the door behind me.

Footsteps hesitating. Then walking slowly toward the wing intersection. They come my way, quietly, purposefully. Coming for me. Panic threatens to strangle me, but I push it away, or maybe I channel it elsewhere. I didn't go down like a chump in my underwear earlier, and I'm not going down now. I have nothing to use for a weapon but unrestrained insanity, but that has worked for me in the past.

This is the me that shows up once in a while—like with the exploding toilet, the fights, the stealing and lying. The me that protects me, if you get what I'm saying. In a moment of inspiration, I stuff the BlackBerry and the school keys down the back of my pants. They're so tight I know that nothing will fall out. I stand up, and when the silhouette of whatever is coming for me appears in the office doorway, I shine the Maglite directly into its face.

"Get that out of my eyes!"

My assailant turns out to be no assailant, only Ms. Viola.

I switch off the flashlight. "Oh. Sorry," I say. "Hi."

She stalks past me into the office, her eyes darting all around. "'Oh, hi.' Are you kidding me? What are you doing back here? How did you get in the school?"

"The door was unlocked."

"Bullshit," she snaps.

I shrug. "How else would I have gotten in? Isn't there an alarm?"

"It was off. And I *knew* I saw somebody go in the school. Mr. Downie tried to convince me I was imagining things. So what are you doing in here?"

I put on my embarrassed face (not so hard, really) and say, "I'm telling you, Ms. Viola, the door was open. Some of the seniors outside were humiliating me." I turn around, showing her my stapled pants. "See? My pants ripped, and some kids were after me. I ran away from them, and I was desperate, so I tried the door."

She doesn't say anything, and I know I've got her. I hit all the right notes.

"Well, what are you doing in the office?"

I whip the ministapler out of my pocket and show it to her. "Looking for something to fix my pants. It was in the desk here. I mean, it's not much, but I think I did a good job."

"So why is it still in your pocket?"

I can't come up with a good answer. Dammit.

"What else is in your pockets?"

There is absolutely nothing I can say, so I don't try.

She rubs her temples. "Like I don't have enough on my plate right now. Okay, let's see it. Empty your pockets."

I don't make a move.

She shoves her chaperone-issued walkie-talkie in my face. "Do it, or I'll call Mr. Downie to come here and give you a hand. Your choice."

I empty my outer pockets. The BlackBerry device is snug against my butt. It's going to need a good swab of rubbing alcohol when I get home.

"What is all this?" she asks, sifting through the junk.

"I kind of have a hoarding problem."

She ignores the USB drive, bent paper clip, money, peppermint candy, crumpled notes, and cell phone—all of which I took from the office—and zeroes in on the things that are actually mine: a bottle of prescription pills and a vial of liquid medicine.

She picks up the pills first. "Luvox," she reads. "What's this for?"

"Antianxiety meds. They're my prescription. My name's on it, see?" My mom expects me to have them on hand constantly and she's gone through my briefcase and coat before, making sure that I do. I carry them to keep her off my back.

Ms. Viola grimaces at the mention of "antianxiety meds." Sometimes I milk this glitch in my brain for all it's worth. She moves on to the vial. "Syrup of ipecac? What is this for?"

"Ipecac is a plant extract that, when swallowed, stimulates the central nervous system and the stomach, causing vomiting, usually in about twenty minutes," I recite from memory.

"I know that. What I don't know is why you are carrying it around with you."

"It's part of my first-aid kit. I also carry Band-Aids and antifungal cream."

She stares at the bottle. Then she says, "A few people got sick tonight. You know that, I assume."

I shrug.

"Did you slip this in the cider? I saw you hovering at the kiosk before."

"No." I know she's trying to get me to knot my own noose, so I don't say anything else—I learned a thing or two from my stint in lockup at Twenty-Sixth and California.

She asks, "Did you get sick?"

"No." I am totally at sea here. I was expecting to get busted for the phone or the stolen USB. I wasn't counting on getting grilled about my embarrassing first-aid supplies.

You can see her brain switching gears. "Okay. So tell me: How did you really get in the school? It's always locked."

"It was unlocked," I say.

She gives me a withering look.

"I didn't do anything," I say.

"Have you poisoned the student body, Bud?"

"Poison? With ipecac? Believe me, if I wanted to poison

everyone, they'd be in the hospital right now." This does not come out as reassuring as I thought it would.

She's turning the bottle over and over in her hand. You can practically see her mind turning over, too. She murmurs, "If it's just syrup of ipecac, then everyone will be all right. McNeill already called the paramedics, so they can figure out for sure." She looks at me. "Were you trying to hide this in Mrs. Kobunski's desk? Why? Half the school thinks you're responsible for those anonymous letters, and now this?"

"I didn't do anything," I say again. "I was stapling my pants."

She tries another tactic. "Is it because people bully you here?"

This throws me a little. "Nobody's bullying me."

She doesn't believe me, which is understandable. "You're only sixteen, so maybe you don't realize the repercussions of pranks—"

I interrupt. "I may only be sixteen, but I'm smart enough not to pull lame pranks like posting mean videos on YouTube or making people barf."

"What sort of pranks *do* you pull?"

I laugh. "Don't try to hook me." I can't believe I'm speaking to a teacher this way, but she brings out the real me. Is it because we're so alike?

She sighs and closes her eyes.

I go on. "I haven't spiked the cider, but you know what? If you want to turn me in, go ahead. My life is already heading down the drain."

She opens her eyes. "Principal McNeill starts off each term with a faculty meeting about the need for vigilance in what he calls these 'post-Columbine days.' His motto is 'Arrest now; ask questions later.' He believes it's better to look alarmist and overprotective when faced with troubled students than to have the media and parents accuse us later of standing by idly, ignoring the signs. I disagree with this tactic, but listen: poisoning people is wrong, no matter how you spin it."

I shake my head. "I am not pro-poison. I am antipoison; ask anybody!"

She holds up her hand. "Enough. I think turning you in would be a mistake. Things would only get worse for you. I don't believe that every unhappy young person is a potential murderer."

"So . . . can I go?"

"I'll walk you out," she says, nudging me into the hall.

When we reach the east-wing exit, she resets the alarm. I hold open the door for her and I think she's going to say thanks, but what she says is "Tread carefully. I'm watching you."

Does Viola still wonder if I'm responsible for the vomiting? It strangely seems better than her knowing about the keys, the BlackBerry, and the other stolen items, which, by the way, I have happily transferred from my pants to my jacket pockets. The paramedics took the remains of the cider and doughnuts to be tested, but at that point kids were already feeling better and leaving.

Nikki and Reggie are waiting for me in the parking lot. They ask where I've been, and I say nowhere. Nikki frowns and cocks her head at me, but I am not offering up any more info, sorry.

Nikki says, "I'm superhappy about the barfing, but now that it's over, Bonfire Night just sucks. Let's blow."

"Can either of you give me a lift?" asks Reggie. "My dad said I should call him and he'd pick me up, but I'm not in the mood." He shifts his enormous keyboard from one arm to the other.

"Sure," says Nikki, even though it's my car. I mean, of course I was going to offer him a ride, but it would be nice for her to look bummed out that we can't be alone. But who am I kidding?

Ms. Viola walks by and eyeballs us. "What are you hanging around here for? Move along."

We meander farther down the sidewalk. After Viola's out of sight, Reggie says, "She's just pissed they're taking away her archery team."

I stare at Nikki. "You told him?"

"Well, yeah. What? It wasn't confidential, was it?"

I thought it was just between us, I want to say. But then I was hoping a lot of things were between us that aren't.

I say, "Well, she doesn't want the archery team to know."

Reggie says, "It's cool. I won't tell anybody." And he probably won't, which for some reason pisses me off even more.

"Where's that Mila girl?" Nikki asks.

"I don't know." Probably somewhere making a screenplay out of all this.

As we near my car, Reggie slows and mutters, "Shit." A tall black man is standing with his arms crossed at the end of the sidewalk. He's staring at Reggie. He's wearing plaid flannel pajama bottoms and a wool coat but still manages to look menacing.

"Hi, Dad," says Reggie. His dad doesn't say hi or smile

or anything. Jeez, even *my* dad puts on a show when other people are around.

His dad says, "You were supposed to call. I've been waiting here half an hour."

"Well, the bonfire got kinda screwed up. Our singer lit himself on fire—his sleeve anyway—and then a bunch of kids came down with food poisoning or something, so—"

His dad repeats slowly, "You were supposed to call."

"Sorry, Dad."

"And I've been calling you. You never answered."

Reggie takes out his cell phone and examines it. "Oh. I had it on silent." He swallows and glances at Nikki and me. "Uh, these are my friends—"

"Mm-hmm," his dad says, his eyes never leaving Reggie's face. "Let's go. I have to get up in six hours."

"Sorry, Dad," Reggie says again. I am embarrassed for him, at the pleading tone in his voice.

His dad glances up at the red turban still on Reggie's head. It's like Nikki and I are watching a tennis match: our eyes follow his gaze to the turban, then down to Reggie's eyes, then back to his dad, then back to the turban again. His dad's mouth curves down. Lightning-fast, Reggie reaches up and yanks the turban off. No one says a word as they walk away. Their figures recede into the night until I can't see them anymore.

Nikki and I are quiet as we get in my car. Ordinarily when parents are dicks, you'd laugh about it and mock them when they're gone. But this has been a long night, and Reggie's dad seems dick-like in a way that is not funny.

Nikki stares straight ahead as I drive. She looks disappointed.

"Too bad Reggie couldn't ride with us. Sorry it's just me," I blurt out.

"What are you sorry for? Jeez, Bud. I know what you're getting at, but it's not like that between me and Reggie."

I feel like an idiot. This anger wells up in me, anger at myself and at people and situations and life. I pull over on Sheridan, turn off the car, and look at Nikki. Maybe I did imagine her disappointment. Maybe I imagine a lot of things. But I'm not imagining what I feel for her. That's real. It's the one thing I don't have to lie about.

I can't look away from her.

"Your eyes are hazel." Her voice is low. "I thought they were brown."

I reach over and brush a strand of hair off her cheek, tucking it behind her ear. Her skin is so warm. I stroke that little lick of hair and that incredibly soft skin right below her earlobe.

Her gaze is locked on me and *she shivers*, and I swear I am not putting the moves on her. It is just an electric thing between us, and now I know she feels it, too.

"Don't," she says softly.

"Why?" I ask. I don't come closer, but I trace the line of her jaw with my thumb.

"Because I am a very confused person right now."

Nikki almost leans toward me, but then she turns back to the window and everything shifts. I am not going to make her do or say or admit anything. But I know she feels something, even if it's fleeting, even if it disappears tonight. I wish the rest of my life could be this moment.

I ease the car back into traffic, and we say nothing else. My thoughts are jumbled. They crash into one another until

I don't know what they are anymore. This night is killing me.

I'm torn between happiness and frustration and anger—at school, at home, with Nikki, everywhere. The back-and-forth I've done tonight—the stealing, the sneaking, the lying—is exhausting. I can't figure out whether it makes me feel like I am one-upping everybody or whether it makes me feel more alone. Does it matter if Nikki feels something for me if we cannot be what I want us to *be*? The line between reality and illusion is getting blurry. Sometimes I really do think everyone hates me. Sometimes the crazy is all I've got. My head's pounding again. I *hate* all this: the pathology and the defiance and the confusion about whether I'm getting better or worse. And yet it is so totally *me*. I know that none of it ends here tonight. Not by a long shot.

CHAPTER SIXTEEN

In homeroom on Monday, I walk up to Sister Tim and plop my two unopened, unsold boxes of fund-raising chocolate bars on her desk.

"I'm not going to be selling these," I say.

She looks down at the boxes, then back at me, then down at the boxes. It's incomprehensible to her that anyone would refuse to sell the chocolates.

"You have to," she says.

"No, I don't. I'm a conscientious objector. Like in a war."

"This isn't a war."

Oh no? I shrug and turn away from her baffled face. I get a guilty twinge because, as an individual, she is not the enemy. But generally speaking, she's over on that side with *them*, and I'm over here by myself.

By now people have stopped their conversations to watch us. Some whisper, "Did you hear that? The new kid's not going to sell the chocolate bars!" I sit at my desk, wishing I'd timed this differently, maybe at the last possible second before the bell rang instead of having to sit here under the silent scrutiny of my classmates for four more minutes.

My Homeroom Buddy saunters over. "What's your problem?"

"I don't have a problem."

"The hell you don't," Dylan says.

Mercifully, the bell rings, and I escape into the hallway. Dylan and his buddies stalk me. Pushing through the crowd, they run ahead of me. They block my path as I get near the bathrooms and then slowly walk toward me.

I consider turning tail and running the opposite way, but what's the point? Not just because they would catch me with no effort at all, but because I am on a path now, and I intend to see my way to its end.

I stand still and wait for them.

When they get in front of me, one of the guys—it's Jason Amato of the Salisbury Steak Incident—holds up his hands, palms outward, as if to say "We come in peace."

He tells me, "You're new, so maybe you don't get how important the chocolate bar sales are to our school."

"Oh, I get it," I say. "I'm just not selling them."

"Why not?"

"Personal reasons."

Another guy, I don't know his name, says, "This is a big tradition at Magnificat. It unites each class. The seniors always win, but the juniors plan on beating them this year. We need everyone to cooperate."

"I'm not selling them."

"Don't you understand?" says Jason. "We get a free day if we win!"

I don't get what motivates people. I really don't. A free day?

"It's just twenty chocolate bars," I say. "I'm sure between

the six of you, you can make up the difference."

Dylan finally speaks up. "You're a complete ass to come here to *our* school and mock *our* traditions. Why don't you go back to Sullivan where you belong?"

"They expelled me." A lie, but I had to bring out the artillery.

They laugh. The idea of a geek like me getting expelled has them in hysterics. "Oh, yeah? For what?"

I say, "I tried to kill a guy."

They stop laughing then. They don't look afraid, as I had hoped, just annoyed. Nobody takes me seriously.

Dylan says, "Right, then why are you here instead of in jail?"

"It's complicated." And it is. Because I am telling the truth about that guy. But the guy, of course, was me.

One of them has had enough of me. He grabs me by the neck and shoves me against the bathroom door. The universe, always my friend, has seen to it that no teachers are around. The guy doesn't push me that hard, but I fall to the floor as the door swings in from my weight. In that split second, I see uncertainty in their eyes. They want to leave me there and be done with this. They're all decent students: jocks, not bruisers. But the thing is, I laugh when I look up at them. I don't mean to, but it just strikes me as ridiculous that 1) I am being assaulted over a fund-raising event, and 2) so many of my fights with people end up in the bathroom. They don't like that I laugh, so they advance.

"What the hell happened to you?" Reggie jumps out of his chair when I walk up to the lunch table. I skipped Chemistry, and he hasn't seen me yet this morning.

"There was an incident," I say, gingerly seating myself next to him.

Nikki stares at me, speechless. The other people at our table look up and then look away. They don't want to be mixed up in any of my weirdness.

"It looks worse than it is," I say, which is accurate. Somebody got in a swift kick to my jaw, and somebody else nailed me in the ribs and the shoulder, but that was all. They didn't want to be marked tardy for first period.

"Who was it?" Reggie asks.

I don't answer. I can't have them following me on this path.

Nikki says sharply, "Tell me."

"Look at your face!" Reggie sputters. "You look like a busted pumpkin. Your jaw is swollen, and it's turning purple."

"It is?" I ask. I take out my first-aid kit and put a Band-Aid on my jaw. "I don't need more people noticing my face. I'll just say I cut it shaving."

Nikki says, "At least tell me why they did this. Is it because of Bonfire Night and the pictures we took of people barfing, or the anonymous letters, or—"

"No, none of that. It's the chocolate bars. I decided not to sell them, and some of my classmates found out and took offense."

Nikki shouts, "Who the hell cares that much about chocolate bars?!"

Scents waft up from my lunch tray . . . meat loaf, unspecified vegetable mush, apple cobbler. These things shouldn't smell bad, but they do. And their appearance reminds me of the bonfire upchuckery. I push away the tray.

I say, "You know it's not just the chocolate bars, or any one thing. People cannot even define why they hate me."

"Screw them, Bud," says Reggie. "They suck, and none of them will amount to anything. They'll be selling salami one day while we're pursuing our dreams. We're the ones who count. *We* are totally on your side." As he says *we*, he puts his arm around Nikki's shoulder. It strikes me as a possessive, predatory gesture.

I hate myself for feeling like this about Reggie. But I'm starting to hate him, too. Maybe *he'll* pursue his dreams one day: he's got guts, whether his family is behind him or not. But I'm not like that, or maybe my family is worse. Or maybe Reggie's just far more talented than I am. In addition to his jazz/death metal keyboard–playing ability, he maintains a 3.9 GPA while defending his ranking as a national chess champ. He placed first in State and was the Illinois representative at the Denker Tournament of High School Champions, placing first. Another first this year would guarantee him a full ride to his first-choice college, Texas Tech. What do I have to show for myself? A C average, an exploding toilet, and an article on the annual Chicken Barbecue.

"I can't believe that happened to you on top of everything else," Nikki moans, her head in her hands.

"What everything else?"

She picks up her head. "You know, right? You saw it, didn't you?"

"What?"

The pity on her face alarms me. "The scumbags posted that video." She takes out her phone and pulls up someone's Facebook page. It's not the deadhead guy, but apparently it *is* one of the fifty people who've linked to the YouTube video he posted, which has had 541 hits in less than two days. Now 542.

"Oh God," I say.

You should see me on that video. It's so much worse than I imagined. You can see me swatting at the camera and trying to cover my ass. The worst part is the panic in my eyes, like an animal caught in a net. I look utterly afraid. In the background of the video, you can hear thunder roll in the distance.

Just then a freshman—a *freshman*—walks by our table with his friends, points at me, and says, "That's him! That's Thunder Pants!" Seriously. The video is called "Thunder Pants."

Get up, leave, go. "I'll see you guys later," I say. Nikki reaches out to grab my sleeve, but I pull roughly away from her and sprint toward the exit.

I am so out of here, I almost go straight through those glass doors without even opening them.

I get dirty looks in the hall on the way to Modern Lit. It seems Dylan and his buddies have been busy spreading stuff about me, not just about my conscientious objector status, but a bunch of half-truths and outright lies. I guess it's hard to fact-check all your accusations when you've got a witch hunt to conduct.

The class-wide tide of opinion has turned against me, not that it was ever *for* me, but before all this, I was a neutral nobody. My chocolate bar stance has inflamed the Magnificat junior class and propelled me into its center.

Ms. Viola does not lecture during sixth period but merely assigns us some goofy essay to write about how *As I Lay*

Dying affects us personally. She's sitting at her desk tearing her cuticles to bloody bits. So far I've written down the title.

When the bell rings, Ms. Viola stops me as I pass her desk. Everybody watches us as they head toward the door.

When we're alone, she says, "What's this?" pointing to my jaw.

"I cut myself shaving."

"And the bruise?"

"Oh, that. I fell off the trampoline in Phys Ed."

"I wanted to talk some more about what happened during the bonfire, but all I've been hearing today is how you refuse to participate in the chocolate bar sale, and now I see what happened to your face, and I don't know where to begin. So why don't you start by telling me what's going on."

"Nothing's going on. I fell off the trampoline, and I don't want to sell the chocolate bars. I mean, I don't have to, right? It's not like a written rule."

She passes a hand over her eyes and then squeezes the bridge of her nose. A million wrinkles spring out around her eyes, and I feel sorry for prematurely aging her with my shenanigans. After a big sigh she says, "I like that you question authority. But maybe I shouldn't be encouraging that. I don't think the chocolate bars are your enemy here, Bud. You have to pick your battles."

"I have," I say. "And I've picked this one."

"People are saying things about you. You guys may think teachers are clueless about what goes on in school, but I've been hearing some unkind and downright vicious things about you today. I don't like where this is heading," she says. "Please sell the chocolate bars."

"I can't," I tell her.

I feel a cold wave of fear wash over me. I know where this is headed, too. But in a way, I'm kind of comforted by my resolve, by my decision to act, no matter what the consequences are. I may be a conscientious objector, but if I'm going down, I'll go down in combat.

The tardy bell rings. "Can I hand in my essay tomorrow?" I ask.

Ms. Viola looks at me helplessly, like she can't believe that's all I have to say. It's not all I have to say, but it's all I can say at the moment, because she's now one of the few people I feel I have to protect.

The only bright spot is in eighth period. Mila from Bonfire Night had switched with my lab partner in AP Bio—not difficult since my old partner practically leaped with joy at the chance to get away from me—so the teacher gave us permission to meet during eighth-period study hall to catch up on our lab.

In the middle of dissecting our fetal pig, Mila says, "I saw it. I saw those boys gang up on you outside the lav. And I just stood there like a jerk and didn't do anything."

"What could you have done? Anyway, it's not a big deal. Guys like to fight."

"But it was an unfair fight. It made me so mad, the way they swaggered down the hall toward you, six in a row, like the Reservoir Dogs. And now look at your face." She almost reaches over to touch my jaw, but then she seems to think better of it and takes her hand away.

"There's so much crap going on right now, getting beat up is the least of my problems."

"You mean . . ." She hesitates. "Thunder Pants?"

"So you've seen it."

"Cinematically and morally, it is a piece of garbage. Don't waste another minute worrying about it. But I just want to say that even though you got beat up for it, I still admire you for not selling the chocolate bars."

"Thanks," I say.

"You must feel let down by the school," she says quietly, lowering her gaze, intent on the pig. "Me, too. This is the first year that Computer Club isn't going away to Computer Camp. No money, they say. There seems to be plenty of money around this school for other, more 'important' things."

I look at her, but she doesn't raise her head. We don't speak anymore about it. We just poke our pig in his underdeveloped brain in silence.

During the end-of-the-day announcements, McNeill gets on the loudspeaker and says they will be sending notes home with us and e-mailing our parents about the Bonfire Night food-poisoning episode. We are not to worry, he assures us: the reports from the lab came back, and it was just some almost-harmless bacteria in the doughnuts. A couple of people turn around and gawk at me, and I want to shout, "It wasn't me! Weren't you listening to the dumb announcements?"

My classmates look disappointed that I didn't try to poison them. I wish I could tell them that it's not that I *couldn't*, it's just that I didn't.

There's a *Vox Populi* meeting after school. We're supposed to hand in our articles and kick around ideas for the next issue. On my way there, I pass Sister Tim coming out of our homeroom. She squints at me and then asks, "What happened to you?"

"I fell off the trampoline in Phys Ed."

"Are you all right?"

"Yeah, I'm fine, Sister. Thanks."

I walk on before she can say anything else. You can't expect teachers to help you when you don't tell them the truth. But then I don't expect them to help me at all.

Nikki stops me in the hallway before we go into the newspaper room.

"So it wasn't you," she says.

"The food poisoning? Are you serious? Why does everyone think that?"

"Oh, you know why. Anyway, I'm glad."

"You should know me better than that," I say.

"Sometimes you're hard to read. I thought maybe it was what those idiots did, filming you in your underwear, that sent you over the edge. Or you were unbalanced because of that skinhead beating you up. Or I guess I thought for a second that maybe you were mad at me, and it made you flip out and try to poison the student body."

"Why would I be mad at you?"

She blushes and doesn't answer. Oh right, I lost my mind and tried to poison people because she doesn't think of me *that way*.

"Are you kidding? You thought that even for a second? You don't know me at all."

"I'm trying to."

I cross my arms. I knew it would come to this. "You're against me," I say.

"Against you? Dude, I am *against you* back-to-back, surrounded by infidels," she says. "I am *for* you. I want you to succeed and be happy, even though being happy seems completely unrealistic for people like you and me. I'm getting concerned here. Scared. I'm afraid something bad is going to happen to you. It's making me not see things clearly, and I'm sorry."

The meeting is due to start, so I go in and leave her behind. I hate to do it.

Everyone stops chatting when I walk in. Trevor stares at me with unabashed hatred in his eyes. Why? What have I ever done to make him feel this way? Ms. Viola is late for the meeting, so Trevor takes advantage and corners me by the computers.

He says, "Yo, Thunder Pants, I heard about you and the chocolate bars. I thought you were just talking smack when you first said you weren't gonna sell them. But I guess you weren't bullshitting, huh? You think you're some big rebel."

"No, I don't."

"Yeah, right. But you know what? On this staff, we are proud of our school. We *want* to do what we can to support it."

"Only because it supports *your* cause: the newspaper. Maybe you'd feel differently if you were in the Computer Club. The school took away their camping trip. So, see, not everything works out for everybody here. And I'm not the only one who thinks that."

"But you're the only one on *my staff* who thinks that. We don't have room for people like you, and when you pull stupid shit like this, it reflects badly on the rest of us."

"Are you trying to fire me? Because you can't. You're

not my boss. I'm a volunteer, and I haven't done anything wrong."

"We'll see about that, Badi." He pronounces it *baddy*, and I almost correct him—*Bah-DEE*—till I realize he shouldn't be saying it at all.

"Uh-huh. I know all about that. Remember my friend Brad Bates at Sullivan? I figured there must be a reason he'd never heard of you, of Bud Hess. So I described you to him and asked if there was a sophomore there last year who left and who looked like you. 'Oh, *him*,' he says. And he told me everything. You didn't leave; you got kicked out. He said you're like some wannabe Arab terrorist."

"One, I wasn't kicked out. Two, Iranian is not the same as Arab. And three, I don't terrorize people, even jackasses like you who deserve it."

"Sure, whatever. God, are you stupid. First the anonymous letters and now the chocolate bars." He peers at my swollen jaw. "Who beat you up? I'd like to congratulate them."

"You don't know the first thing about me. Nothing. And as far as those letters go, I've spoken to people who think it's *you*."

"Me?" His face goes pale beneath the freckles. "You're lying."

"Those letters really raised the profile of this newspaper. Nobody looked at it before. Now it's all anyone talks about."

Ms. Viola walks in, and her gaze flicks between Trevor and me. "What's going on here?"

"I was just leaving," I say.

I walk right out of the meeting, and the next thing I know, I'm on the 290 Touhy bus. There is a large chunk of time that I've completely blacked out. I don't know how I got on the bus. I don't remember walking down the sidewalk or being at the bus stop. My face hurts, the back of my head still hurts. I've been beat up twice in three days, had a video of me in my boxers posted on the Internet, and been accused of poisoning people. My ribs are throbbing, my brain is vibrating, and I am in danger of completely losing it here on public transportation. Why don't I remember leaving the school or how I got on this bus? I'm shaking. *I am getting through this . . . I am not losing my mind on the bus.*

But it doesn't work. Because that's one of the big signs of mental breakdown: losing chunks of time, time that you cannot account for. It happens to schizophrenics and other people for whom there is no return.

CHAPTER SEVENTEEN

ariush has his things piled up outside our apartment building, waiting for his friends with the truck to come by. I knew he'd been looking for a place to crash, but I didn't know he'd found one.

I see all this from a block away as I walk home from the bus stop. His futon, his milk crates full of books, his chrome-rimmed kitchen table, the chairs with the duct-taped legs.

"Dad is making you leave *now*?" I ask when I reach him.

He shrugs like it's no surprise. "Mom's cousins, the Elghanayans, are moving into my apartment in a few weeks."

"Oh no, not them! They don't even play croquet."

"It's okay," he says. "I'm ready to go. My friends have an extra bedroom in their apartment, and the rent is cheap. I'll be fine."

"Where is it? Can I come visit?"

"Of course, any time you want. It's in Pilsen. My friends have a café where they'll let me wait tables for a while, until I figure out what I should be doing."

"Pilsen? But that's the South Side. I don't know my way around there. I've never been south of the planetarium."

"It's easy," he says. "Take the Red Line and get off at Chinatown, then take the number 21 bus to Cermak and Ashland. Not much more than an hour, door-to-door."

"I'll never see you." And despite his protests, I know it's true. Sure, we'll both make an effort in the beginning, but between school and the slacker café and the new friends he's sure to make, that hour-plus train/bus ride is going to look pretty grim.

He doesn't seem upset. He actually looks excited. I mean, who could blame him? He must be thrilled to get out from under our dad's thumb. But the prospect of living here with no buffer between me and my parents, Azita, and the whole rest of the family makes me feel totally alone and crazy.

"Well, I guess this all works out for *you*," I say.

I try to walk past, but he puts his hand on my sleeve. "Badi-jan, everyone has to leave home sometime. I've had a good run here for twenty-four years, and many of those years were spent happily unemployed and playing croquet with you. But I'm ready for the next phase of my life. You'll understand one day when you move out."

Standing so close makes him notice my beat-up face. His eyes open wide, and he says, "What's this? Have you been in a fight?"

I don't answer his question. I hardly hear it. Everything sounds like it's being broadcast from a loudspeaker ten miles away.

"Dad made this happen," I say. "You were happy living here, but he made your life so unbearable that now you're glad to leave."

"Not quite. And you didn't tell me how you got these bruises."

It feels like a volcano of rage is about to erupt out of the top of my head. A panic attack but different, because there are sharp stabs of anger running through it and my thinking is even more rapid and disjointed and screwed up. I just walk right by him, and everything I see looks like a series of photographs instead of a moving picture: the pumpkins, the black wrought iron gate, the sidewalk with a thousand cracks. The jack-o'-lanterns my mother carved are falling apart like I knew they would. I kick one over. Its face is evil and leering, and there are ladybugs crawling inside its rotten head. Rex next door is crying. I can't see him, but his howl is the soundtrack to the ugliness around me. Even the chrysanthemums my mom bought are dried up because nobody watered them. They belong in a winter field, lifeless and fallow, with pumpkins decaying all around and cornstalks brown and bent, awaiting the thresher's blade.

"You must eat something," my mother says.

"I'm not hungry," I tell her. "Anyway, I have to leave soon for my appointment with Dr. Elliott."

She winces when she hears his name. It's like somebody has belched in front of her and she has to look away, pretending it hasn't happened. She never, not once, has asked how my sessions are going, if I'm feeling any better. Neither has my dad.

"It's quiet here without your older brother," Dad says, looking around the dinner table at our sullen faces. Arman and Dorri are sulking because he made them turn off the Xbox, and Azita's natural state is surly. I'm the only one who misses Dariush.

I look at Dad, like, Are you kidding me with this? God,

how I want to say something, stand up for myself, for my brother. I want to say, "How could you kick out your own son?" But I don't know how to start. It's not that my dad has a bad temper; it's that every time I open my mouth, I can't stand his disapproval and disappointment. He doesn't hit us, but I still fear him.

He asks me, "How is school? When are report cards? Grades getting up there, yes?"

"I'm doing okay," I lie.

"Okay means average." He says it mildly, but the arrow finds its mark.

Mom tries to rescue me. "Javeed, please do not *derange* him." She winks at me. "Bud fell off the trampoline at school today. Look at his face. I cannot believe it, this injury."

"Hmm. I noticed that."

"Fool," Azita mutters under her breath.

"I'm really going to miss Dariush," I say. My mouth feels dry, and I gulp my milk.

"Do not drink so fast," Mom says.

"Yes, well," Dad says, leaning back in his chair. I wait for him to continue, but that's it.

"I wish he hadn't left," I go on. "Will he play in our Halloween tournament?"

He ignores my question. "Everyone must pull his own weight. Perhaps this is just the push he needs. You could learn a lesson from this, Bud."

My mom absently stirs the *mejadra*, a lentil-and-rice dish, sadness sinking into her features. She startled when I mentioned our Halloween family croquet game—I bet she hadn't thought about that—and maybe now is visualizing the contest without my brother there. And I realize she misses

Dariush and wishes he were different so that he could be with her, with us, right now.

"I'll have some more, Maman." I offer her my plate, and she scoops some *mejadra* onto it, looking grateful that she can still give me something.

I wolf a few bites and check my watch. I have to leave right now to get to Dr. Elliott's on time. It makes me brave, knowing I can speak and then run out the door to escape.

I stand up and turn to my dad. "It feels like you kicked him out of the family, Baba. Who cares if he was unemployed? What does it matter if he can't pay you rent? You make enough money."

"I make money to support my children who are in school, not a grown man who has the SpongeBob tattooed on his ankle." Dad turns his eyes toward the front window, where we can hear my brother and his friends on the sidewalk. They are laughing and loading up the few trappings of his life.

"Dariush," Dad whispers to himself, eyes still on the window, "with your engineering degree and your big, wasted brain."

I try to say something else, but Dad raises his hand and flicks away my words.

Dr. Elliott sits there waiting patiently, his hands folded in his lap. We got through the preliminaries, discussing the bus ride and how cold it is for this time of year, and he asked what's going on with me, and I said, "Nothing," and now ten minutes pass while I stare at the bonsai tree.

He gives in. "You're quiet tonight, Bud. What would you like to talk about?"

"I don't want to talk about anything." I wonder if he trims the bonsai tree himself. Don't you need specialized knowledge to take care of one of those things? Not my area of botany expertise.

"You have a bruise on—"

"I fell off the trampoline at school." If I have to say it one more time, if I even have to hear the word *trampoline* in some other context, I will flip out. Yet I can't seem to stop saying it. "*Trampoline. Tramp-o-line.* Say it enough times and it doesn't make sense anymore. It sounds completely made-up."

"You seem anxious, restless. Do you think the Luvox is helping at all?"

Oh, you mean the drug you think I'm taking but in reality I haven't touched in three months? I say, "Yeah, it's fine." Mom picks up the prescription every month, and I stockpile the bottles in a locked chest in my room.

He talks for a while about other drugs we can try if we think the Luvox isn't the right one. *We*, right.

Another five minutes go by. Can you imagine the size of the pruning shears you'd have to use on a bonsai? It's all I can think about.

He asks a few questions about home and school, and I lie and give some one-word answers. If I told him the truth, he would know I wasn't taking the Luvox, and he'd probably want to lock me up, or, even worse, he'd try and set up some "family counseling" with my parents, and I swear to God if he did that, I would never stop throwing up.

I don't want to be here anymore.

"What's that?" he asks.

"I didn't say anything."

"It sounded like you said you didn't want to be here anymore."

I said that out loud? Whoa.

He's looking at me curiously. He passes his pen around all his fingers, over and over again. It's his nervous habit. You pick up on these things after a few months, even when you're mostly staring at a bonsai tree.

"When you say you don't want to be here, do you mean therapy specifically or—"

"I'm not making some veiled suicide threat," I snap.

"Why do you think that's what I meant?"

"I don't want to come to therapy anymore," I say. I rise up and put on my coat and head for the door.

"Please, wait just a second—"

"No. My parents said I could stop, and I'm really busy with school and it just isn't helping. I mean, I feel okay now and want to try things on my own. You're a good shrink. It's not that you haven't helped at all, you have; it's just that I feel done. I'm done here."

"Ending therapy isn't quite that simple—" As he stands, he bonks his bald head on the lamp, and he suddenly seems so clueless and inept that I have to get the hell out of there.

The bus ride home is ridiculous. Everyone reeks of meat and wet wool. It makes me sick. The overhead lights cast a disgusting green color on all the faces. My bus partner has a mole on his cheek that is shaped liked Thomas Jefferson's profile. I cannot get over it, I have never seen anything like it. You can almost see its mouth moving, saying, "A democracy is nothing more than mob rule."

"What you looking at, *maricón*?" the mole spits at me. I mean, I know it must've been the man who said that, the mole's owner. It couldn't have been the mole. But it was.

I get this feeling that something bad is happening, like I'm going to come home and find our building burned to the ground or white supremacists chasing my family around with baseball bats, or that this bus is going to crash into the bodega on Clark Street. My head won't stop with this shit. I know it's all anxiety. It pummels my brain with thoughts and images of horrible things going down. What is the matter with me? I'm sick of talking about myself. I'm sick of thinking about myself. I'm sick of myself.

I can hardly breathe by the time I get home. *I am getting through this. I am open to happiness.* Yeah, this voodoo doesn't work, Dr. Elliott. You should have come up with something better.

My hippie neighbor waves to me from her porch. She's sweeping leaves off her steps as Rex cowers at the bottom, afraid of the broom.

Inside my apartment, everything's normal: the building hasn't burned down, everyone's still alive. Do my parents even see me come in? I go straight to my room and shut the door. King Sargon snoozes on my bed, all curled up. I sit down next to him, and he purrs as I scratch behind his ears. I'm glad that his pleasure receptors still work.

I call Nikki.

"What's up?" she asks. "How come you didn't stay for the newspaper meeting?"

"I had a headache." I hadn't planned on anything else to

say. I think I mostly want to hear her voice. We talk about I don't know what. And then I hear myself inviting her to our Halloween croquet tournament.

"It's kind of fun. We play in costume and my dad usually tries to rig up some spooky decorations and there'll be a ton of food." It's so lame the way it comes out, even though I actually like the tournament. The thought of playing this year without Dariush makes me feel lost.

But she says, "Sure. I was dying to get away from my house and the cuteness of the twins in their princess costumes. Do you know my stepmother hands out little boxes of *raisins* on Halloween? I could just puke. No wonder we get egged every year."

I tell her she doesn't have to wear a costume if she doesn't want. She says she might, and then she adds, "Should we ask Reggie?"

"Oh. Oh, yeah. Of course. Give him a call."

When we hang up, my emotions are all out of whack. This sucks. If Nikki doesn't have a thing for him, why does it feel that way to me? I want Reggie there but I don't. It's exhausting to feel like this every day about someone you actually consider a friend.

I can't read or study now. My brain is frizzling, if that's a word. Like frying and sizzling and vibrating at once. Do you have any idea how behind I am in my homework? I can't even think about it right now. How many days or weeks can go by until it's impossible to catch up?

I tell King Sargon about that mole on the bus. "You would not have believed this thing," I say. Then something bad starts happening: I feel an itchy spot on my cheek. I scratch it and feel something . . . *bumpy* there. Oh no. It itches like hell. I'm not getting up to look at it, no way. But I scratch until it bleeds.

I glance down at the floor where I store my music collection of three CDs and one vinyl album. Right there in front of the Chet Baker record is a turntable hooked up to some old speakers. Dariush's turntable.

The note taped to it says: *This is yours now, Badi. Keep listening to jazz, but don't forget to listen to New Wave sometimes. Your loving brother, Dariush*

He's left me another present, too: Car Wash of Death's only recorded twelve-inch single, "Car Wash of Death." I have the MP3 of the song on my iPod, but they actually made a hundred vinyl pressings. So it's a collector's item. I put it on and sing along with the familiar first verse.

Azita complains as she stomps down the hall to the bathroom, "I'm trying to *study*, which is kind of *difficult* with someone's music being so *loud*."

I don't turn it down. In fact, I turn it up. Unfortunately, nothing drowns out Azita's whiny voice. King Sargon hears her and stops purring. It's just an automatic response with him. Like Rex next door with the broom. The neighbors had told me that they'd rescued him from an abusive home where he was regularly beaten with a broomstick. It's been years and years, but he still wigs out when he sees one, afraid the danger has returned.

CHAPTER EIGHTEEN

To Whom It May Concern:

Am I who you think I am? Not that it matters to me. Lynch whomever you want.

You were there: Bonfire Night. The Magnificat Sheep were sacrificed to the Gordon Tech Rams. Who would have thought ovine creatures could be so violent? We are all sheep-like in our mentality, our stupidity, our willingness to follow.

Well, what's one more loss to the football team? They still get to keep their new uniforms. Other clubs don't have it so easy. For example, did you know that this is the first year that the Computer Club will not be going away to Computer Camp? They thought they'd raised enough from their popcorn sales, but apparently there was a discrepancy in accounting: the amount missing equals the cost of new football uniforms. Coincidence? I think not! You'd be amazed at the kind of information people leave lying around in their e-mail folders.

What's next? Will your organization's funds suddenly disappear? Will your meeting place be usurped by larger mammals in new sports attire? Chew on this:

Whatever happened to the old Mah-jongg Club? The Kite Flyers? The choir? They're gone, all of them, and not because enrollment or interest was down. They were systematically exterminated because they did not generate cash flow like the athletic clubs. Students have been kept in the dark. Now that Regionals are almost upon us, I hope nothing happens to the Checkmates. Or the Archery Club.

Homecoming is soon. The football team will be celebrating at Loyola Beach. It would be a shame if something ruined their good time as they crowned their Gridiron Queen.

Sincerely,

Anonymous

The school is in a total uproar. My chocolate bar transgressions have been pushed to the side, which is actually a little disappointing. I mean, I don't want to get beaten up over that again, but it was a nice feeling to stand up for something. Anonymous is stealing my thunder. He has stolen Thunder Pants's thunder.

Most of us dive for the *Vox Populi* as soon as we get to school. The issues have magically appeared on our desks before anyone enters his or her homeroom. I heard that Principal McNeill always checks over each issue before it goes to press. All I can think is that whatever he's checking over is a dummy copy and not the final layout. But isn't Trevor the one who hands it to him? How deep does this conspiracy go?

As we're all reading, another nun comes in and whispers

to Sister Tim, who then stands up and confiscates all the copies. I hear the nun whisper something about "orders from above," and for a second I think she's talking to Sister Tim about God, but then I realize she just means McNeill.

I can't tell from my homeroom who they think Anonymous is. Except for Dylan—it's clear who he blames. Lots of rumors are flying. It looks like I'm not the only anarchist in school.

In Chemistry, the girl who was possibly checking me out that day at Charmers Cafe is sitting there with this weird expression on her face. I jerk my head up in greeting the way guys do, and she frowns a little and looks away. I have to sit next to her, so it's awkward. She steals glances at me.

When we're doing our lab and Ryndak's occupied on the other side of the room, she says, "I heard some wild story about you and your old school."

I keep my head down, concentrating on the experiment. "Do you want to add the hydrogen peroxide or should I?"

She takes the peroxide and adds 30mL to the bottle. "Is it true you got kicked out for blowing up the locker room?"

"No," I say, "and you should be wearing safety goggles and rubber gloves. Hydrogen peroxide at this concentration can cause burns."

She puts them on and then hands me the tea bag, which I fill with solid potassium iodide, and then I place it in the bottle and secure it with the stopper, making sure the tea bag is not touching the peroxide within. This experiment is really simple but kind of fun. I wish she would shut up so I could enjoy it.

"But what happened? And didn't they make you change

your name or something? Because it was Middle Eastern?"

I stop and look up at her. "What are you talking about?"

"That's what they're saying."

"Who?"

She shrugs. Protecting Trevor, no doubt. My hands shake as I remove the stopper and let the tea bag fall into the hydrogen peroxide. I am seized by this mad desire to point the bottle right at her face, but of course I don't. I point it away, in a safe direction. Within a few seconds, an impressive cloud of oxygen gas and water vapor escapes from the bottle.

"Exothermic reaction," I say, scribbling it in our notes.

"The 'Aladdin's Lamp' reaction," she says. I just look at her. "That's what the experiment's called. The cloud from the bottle is like a genie." She narrows her eyes. "You remind me of him, from the cartoon. Aladdin."

"Oh, *I* get it!" I feign hilarity, slapping my leg, which jolts her. "Like, 'cause Aladdin is Middle Eastern and I'm Middle Eastern! So it's a joke! Good one."

"Thunder Pants," she mutters.

"Oh, blow me," I say. People are listening to us. Then the bell rings.

In the hall I am bashed into with more than the regular frequency. Maybe I'm imagining it? I feel really paranoid. People are making more eye contact with me than normal; I'm pretty sure of it because usually nobody makes eye contact with me. Their looks tell the story; I see all the fear and curiosity that come from hearing rumors about someone you don't even know.

In AP Bio Mila is still my lab partner, and she's still

committed to ripping apart our fetal pig, but she's quiet the whole class.

"Did you read the paper this morning?" I ask, making sure no one else is listening.

She lifts her eyes to me. "Yes. Why?"

"Well, that stuff about the Computer Club. I thought—"

"What? You thought what? You thought I wrote it?"

"I didn't say that. It just seems like maybe other people in your club are angry about not going to camp, too."

She looks miserable. "I'm sure we all told our friends. There's no way to know who leaked that info. The only person I told was you." But she doesn't say it accusingly.

I think but don't say, *Yes, but then I told someone.*

Mr. Downie tells us to quit yammering and get back to work. When the bell rings, I ask Mila to wait.

Her eyes focus on me. "Your jaw still looks horrible. And what's this? What happened to your cheek?"

I rub the scratch there. The Thomas Jefferson mole from the bus has been haunting me. Can you catch moles from people? Because I swear I have. It itches constantly, and I can't keep my hands off it.

"I fell off the trampoline. . . . ," I say. I picture myself falling off the trampoline, and for a second I believe it really happened. My various deceits and half-truths are beginning to mutate into some sort of bizarre reality.

"It's bleeding."

I reach up and touch the mole—or whatever it is. I shrug. I'm not crazy enough to tell the mole story.

"Are you okay?"

"I think so." Am I? I don't know. "Are you?"

She shakes her head. "I think I might have done something really stupid," she says, and then tears out of the classroom. I want to follow, but I lose sight of her as she disappears into the mass heading to third period.

At lunch, Reggie and Nikki are poring over her chart of people who hate me. They wave me over and insist I put aside my lunch and brainstorm with them.

"All right," Nikki begins. "What have you heard?"

Reggie says, "The printing of the newspaper is suspended until further notice. That's not gossip. I know it for a fact because I heard McNeill yelling that at Ms. Viola in his office."

Nikki makes a note of this. "I heard Trevor was taken into McNeill's office for questioning."

"Cheerleaders are issuing hot denials to anyone who will listen that there never was or will be a Gridiron Queen," Reggie says.

"Ha, as if. Now, here's my take on things in this letter," she says. "First: who cares about the old Mah-jongg Club? Second: this Computer Club stuff throws a whole new light on Anonymous. You know the president of their club was seen crying when he came out of McNeill's office after second period?"

"Doug Lee was in McNeill's office?" Reggie says. "I don't believe he had anything to do with it. Doug's on the Checkmates with me. He's like the most mild-mannered, quietest kid you've ever met."

Nikki drones in a voice of doom: "It's always those quiet ones."

"I don't mean to be harsh," Reggie says, "but Doug's only been in this country for a few years. His grasp of English is far from perfect. No way could he have written the letters.

It's got to be someone else, someone who can write well—in English—and who is either in Computer Club or is smart enough to figure out the layout software."

I stare at him.

Nikki shoots me a glance. "What about your friend? Isn't she in Computer Club? She wears that sweatshirt of theirs, 'Computers can never replace human stupidity.'"

"Who, Mila? It can't be her. She's not out to get me," I say. Then I hesitate, because I'm not sure of anything anymore. "Is she?"

"Don't forget," Reggie says, pushing his food around on his plate, "column B: people who have grievances against the school. They may not have anything against Bud—maybe they were even inspired by Bud's chocolate bar rebellion—and may not be trying to implicate him at all. But he's just sort of . . ."

"Collateral damage?" I offer.

"Exactly."

"This list keeps getting longer instead of shorter." Nikki groans. "Do I add Doug and Mila to column A or B?"

"Don't add them at all," I say.

"Why not?"

I can feel Reggie's eyes boring into me. I don't look at him. "Because I think it's someone else," I say.

Nikki ticks off each name. "Trevor, Dylan and his do-gooder zombie army, Colin, Jason, the Religious Activities Committee, Doug, Mila—"

I interrupt. "Am I just being stupid here, or is it unclear what Anonymous is threatening? There are these red flags that something *might* happen at Homecoming, or after, at the Loyola Beach party. But he hasn't said anything specific or violent. Only stuff like 'people fade away' and 'I hope nothing ruins their good time.' They seem like empty threats to get people stirred up. Everyone knows McNeill's alerted the police already, if for no other reason than to make the parents feel he's not ignoring all this. Anonymous would have to be nuts to try anything violent."

"Well, aren't you curious to see what Anonymous has in mind?" asks Nikki. "I know I am."

"No," I say flatly. "I'm pissed that someone is trying to get me in trouble."

Reggie says, "Bud's right. Anonymous hasn't actually threatened *anything*. McNeill obviously just resents that somebody is pulling the same prank over and over, and nobody can stop him." I note the admiration in his voice.

We sit there ruminating. And the more I think about Nikki's chart and the ever-growing list of people who have it in for me, the more miserable I feel. I started this school year with good intentions. I really tried hard not to be a spaz, to fit in, to make progress in my treatment with Dr. Elliott, to make progress in general as a human being, and it's all just going to hell.

Days pass. Not in a blur, like the cliché goes, but rather like a series of isolated photos that have nothing to do with each other. I feel like I'm watching a documentary narrated in Swahili.

Ms. Viola assigns another lame "write about your feelings" essay and never once raises her head from her desk.

I'm trying to do the assignment when someone flings a folded-up note that lands at my feet. I pick up the paper and unfold it. On it is drawn a crude rebus puzzle:

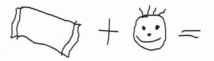

Badi Hessamizadeh

Towelhead. Oh, not again. It follows me like a hungry dog. Then I catch it—my name. My real name. First the girl in Chemistry, now this. Trevor's not in this class, so he must have spilled it to someone else. But who? And how many of them know?

I turn around, and I see many eyes locked on me. And I think, *They all know.*

Nikki is hissing at some dude in the back. I miss what she says, but the guy hisses back at her, "Shut up, lesbo. You only think that 'cause you're friends with the towelhead." He points at me, but his eyes don't leave her face. "The loser who won't sell our chocolate bars."

Everyone within earshot—so that's everyone—looks at me now. I wait for my heart to start racing and for the sweat to come pouring out of me, but it doesn't. I feel strangely calm.

The guy now asks me, "So why aren't you selling the chocolate bars?" He doesn't even whisper, just says it like we're alone here. "Yeah, you, Mohammad. Camel jockey."

At this Ms. Viola raises her head, but her gaze is weary. I know I'm on my own. I don't respond, but I don't look away either.

The bell rings, and I bolt from my desk. I don't want to talk to anybody. Nikki calls for me to wait for her, but I don't. As I try to leave the room, the camel-jockey guy and two of his friends block my way. Not in a big, aggressive show. If you didn't know better, you'd think it was the normal bottle-neck that arises from slow-witted dudes trying to fit through a doorway. But I do know better.

When I change my course and try to walk around them, they shift as a group and block that way, too. You see where this is going, right? They part to let other students through but not me. These guys all wear pins from the tennis team on their uniforms. Tennis-team thugs. Did you know there was such a thing? They ought to stage a rumble with the golf team from Sullivan.

"Move it," Nikki says to them from behind me. Oh no. I cannot let her rescue me. Not just because the tennis thugs would tear me apart, but because I don't want her seeing me like that. So I have no other choice but to head-butt my way through them. I knock the camel-jockey guy to his knees. Physical fights are automatic grounds for suspension at Magnificat. Head-butting probably falls into that category.

"Ms. Viola! You saw that, didn't you? You saw him hit me," he complains from the floor, rubbing his knee.

I stop in the doorway. I don't say anything to Ms. Viola. I don't rat on the tennis thugs. I just look down at the kid on the ground and feel nothing.

"Aren't you going to do something, Ms. Viola?" the guy says. "I banged up my knee, and we have a match against St. Ignatius in two days. Coach is counting on us to get to State this year."

But all Ms. Viola says is "I'm sorry, Ben. I didn't see any-thing. That's the late bell now. Off with you."

The tennis thugs leave. They look back at me with icy smiles.

"Bud, wait," says Ms. Viola.

"I'll be late for study hall."

"I'll write you a pass."

Nikki lingers, but Ms. Viola says, "No pass for you, Vrdolyak. Get going."

When we're alone, she says, "I saw them block you, and I saw you head-butt John McEnroe there. You should all be suspended."

"So do it," I say.

"Don't call my bluff, friend."

Why is this woman in the sweater vest on my side? Why does she take such an interest in my welfare? Why does she freaking *care* so goddamned much? It makes me want to punch a hole in the wall.

"I know you're being true to yourself, Bud, but if you're not careful," she says, gesturing toward the students filing through the hallway, "they'll kill you."

"No, they won't."

"Yes, they will. I've seen it. Not kill you in a literal sense, but—"

"It doesn't matter. Let them try."

"A lot that was good about this school is gone," she says. "Archery is on its way out. The choir is gone. I don't want them to get you, too."

"That's what Anonymous said in that letter last week. I never knew we used to have a choir."

"I knew," she says sadly.

"You remember the choir?"

"Yes," she says. "They had beautiful voices."

We stand there looking at each other. We're each

waiting for the other to break. But neither of us does. She is a lot stronger than she seems, but then, so am I.

Nikki is waiting for me in the cafeteria. "Dude," she begins, "what is going—"

"I need to get home," I say. I'm finding it harder and harder to be alone with her, even in the hideously unromantic gloom of the cafeteria. I can barely keep a lid on my feelings about her, and I *can't* tell her how I feel because once you spew something like that, you can never take it back. You cannot unhear those words; they'll ring in your ears forever. She'll look at me with pity, then she'll just get uncomfortable, and eventually she will stop hanging around me, and if that happened, I don't think I could take it.

She grabs my arm and won't let go. "What did Viola want to talk to you about?"

"The *As I Lay Dying* essay. That's all."

"Oh. I thought it was about those tennis team dickwads."

"No. It wasn't about them."

"God, I hate them. Makes me want to climb up into a tower with a rifle. Just start picking them off."

I turn to her. Her hand is still on my arm, and it makes me feel hot and cold. "Nikki. You don't know what the hell you're talking about, so don't say stuff like that. For one thing, you don't have any idea what it's like to— You know what, forget it."

"What? I don't know what *what's* like? Believe me, I know all about those jerks. They've surrounded me all my life. I'm going to put their names down on my chart."

I shake my arm out of her grasp. The anger that I carefully keep in check is seeping out. "Is that all you care about, the chart? Column A, column B, and don't forget X, the unknown factor. We're real people—me and Ms. Viola—and we're getting stomped on. *You* just want to 'win,' don't you? You want to be the one who guesses correctly, even if I get pummeled in the process."

"You and *Viola*? Who gives a shit about her? And this chart, all of this, is for you. This is because I'm on your side and want to help you."

"I don't want help. I'm not a little puppy that needs to be rescued."

She wants to yell at me more, I can tell, but she stops herself. I turn on my iPod and jam the earbuds into my ear canals. I crank the volume to drown out whatever Nikki is saying. The mole is itching again. I know Dr. Elliott would say it's psychosomatic, that I'm transferring my anxiety onto a nonexistent mole. Except this is *real*. I can feel it taking over my face.

Nikki lays her hand on my arm again. I can't stand it, it honestly drives me insane, that physical contact that means so much to me and that is obviously something she does without thinking. Then she yanks out my earbuds.

"Again with Car Wash of Death?"

The lyrics, small and tinny through the earbuds, buzz around us.

> *I walk through the valley of the car wash of death*
>
> *I'll punch the clock till my last dying breath . . .*

"What is it with you and that song?"

I swallow the anger. Half the time, I'm not sure where it comes from. "I don't know, it's been in my head all the time lately. It's based on Dariush's old job, and trying to do what you're supposed to do in life, but it all explodes in your face anyway. Just another sad and bleak story that I am drawn to," I say. "Like *The Chocolate War.*"

She sighs. "Bud, listen: I don't think you're a puppy that needs rescuing, okay? I want to help you because that's what friends do. I've always been kind of a loner, but I haven't been a loner this year. I've been with you and Reggie, like we're a . . . a . . .oh, Jesus, a *team*. You know I hate the concept of teams and joining shit, but somehow, with you guys, it seems like a totally positive thing. It's good. It can effect change."

"I don't really see how," I say.

She says, "I'm not selling the chocolates either."

I get home at my usual time, 3:45. It's cold. I don't have my stupid hat and gloves, so I freeze on the walk home from the bus stop. The sky is an ominous gray. Halloween is tomorrow. In front of our building, the dead chrysanthemums welcome me, and my mother's rotting jack-o'-lanterns lie smashed on the sidewalk.

I sidestep the pumpkin guts and have my hand on the gate when I notice something ten times worse than the murdered jack-o'-lantern: my dad's station wagon parked on the street. He is never home before six. Why is he here?

I take the stairs two at a time. My heart pumps like mad, and images shift through my mind: something has happened to my mom, my siblings. Dariush.

The door is unlocked. I burst in. There's no carnage in

the living room, so that's good. Arman and Dorri are sitting on the couch. They are not watching TV or playing *Halo*, so that's bad. My mother and father are standing in the kitchen—alive. Where's Azita? In class? Where's Dariush? I see my parents' faces.

"What's the matter?"

My dad is only slightly taller than me and a bit heavier, but he gives the impression of being an incredibly powerful man. He approaches like a prizefighter charging out of his corner. I can see the spidery, bloodshot threads in his eyes and his extralarge pores, and he raises his fist to me with a right hook that stops just short of connecting with my head.

My mom shrieks, and my little sister and brother look at each other nervously. But Dad doesn't hit me. He does something far worse. There's a low, keening moan. It's coming from him. He is *crying*. And it sounds like a wounded animal, like he has never cried before and doesn't know how to do it right. He screams at me in Farsi and then switches to English, which is more disturbing, because when he gets upset, his English becomes more broken, and he sounds broken, too.

"Why you are doing this?" he screams. "Why you are doing this to me?"

"What? I'm not doing—"

He reaches out to grab me, then thinks better of it and grasps his own hands in a pleading gesture. "You are so stupid, Bud, with this chocolate bar refusal. You are ruining everything we plan, everything I work so hard for. To get you into that good school, hoping you have no more problems; but no—we get phone call from the vice principal today, to your mother, saying you refuse to sell those chocolate bars. They are displeased, they want to know why, they ask, 'Is there trouble at home?' Always this is how it starts. They ask is there trouble, and then if you don't shape up, they throw you out."

I hold up my hands to calm him down. "Look, just let me explain—"

"Shut up. Nothing you say makes any difference. You will not get good grades nor good transcript notes, nor have a good record for applying to university. You don't see this now because you are too young, but you are destroying your future on a . . . a *whim*. A silly, rebellious idea that is for nothing."

"I'm standing up for something I believe in. The money that comes from fund-raising doesn't go to the right clubs. Baba, you don't understand how my school ostracizes everyone who is different."

"Ignore it!" he shouts. "You think I have not been ostracized, intimidated, assaulted all my life in this country? Especially since 2001? Be better than that. Hold your head up, say nothing, move on. Just take care of your own business."

"This *is* my business," I say. "It's the only thing I believe in or care about. Your plans for me are not my plans. You can't control me!"

I've never talked like this to Dad before, but then he never usually listens to me when I talk to him. Again he raises his hand to me, and I can feel this earthquake of rage boiling up to my brain. My dad always told Dariush and me how his own father hit him—not just light spanks, like what he gave us when we were kids, but full-on beatings—and how our grandfather could not handle problems in an intellectual, rational manner and lashed out in a "barbaric" way instead. And yet now he's standing here, ready to pound me.

"Go ahead, hit me," I say. I'm shaking and my fists are balled up, as if I could actually defend myself.

Oh, how he wants to. He hates me—you can see it, feel it. But then the anger disintegrates in his eyes.

"You are not worth it," he says. "Even a dog learns a lesson if you hit it, but you are too selfish and foolish to learn anything." He turns his back on me and walks to his bedroom, where he closes the door quietly behind him.

My mother stalks up to me. "You should be ashamed of yourself."

"I'm not. I'm not ashamed of who I am anymore. You've always made me feel like a failure, but I don't care what you think."

She slaps me across the face. Not really hard—she doesn't want to hurt me—she just wants to put me in my place. Arman and Dorri look away.

She says, "Baba is right. You have caused more problems than you are worth."

Parents say these things sometimes, okay. But when I look in her eyes, I know she means it. And it makes me want to disappear for good.

I run for the door, and that's when it hits. My entire body breaks out in rivers of sweat. My vision vibrates as I turn the doorknob, all the spots rush into my eyes—blue, neon yellow, black—I can't feel my hands or legs—I'm suffocating, blackness everywhere, it covers my mouth like a hand, and . . . *I am not getting through this, I am not surviving this, I will never survive this*, I think I'm dying, help me, Mom Dad Dr. Elliott anybody for fuck's sake God help me out of this don't leave me alone abandon me alienate me hate me destroy me—floor rushes up to me—my little brother and sister are crying, everyone's crying but me. I can't cry because I can't breathe. I can't breathe because everything inside me shuts down.

CHAPTER NINETEEN

I come to later, much later. I didn't call Dariush, but some-one must have. Mom, I guess. He's sitting on the edge of my bed. He puts an ice pack against my nose. No one else is allowed in here.

I don't remember going to my room after I passed out. Maybe Mom or Dad helped me. What I remember is open-ing my eyes and seeing Mom sitting on the side of my bed. I was under the covers in my clothes, a bloody mess. She felt my forehead as if I might have a temperature—as if I were merely sick instead of blacking out during the most murder-ous panic attack of my life.

"You should have sold the chocolate bars." She actual-ly said this, actually returned to this topic. "Why must you do these things? What harm would have come from selling them? And then, not one hour after your vice principal calls, we get another call, now from Dr. Elliott, saying you quit your therapy! You cannot do that without asking. That was one of the stipulations from the—the incident last year."

Oh right, the incident. It had struck me that during Dad's tirade, he'd never once expressed concern that I had quit therapy. No, he only mentioned the chocolate bars. I said, "Go away, Mom." And finally she did.

Now Dariush is here, and I don't know where anyone else is.

"I can't believe you fell flat on your face like this. You're lucky you didn't bust your head wide open." My brother adjusts the ice pack gently. "Hmm . . . your nose is bleeding, but I don't think it's broken. Anyway, it makes you look like a badass. I wonder if we should go to the ER, though? Can you breathe okay?"

I don't answer. I don't care.

We've been playing the Chet Baker album over and over. I don't want to hear anything outside this room: not my family, not the phone, and not Rex howling up a storm in his yard.

"Tell me why," he says. "About the chocolate bars. Between you and me?"

I don't know if he's ever read *The Chocolate War*, but I'm too out of it to explain it right. "All I wanted to do was disturb the universe."

I turn away and let numbness wash over me. If he's waiting for me to make sense, he's at the back of a long line.

He says, "I know you didn't ask to be transferred to Magnificat, Badi. None of us ask for any of the things Dad forces on us. But you couldn't have stayed at Sullivan. You had to go somewhere. And now he's afraid you're going to have to leave again. I'm not defending him, not at all. I'm just explaining why he freaked out."

His words settle on me like snow. They melt until they're nothing.

"Just get through high school, and then you can be unemployed and come live with me."

I hear him, but I feel like someone is playing me a recording of what my brother would say if I were really here. I mean, I know I'm here. I'm confused.

The Chet Baker record ends. Dariush looks at me. I don't respond. He puts on "Car Wash of Death" instead.

I think about tomorrow. School. It makes my stomach seize up to think that people hate me, that people I don't know are out to get me, when all I've done is be myself.

My brother shoves a towel under my door and lights a cigarette. "You mind?" he asks. He cracks the window and exhales into the chilly air. "What are you gonna be for Halloween?"

I say, "A ghost."

He sings along with himself on the record.

"Use the pre-soak to loosen crap from the road

I aim the foam brush like a gun and reload . . ."

He cocks his hand like a revolver, squints, and aims at me. *"Boom,"* he says. He grins then because of course he is just joking around, and it is just a song.

Halloween

Everybody stares at my face. Now I have a swollen, blood-crusty nose to go with the yellow-green bruise on my jaw from my Homeroom Buddy and his friends. I remind myself that I look like a badass, but it's not really that comforting.

As I pass the front office, Mrs. Kobunski says, "Oh my. What in the world—"

"A minor car accident last night," I say. "I wasn't wearing my seat belt. But I'm fine."

"Honey, you should turn right around and go home. Let me call your mother."

"No!" I shout, and she flinches. "I'm sorry, please don't. She got pretty banged up, too—in the car accident—and my dad is taking care of her, and really, the doctor said I'm okay and could go to school if I took some Tylenol."

I leave before she can detain me. I can't say why I have such a mad need to be in school other than 1) there's no way I could stay in our apartment a minute longer, and 2) I have a feeling—call it intuition—that everything is about to come to a head, and I want to be here when it does.

The halls are quiet this early. It's a long time before people start trickling into school. I exit the south stairwell by the library and see Nikki at her locker. I go to her, determined to show my face and tell the truth about me and my dad and how my mental problems are only getting worse.

She doesn't say anything. Her eyes search mine, and I don't lower my gaze. Then she hugs me. It's a long hug, especially for someone like Nikki who despises hugging, and it feels like she is about to fall apart. Not cry, but fall apart; there's a difference, and if you don't know what I mean, then I can't explain it to you. She draws back and touches my face in the only unbruised area, I think it's about an inch of skin in the middle of my cheek, although I can feel one of the underground zits there gathering strength. Beneath the mole.

"I fell," I say.

She nods and looks down at her hand, which is holding the laminated folder containing all things pertinent to the anonymous letters. She says, "I wanted to tell you something important, but this doesn't really seem like the right time now."

"Go ahead. I want to hear it." Do I?

"I stayed up half the night going over my chart. I know who it is."

I wait. The blood roars in my ears. What will we do with her information? Who will we take down?

The halls are filling up now. She shifts from one foot to the other, looking unsure.

"Nikki," a voice calls out from about twenty feet away. The tall boy gazes out over the tops of everyone's heads. He's wearing a black plastic mask, the kind I was going to pick up at the Dollar Store back when I wanted to be a cat burglar for Halloween. It's Reggie, and his mouth smiles, but I can't tell if it's genuine because his eyes are hidden. "Boo."

"Never mind," Nikki mutters, her eyes flashing a warning at me.

"You mean . . .?" My eyes cut to Reggie. *Him?*

"Shut *up*," she snarls.

"What are we talking about?" he asks. He doesn't lift the mask.

Nikki says, "Nothing," and Reggie starts to ask about my face. He doesn't get to finish because shoved inside the ventilation slats of Nikki's locker is a piece of paper, and she gasps as she unfolds it. And all around us the same thing is happening; not every locker, but here and there, people are unfolding pieces of paper slipped between their locker slats.

I look over her shoulder and read it.

> *The scene of the crime will be the scene of the crime.*
>
> *Who is alive, who is dead? Is it someone you know, or me: the stranger?*
>
> *Who is reflected in the eyes of the dead?*
>
> *Happy Halloween.*

The three of us stand there reading it and rereading it, and our eyes are darting from face to face to paper and back again. Everyone in the hall is reading one or talking to someone who is reading one. All the notes are the same.

"What's this supposed to mean?" a kid next to us asks. "Is it a Halloween trick?"

A girl says to him, to us, to everyone really, because we are together in this mess now, "Who could put these in the lockers without anybody seeing?"

"Somebody who flies under the radar," I say.

Reggie looks at me and then glances at Nikki. "That could be a lot of us."

I say to him, "Lift your mask."

He says to me, "You first."

This is a day when nothing gets done. People are fixated on Halloween, Homecoming this weekend, and the notes in the lockers. The students have managed to keep the notes secret from the teachers. I'm not sure how or why. Maybe sometimes we just want our own little dramas without adults getting involved and taking them over, or McNeill putting the entire school on lockdown. My beat-up face hardly gets any notice.

On the way out of Chemistry, I hear that girl from Charmers Cafe say to a friend, "It's true. I heard it from Trevor. He brought a gun to Sullivan and was arrested and had all this Muslim shit taped up in his locker."

The other girl goes, "Aw, Thunder Pants? No way."

"I know! He seems so harmless. Too bad, because he's kind of cute in a Harold & Kumar way, right?"

Unbelievable, the stories that are circulating about me. I'm the last kid who would show up at school with a gun. Everything about my arrest was difficult and scary, but I know that doesn't make for exciting rumors. And the "Muslim shit" in my locker? It was a quote from the Middle Eastern poet Kahlil Gibran:

I prefer to be a dreamer among the humblest, with visions to be realized, than lord among those without dreams and desires.

There was an Arabic translation underneath it because he was, you know, an *Arab*. Big deal. Could there be anyone less threatening than a poet?

In AP Bio, Mila brings the fetal pig tray to our table. There's not much left to him anymore except ears and formaldehyde. She stares at me.

"Are you looking at my mole?"

"What? What happened to your nose?"

I say, "Don't ask."

I keep thinking about what Nikki said, that Mila belongs on the chart because of Computer Camp. I don't believe it. Honestly, I don't think Nikki knows who she suspects anymore. I can't see Mila as a villain. She's so gentle with our fetal pig.

She sits down. "How about those notes, huh? Was there one in your locker?"

I blurt out, "I never thought it was you, I just want to make that clear."

"Me? Who thinks it's me?"

"And even if it was you, I wouldn't blame you. I'd support your decision to freak out, as long as no one was killed. And even then, there are probably instances where it could be justified."

"Oh, the newspaper letters. Okay. But it's not me. Or the locker note. Really. I mean, thanks, though. I guess I'm kind of flattered." She taps her pen rapid-fire against her notebook and mutters to herself, "Like a teenage, female Clint Eastwood . . . got it," then scrawls on a fresh page: *Note to self: idea for screenplay—girl opens fire on school but is exonerated due to raging PMS . . .*

"Some people thought it was me," I say.

"Why? Because of the chocolate bars?"

"I'm not sure anymore," I admit. "It's sort of complicated."

She says, "Remember when I told you I was afraid I had done something stupid? Did you think I meant the letters?"

I shrug. She sighs and lightly drags the scalpel over the hole where our pig's heart should be. "I meant the chocolate bars. I told my homeroom teacher I refused to sell mine, too. But I didn't really mean that was *stupid* stupid. More like . . . dangerous."

"You did that? Why?"

She doesn't answer, but she scribbles again in her notebook: *Note to self: idea for screenplay—girl meets boy . . .*

Lunch is incredibly weird. Nikki is sitting off to the side by herself, hypnotized by her charts and laminated folder. Reggie sits at the other end with one of the guys from the chess team. They have a board and pieces in front of them and are discussing strategy for Regionals. He has removed his mask—costumes aren't allowed in school—but he has not said a word to me.

"What's going on?" I ask Nikki.

"I don't know," she says. She lowers her voice and shoots a quick look at Reggie. "The note in the lockers has really thrown me. It doesn't sound right to me. I'm missing something, but what? I've got to figure it out, and I hope I'm not too late."

"Too late for what?"

"To keep some idiot from getting killed or beaten up at Loyola Beach after Homecoming. I think that's what the note this morning has got to mean: 'the scene of the crime will be the scene of the crime,' meaning the scene of the first crime—gangbanging the Gridiron Queen, the rufies, the alcohol—will be where the next crime is, whatever that will be. I thought it meant the note writer was going to humiliate or beat up someone, someone who deserves it, but now I'm not sure. Whatever it is, it'll be bad."

I watch Reggie as he talks chess strategy. He uses words like *annihilate* and *carnage* and *forced surrender*. He has a strange light in his eyes.

"I wouldn't talk to him if I were you," Nikki says.

"Is he mad at us or something?"

She says, "We had words."

But she won't tell me what the words were.

She studies her notes, and I start to hum "Let's Get Lost," but it's hard to hum jazz, plus it bothers everyone at the table. I switch to singing "Car Wash of Death" under my breath.

> *"I walk through the valley of the car wash of death*
>
> *I'll punch the clock till my last dying breath*
>
> *A dark-skinned stranger with an engineering degree*
>
> *Wipes down your car, his diploma is a chamois . . ."*

Nikki murmurs, "That's funny."

It is funny. But it's also true. It was the only way Dariush could tell people who he was. Sometimes *I* feel like I'm dying to tell the whole world who I really am: Badi Hessamiza-deh—the "Arab," but not an Arab, just an Iranian American boy who is drowning. Why shouldn't I tell everyone? But telling people the truth about yourself is like daring them to screw with you.

Nikki says, "Why'd he quit his band?"

"My dad made him. I mean, he didn't force him, but he made Dariush's life so miserable, complaining and making fun of him, that Dariush just gave up."

She peers at me through her glasses, her green eyes sharp and inscrutable. Suddenly they widen, and she looks down at her chart. What is she figuring out?

She jerks her head up. "Bud, the notes in our lockers and the letters in the paper were not written by the same person. They don't sound the same. And it's not Anonymous's MO to put notes in lockers. He always uses the newspaper."

"His 'MO'? Is this *CSI: Magnificat*?"

"Just listen! The newspaper letters—I think they have nothing to do with you. The author isn't out to get you. They were written by someone desperate, but they never actually threatened anything. The notes in our lockers did. And those notes weren't signed 'Anonymous.' We just assumed it was the same person."

"But what exactly do the locker notes threaten? What crime are they talking about?"

Nikki shakes her head. "I don't know yet. Maybe it's not a *real* crime, not in the illegal sense. Maybe it's more of a crime of, I don't know . . . injustice? A tragedy. A crime against humanity."

I don't say anything. Her mind is moving fast. Too fast.

She goes on. "'Who is alive, who is dead? Is it someone you know, or me: the stranger?' Jesus. Should we tell a teacher? Viola? I don't know what to do."

"How could a teacher help? How could anyone?"

She mutters to herself, "It's familiar to me. . . ."

Reggie's voice breaks through, speaking to his teammate. "Don't get suckered in by the queen's sacrifice." Is it my imagination, or does he flick an angry glance at us when he says this?

His teammate dutifully jots down notes.

Reggie continues. "It's a trap—a seemingly careless move allowing for the queen's capture—that tricks the opponent into opening his defense."

His friend snorts. "I would never fall for that."

"You'd be surprised what you'd fall for when you think someone is vulnerable," says Reggie.

Nikki turns to him. The look she gives him is long, cold, and cruel.

Ms. Viola stops me before I even walk into her classroom. She pulls me aside from the line of students filing in and propels me a short distance away.

"This," she says, swirling her finger in circles around my face. "What is this?"

"You can see it? My mole?"

"Your what? I'm talking about your nose. First those bruises, now this?"

"Oh, that. Car accident."

"Trampoline *and* car accident?"

"I'm very unlucky," I say.

"Tell me who it was."

"It was a Ford Taurus."

She ignores me. "I know it wasn't a trampoline. I know it was some students. Just tell me who it was."

I look away. One more lie and I'm going to spontaneously combust.

She says, "I hope you hit him back, at least."

I say, "Fistfights aren't allowed at Magnificat."

"Was it the tennis team? You know, you could have smacked that kid Ben after I sent him packing. You wouldn't have gotten into trouble. I'd have lied for you."

"I'm not going to fight. I'm a conscientious objector." My voice sounds thin.

"Are we talking about a war here, Bud?"

"You would lie for me," I say, "and I would lie for you."

She says, "You don't have to lie for me."

The bell rings. We should both be in the classroom now. She opens the door and waves her hand ahead of her: *After you.* But I'm not going in. Out of all my classes here, I'm most sorry that I'm skipping hers. I turn and head quickly toward the north wing. The corridor is empty except for lost items, a pencil, a wadded-up ball of paper on the floor, a rubber bracelet, all gathering dust like dry, dead things.

My mom is in Khaleh Rana's apartment when I get home early, using my aunt's oven to prepare extra dishes for tonight. Our apartment is empty. I put some things in a backpack, I don't even know what. I don't know what I'm doing. Running away is pointless—where would I go? But I want to run. I riffle through my parents' desk for cash or candy or something useful. I find my dad's checkbook and flip through it.

I look at the check record and see that the last one he wrote was dated this morning. It was made out to Magnificat for five hundred dollars. On the description line he scribbled CHOCOLATE BARS.

He *can't* have. But he did. I add it up in my head: each box has ten bars and costs ten dollars. So he bought fifty boxes of chocolate bars. My father bought the school's silence and squashed my revolution, confused as it was. He never gave me the chance to figure out and explain what it meant to be a conscientious objector. I will never get a chance to explain anything to him because my reasons and feelings don't matter in this house.

He must have delivered the check this morning. So where are all those chocolate bars? Probably in the basement. I really could go for some chocolate . . . no, no. Stop that. I'm ashamed that I thought about it.

I tear through the pigeonholes in the desk, hunting, hunting. Ah, money, glorious. Left over from grocery store trips, lunch money for school, dollar after dollar crammed in there. And now crammed into my wallet.

I stumble down the hall like a zombie. King Sargon waits for me at the end of my bed, and I pet him a little. I go through my nightstand. Inside is my journal—I throw that in the backpack—and then I spy a tiny, folded slip of paper. It's the label from our mailboxes, the one that had our old name on it. I stuff it into my shirt pocket. I want it with me. Next, I hunt through my secret stash in the hidden compartment of my old toy chest. No money there. Just the BlackBerry device I stole from school, the dupe set of keys, the antianxiety meds my parents think I still take, other pills I've stockpiled from the past, names and addresses of those who have wronged me, a dog-eared copy of *The Anarchist Cookbook*, and a map I recently made of the school and its grounds. There's also that photo of Nikki and me on our nonsexual date. I put the drugs, the map, the BlackBerry thing, the keys, *The Anarchist Cookbook*, and the photo in my backpack. Some people might have put such a treasured photo in an album or tacked it to a mirror or framed it or shoved it in a wallet. But I wanted to keep it somewhere safe.

CHAPTER TWENTY-ONE

I need to go someplace and think. Someplace to plan. But I have all this important stuff with me, and I'm too nervous to leave the house. What if I got jumped and they took the BlackBerry device or the school keys? So I go down into the basement, the Pit of Despair with its nasty subfloor and rat traps and mildew. Ha, just as I suspected: there are the fifty boxes of chocolate bars way in the corner, behind a crib and a pile of two-by-fours that have warped from dampness. I'm kind of hungry, but I resist the temptation. There's the wicker outdoor furniture we use in the summer. I sit in a wicker chair for a long time. I take note of all the ordinary household and landscaping chemicals my dad stores down here. It's a veritable arsenal of poison and explosives. I consult *The Anarchist Cookbook*. It has recipes for manufacturing explosives, but it's decades old and unreliable, and I can figure out stuff like that in more scientific ways. Still, it's a symbol for me of what can be achieved when you are pressed, pushed, and put upon for too long.

I hear people moving around upstairs. Mom hired a cleaning service to fumigate the reek of pot out of Dariush's old apartment and to wash the resin stains off the light switch plates. I hear them dragging their industrial-grade vacuums around, obliterating the last traces of my brother. I hear the joyful shrieks of my cousins and Arman and Dorri as they pound up and down the stairs from apartment to apartment. And then I hear footsteps coming down the basement stairs. I peek over the top of a papasan chair and see Dad walk in. Luckily I'm on the opposite side of the room and hidden behind tons of wicker, so I can get my stuff together quickly without him seeing.

"Hey, Baba," I call out, all innocent.

"Bud? What are you doing down here?"

"Oh, just going through some old . . ." I see him hoisting the extra croquet set over one arm and a life-size plastic skeleton over the other. Wow, I've been so wrapped up in this crusade, I forgot for a while what tonight is. "The croquet game!"

"Come help me. You can put this skeleton somewhere outside. I am going to string up the orange Ramadan lights to go with the others." He chuckles at his lame joke about the lights.

I'm not surprised that he can act so normal after our huge fight. That is how it is with us. With him.

"Okay." He sees me rise from behind the papasan chair, and his eyes fall upon the boxes of chocolate bars as I pass them. Neither of us acknowledges them.

"Maman says you are going to be a cat burglar this year. She washed the crotch rot out of your thrift costume."

I take the skeleton from his arms. "I changed my mind. I'm going to be a ghost."

"Well, that's good, too." He hums as he gathers up

more decorations from the Halloween box. He's happy and smiling. It's such an unusual look for him.

Then I remember that I invited Nikki to our tournament, and that she invited Reggie. "Um, is it okay that I invited some friends from school? I asked them a few days ago and forgot about it." I recall the weirdness with Reggie today. "Actually, I don't know, they might not even show up."

"Friends? Really? Well, yes, of course that's fine. I didn't know you had any." Only my dad would say that.

"Is Dariush coming?"

"That I doubt very much."

I hang the skeleton from the garage gutter. Then I go upstairs to lock my backpack in my old toy chest. All my contraband is in there, including the notes I wrote out for the pipe bombs, fireworks, model rocketry, and low explosives. I cut eyeholes in the sheet that used to cover Dariush's futon and drape it over me. I look at myself in the mirror. With everything else covered—the worry lines in my forehead, the nervous smile, the retainer—my eyes look bleak.

I look out my window. Dad has already strung up the lights and fixed a green spotlight on the skeleton. Spooky haunted-house sound-effects blast from the ancient boom box plugged in outside the basement door. Little ghosts made from tissues wrapped around balled-up newspaper, courtesy of my siblings and cousins, hang from the fence posts and low tree branches. Pumpkins dot the lawn around the wickets, an extra challenge to our game. The smashed jack-o'-lanterns have vanished.

Dad is dressed like a vampire. Mom just wears a black

headband with sparkly cat ears on it, and she has whiskers painted on her face. Her costumes are always minimal, thrown together at the last minute. She'd rather spend the day making food. The rest of the family trickles out there. The only person who stays inside is Khaleh Rana, mostly because we need someone to hand out candy. She looks like a witch in her everyday clothes.

The doorbell rings, and I hear Khaleh Rana blathering loudly in broken English, her voice carrying up the stairs. "Here candy! Happy Halloween! Bye-bye!" which is a total sham because she has a master's in biomedical engineering, and her English is fluent and elegantly nuanced. She just hates strangers and avoids interacting with them whenever possible.

Then I hear Reggie's voice above hers: "We're not trick-or-treating. We're here to see Bud."

They came.

I book down the front stairs, wrestle Nikki and Reggie away from my aunt, and lead them around the corner of the building to the pathway that goes out to the backyard.

"Nice sheet, Grand Dragon," says Reggie. "Way to make a brother feel welcome."

"Are you here to play croquet?" I ask. They're not wearing costumes.

"Is the invitation still open?" Nikki asks.

"Y-yes . . . of course," I answer, bringing them through the patio gate. I realize I'm not happy they showed up. I introduce them to my family, get them mallets, explain the rules, show them where the food is, and the whole time I feel like the Bud they knew—the guy they became friends with and who invited them (or Nikki, to be honest) just a few days ago—is gone, and in his place is the guy who spent hours painstakingly assembling explosives recipes and amassing chemical compounds.

The tournament begins. My dad offers to let Reggie go first, and my stomach turns into a small, cold ball. Good Persian culture is insane with politeness and a pretense of being humble. Iranians have a complicated list of things that are considered good and polite in social situations, including treating your guests better than your own family—or at least appearing to.

"Sure, thanks," says Reggie, and he whacks his ball through the first wickets. Dad's mouth sets into a grim little line. How was Reggie supposed to know he should refuse twice before finally accepting Dad's third offer?

My mom explains to Nikki what the dishes are that she's prepared: *shirin polow* (Persian sweet rice), *dolmeh* (grape leaves stuffed with spiced beef), curry potatoes, various kebabs. Everything is laid out on these gigantic folding tables and kept hot in electric warming pans.

"Whoa. When we cook out, my dad just grills frozen turkey burgers from Costco," Nikki remarks. Mom looks stricken at this horrific revelation and pats Nikki's shoulder.

I try to line up my shot, but the sheet is obstructing my view. I remove it and hang it on the fence, feeling exposed. After I take my turn, Reggie stands by me and we watch Azita knock the little kids' balls out of the yard. She loves to make them cry.

"Hey, Bud," Reggie says, "is your older brother coming?"

Dad bends down to tie his shoelace, but I know he is eavesdropping. I say, "No, he has other plans tonight."

"That's too bad. I wanted to meet him. The way you

always talk about him makes him sound like an interesting dude."

Dad does not look pleased that I've been speaking of Dariush outside the family.

When it's Reggie's turn, Dad sidles up to me. "So. You are friends with the black?"

Furtively, I glance at Reggie. "I don't know if he's *the* black. He's *a* black."

"Don't be smart," Dad hisses. "It was just a question. Diversity can be a good thing." Ironically, Dad has a very limited view of the merits of other cultures.

"And the girl? She is his girlfriend? What do her parents think of that?"

"First of all, she's not his girlfriend—I'm pretty sure she's not—and secondly, her family would be thrilled to have her hang out with someone like Reggie." Which I'm not at all sure is true, but Dad drives me crazy.

He scoffs. "That is unlikely, with everything that I know of white America."

"Your turn, Bud!" Nikki calls to me. Again, my dad frowns. He disapproves of women raising their voices.

My anxiety level is at DEFCON 5. I'm sweating, and all I can focus on is a strand of Nikki's hair that is stuck to her cheek, which makes me super OCD, which floods me with angst and adrenaline times a thousand, which makes me want to run over there and rip that lock of hair right out of her head. It reminds me of sitting in the car with her after the bonfire, tucking her hair behind her ear, stroking her jawline, almost kissing her. I swear my lungs are paralyzed.

Reggie stands on the patio scarfing down a lamb kebab, and when my mother offers him some more, all the muscles in my shoulders lock. Mom doesn't subscribe to this anti-quated ritual of offering-and-refusing over and over until the politeness kills you, but I know Dad is listening.

"You bet, Mrs. Hess," Reggie says. "This is awesome." Mom is always pleased when people like her food. She piles a ton of cherry-and-lentil pilaf on his plate. Reggie says he needs to carbo-load because of chess Regionals. I don't think he's kidding.

I'm so tense, I could snap in half like a piece of chalk in Ms. Viola's hand.

After my next turn (I hit my foot with the mallet, that's how gone I am), Reggie motions for me to come over to the food table, where he's pigging out on dates stuffed with crushed pistachios, honey, and orange zest.

"Are you going to Homecoming? It's not too late," he says. He talks with his mouth full. I have to look away because the fully visible chunks of masticated nuts are sending me over the edge. I never want to eat, talk, or play croquet again.

"Why would I want to do that?"

"Well, for one thing, to see what Anonymous has planned for the after-party on Loyola Beach, and for another, Nikki and I are going, and we were thinking you should ask Mila and we could all go together."

My mouth dries up. "You're going with Nikki?"

"Just as friends, I guess." He is disappointed about this qualifier, you can tell.

"You guys seemed to be fighting at lunch. When did all this happen?"

"It was a misunderstanding about . . . nothing. It doesn't matter. We made up. So why don't you ask Mila?"

"What? Because I don't want to go. If something happens at Loyola Beach, I want to be as far away as possible. I'll probably be blamed anyway. And you can't ask a girl to a dance three days before. What about all that bullshit you fed me about Homecoming being so 'rah-rah' and ridiculous? Suddenly it's cool to go, now that some psycho wants to murder a football player or the Gridiron Queen or whoever else and pin it all on me?"

"*What* are you so mad about? Jeez, I thought it would be fun, that's all, mocking people and dressing inappropriately. Sue me for suggesting it."

Mom is trying to get my attention with wild eyebrow gymnastics. I pretend I don't see her, but she doesn't let me go that easily.

"Bud, I didn't know this weekend was Homecoming." She butts right into our conversation. Reggie leaves to take his turn, swinging his mallet with violence. "I heard your friend say it is not too late to ask someone. We will be happy to pay. Why don't you go? If you are feeling up to it, that is." She looks sadly at my bruises and gigantic nose.

"Maman, please. I don't want to go."

"But it is an important ritual of high school. You'll be sorry when you're older if you miss out on it now."

"Are you for real?"

"Badi-jan!" She calls me by my old name, the old, old me, before I became Bud Hess, the guy who hid in the basement cataloging chemical explosives. But let's face it, Badi Hessamizadeh hid in the basement, too, designing detonation patterns for toilet bombs. It's useless to try and escape myself.

"I'm not going to the dance because I have a US History paper I need to start."

She falters here, unsure whether to believe me or just feel sorry that my social life is a black hole.

"You're up," says Nikki as she passes me on the way to the food. My parents appraise her old-lady dress, torn jeans, and black Converse, trying to figure out what her costume is supposed to be, and I long to announce that she isn't wearing one.

I whack my ball into a bush and leave it there and then walk back to the patio and sit at the picnic table to keep from falling off the face of the planet.

Nikki comes and sits by me. "Did Reggie mention Home—"

"Yeah, but I'm not interested, thanks. Have a good time."

"What's the matter?"

"You guys were barely speaking at lunch, and now he's your date for Homecoming? Kind of bizarre, I don't know."

"We're just going as— Listen, who cares, it's not important. What's important is that I had this theory about Reggie and the letters"—here she casts a quick glance around, but nobody can hear us—"that I mentioned to him, but I was wrong and he forgave me. So it's all good."

"Great. Fantastic."

She shakes her head. "My chart, my beautiful chart. What a crock. It hasn't helped at all. At first I wanted to protect you, and then things got murky and I wanted to protect Reggie, and now I have no idea who's behind it, and why am I killing myself to protect some jock? And now the locker note. Could this whole thing be more confusing?"

I don't respond. And it's not just that I'm mad at her about Homecoming, because I'm *not*. She can do whatever she wants, go out with whoever, date or not, go as friends or more, even though *we* are friends and *we* could have just as easily gone together. But I didn't ask her, didn't even *think* of asking her, and she didn't ask me, and this is the way things always go for me.

The real reason I can't talk to Nikki is because I've moved off the path to sanity and fitting in—even with the misfits—and where I'm headed now, she can't follow. I love her and that hurts. Even Reggie, the type of guy I've always admired—cool-geek, comfortable with himself, smart, anti-authority—I can't be friends with him anymore because I'm giving up on trying to get better. There are all those people who stand in my way, who haunt me, dog my heels, from Sullivan to Magnificat. The shit just never ends. I'm giving in to being who I am now.

"I'm up." I say this even though it isn't true, just so I can walk away.

Dad's already finished and he's now "poison," trying to knock everybody into oblivion. I swing my mallet as I walk around the yard, looking at no one, and I see the bare limbs of burr oak and ash. Their branches are thin black fingers clawing up into the sky. Stretches of dying grass in our yard lay open to receive the winter snow. Some flowers blossom still—sedum, autumn clematis, aster—more striking because of all that's died around them. The withered summer roses try to resist the autumn wind but bend instead and lose the last of their mildewed leaves.

Then I see Ispahan. An ancient variety of rose that grows wild on the hills of Iran. Its deep-pink blossoms are long gone, but still its thick canes grow. The Ispahan rose is tough and riotous, like Iran itself. And like Iran, like the Persian people, it is beloved and feared and underestimated.

My parents planted the rose in our backyard in honor of our heritage, but it grabbed hold of our chain-link fence and in ten years has pulled the fence out of the cement foundation. We're going to have to cut it down, but it's a bitch to tackle. The thing is too wild to plant in a yard. It grows frighteningly strong. It gobbles everything in sight: water, earth, air. It strangles other plants. It cuts you when you go near it, bleeds you even when you don't mean to touch it, because it has many, many thorns.

CHAPTER TWENTY-TWO

November

I move through Thursday like a shark in the shallows. I feel that everything is within my grasp. No need to engage in petty confrontations—I have a power they don't have. I can choose to make them my dinner, or not.

I don't talk to anyone all day. I spend the lunch period in the library. In Bio, Mila asks if I'm going to Homecoming and I say no, and I think she wants me to ask her and for a second I feel a surge of the old me, the good kid, a surge that almost makes me feel happy, but I squash it. Being a good kid never got me anywhere. I'm not saying I'm a bad kid now, I don't think I am, but when you cross the line from just standing up for yourself to taking revenge, your moral center shifts a little. I don't know who or what I am right now. I guess I'm whatever they say I am.

In Modern Lit, Ms. Viola hands out copies of *The Stranger*. I've been expecting that for some time. I knew she'd return to the syllabus. Old habits die hard.

After class, Viola corrals me to say I'm getting a demerit for cutting class yesterday. I look at her stonily.

"Did you hear me?" she asks.

"Yes, sorry." And then I get a brilliant idea. I need to be

at the dance and wasn't sure how to crash it without being found out. But maybe I don't need to crash it. A lie can become reality. "Actually, there was something I'd like to ask you: I'd like to cover the Homecoming dance for the *Vox Populi*. I know, I know, the publication of the paper has been suspended, but McNeill has got to lift the suspension sometime, right? There should be an article for when that happens. I'd like to go and take some pictures, write up a little piece on it. Okay?"

"I guess that would be all right," she says, and I nod and walk off. "Don't cut my class again," she calls after me.

Nikki is following me to the door, trying to talk, but I keep moving. I hear Viola ask her, "What is going on with your friend?"

"I don't know," Nikki says. "I don't think I've ever known."

After school I would have to pass by Dylan and his army on my way out of the cafeteria, so I linger behind a post and wait for them to leave. To kill time, I put a leftover orange from lunch in the microwave and turn it on.

Nikki pushes through the tide of kids flooding the caf. She's looking for me. I gave her the slip by my locker, but now she's almost caught up to me. I withdraw farther behind the post. She strides up to the jocks, who are on the other side of my hideout.

I can't hear what she says to Dylan, but I hear his reply: "Now, now. Be nice." His voice has a leer in it, if that's possible. I can picture his eyes raking over her.

"Beat anybody up in the bathroom lately?" she asks him.

Silence. I peek around the post. Dylan's bravado melts,

and he looks around guiltily. He's so worried about his status as a "good guy," but he has no problem with hustling up a bunch of pricks to whale on me.

Nikki takes a step toward him and gets in his face. "I really have a thing for guys who pick on innocent people, especially boys who can't defend themselves against a pack of testosterone-fueled dickwads."

"Innocent?" He laughs.

"Give me a break," she says, about to push by him. He grabs her arm and stops her. Adrenaline washes through my system. There's a metallic taste in my mouth. I want to kill him.

"Why don't you ask Thunder Pants about the kid he tried to kill at Sullivan? He was bragging about it before I kicked that smug little grin off his face."

"Bud? Try to kill someone? You don't know what you're talking about." But a flicker of doubt creases her forehead. She doesn't know what to believe about me, and I can't blame her for that.

"Ask him, then." Dylan lets go of her arm and raises his hands as if to show that he's harmless.

"I don't need to," she says, and stalks off.

He shouts after her, "He's not who you think he is! And it is going to be *all over this school* by tomorrow!"

She flips him off over her shoulder as she leaves.

The orange explodes in the microwave before the timer even dings. The air is filled with the scent of charred citrus. Black smoke pours forth from around the oven door. Why is this so satisfying to me? Because it turns something into nothing? I rush out of the cafeteria, crowded on all sides. We move together like a flock of birds, a murder of crows.

• • •

Our apartment is disturbingly quiet. The little kids are not playing video games; instead they are reading from actual, live books. My mom is sitting at her desk, thumbing through her birding book and looking out the window with her binoculars. I used to think that if it were me, I'd be spying on people with those things, but now I realize that I see enough of ugly humanity without delving into their dark, solitary perversions.

I head toward the kitchen, but my mom beckons me to her. She puts down the binocs and picks up a piece of paper, waving it in my direction.

"Your report card came. You want to see?"

No. "Uh, I guess."

Then, before I even get to her, she says, "Two As, a B, a bunch of Cs, and a D+. These are what you will be taking with you into the next quarter, where you will try and salvage your grade-point average. What sort of college will take you with grades like these?"

"Cool, two As? In what?"

She gives me the look you give a crazy person. "*Only* two As, yes. AP Biology and Modern Literature."

Ah, Ms. Viola. Always on my side.

"These grades are unacceptable."

"I'll work harder," I say in the dead voice.

"Your father will have a stroke."

"Can we not tell him?"

"Your IQ is over 140; you know that, yes? That's genius level."

"I know. I know it's a waste, I know my brain is wasted on me."

"We are the only family we know—the only family in our culture, I mean—that treats the girls the same as the boys. Look at the Elghanayan cousins. The sons are gods to your uncle, and the daughter is basically just a helper for the mother. Barely even there. I always thought myself so superior to them. 'Look how they force those boys to study, to excel, to be all that the parents want. So sad.' Driving them always, always. Your father and I said we would not do that to you or Dariush. Let you find your own way, enjoy your studies, choose your own road to success—"

"Wait, what? You'd let us choose our own road to success? Are you kidding me, Maman? You didn't let us do anything we wanted! You threw Dariush out of the house because he didn't want to go into engineering. Dad flipped out on me because I don't want to sell those chocolate bars."

"You have exactly proved my point. We let you boys make your own decisions, but what came of that? Look at both of you: failing. And look at Azita: we encouraged her to study, to be more than just a helper for me, and she is the only one achieving anything."

"I'm achieving things," I say.

"What? What are those things? Because I would dearly love to know so that I might have *something* good to tell Baba when he gets home."

I turn and walk out of the room, and I think she'll stop me, but she doesn't.

King Sargon sits on my desk and looks out my bedroom window. I close the door and play "Car Wash of Death" ten million times on Dariush's turntable, lying on my bed, staring up at the darkening ceiling and picking at my mole. I don't fall asleep though I'm beyond tired, and I can't eat—

not that anyone calls me for dinner and I can smell that it's orange chicken *koresh* again, my favorite—but my stomach is blocked by a trapdoor that closes whenever the depression hits. And it is hitting hard. The only thing that gets me through is the thought of what I will do to that school on Saturday night.

CHAPTER TWENTY-THREE

Friday flies by in a flurry of who-cares, beginning with a boring assembly in which the Homecoming Court was announced, seniors I don't know, some zit-free robots.

As Dylan promised, the rumors about me have caught fire today. In Chemistry he and his buddies glared at me. The girl from Charmers Cafe, too. I don't remind her of Kumar anymore. Someone across the aisle from me was studying a note with his lab partner. I heard him whisper, "That's Thunder Pants's *name*? Get out! You can't even pronounce that." Then much of the same in Bio and Precalc, except Mila tried to talk to me and I felt bummed out—not for me, but for her. Why should she pick me to be her friend? I will only weigh her down.

By lunch I can't take anymore. The fat, friendless hall monitor silently watches me approach the doors that lead outside. She's looking at me with a combination of familiarity and fear. I keep thinking, *This is the end of my time at Magnificat.* I have that stinging sensation in my eyes that happens right before you cry, and crying would be a relief. It's pure emotion and good for you to get through. But it doesn't happen. My eyes sting and then a dull, flat feeling washes over me, inside and out. Dr. Elliott always spoke of the "flattening of affect" as a symptom of my depression, but now it's more than a symptom. It's all I have: an endless gray parking lot where my soul should be.

The theme for Homecoming this year is *Pirates of the Caribbean*. The gym will be transformed tomorrow into an island paradise with inflatable palm trees, papier-mâché pirate ships, and treasure chests spilling over with Crafts Club–made gold and gems. For a school that takes in a lot of cash through constant fund-raising, they sure go cheap for the dances. For one thing, it's held in the gym. I thought they only did that in movies. Even at Sullivan they had their dances at a hotel.

Anyway, the treasure chests are what I am most interested in. There's some game where they're going to hand out maps to the couples, with cryptic clues to help them find some kind of "treasure" hidden in only one of the chests, probably a gift card to Olive Garden. People will be looking everywhere for it. I'm going to make sure they find something else as well.

After school there's a Homecoming "parade" of floats and cars traveling around Magnificat at old-lady speed. Actual alumni have shown up to watch the parade. *Adults* have left work early to drive over here and watch it. There's lots of clapping and wearing of blue and gold.

I watch from across the street. Nobody sees me. I am X.

Saturday. My parents have grounded me because of my report card, but they're gullible enough to believe that I have a sudden assignment to cover Homecoming for the school paper.

"But you said you had to stay home and do your US History project," Mom says.

"I started that this morning. I got a lot done."

She beams at me, proud to hear how diligent I am.

Before I leave, I stand at the apartment door, backpack heavy on my shoulders with all its precious cargo, and look at them. Mom is cleaning up from dinner (*ghormeh sabzi*, her specialty: a stew with lamb, beans, rice, and secret ingredients, but I could not eat more than a bite); Dad is lying on the couch with the newspaper over his face; Azita's at the Loyola library; Dorri and Arman are watching something inappropriate on TV. I get a pang for Dariush, but he's probably out somewhere having fun with his friends.

"Good-bye," I say.

Dad waves from beneath the newspaper.

I can't find my iPod, and I'm pissed because I need the perfect playlist for this night. So I have to summon my own internal soundtrack.

I walk through the valley of the car wash of death

I'll punch the clock till my last dying breath

A dark-skinned stranger with an engineering degree

Wipes down your car, his diploma is a chamois

Use the pre-soak to loosen crap from the road

I aim the foam brush like a gun and reload

Now get the soap off, rinse and repeat

Spray wax like bullets till I'm dead on my feet.

The two bus rides to school wreak havoc with my ten-
uous grip on things. The bravado I felt earlier is slipping.
My backpack has everything I need except confidence and
courage. My hair is stuck to my forehead in mad peaks due
to the incredible amount of sweat pouring out of me. Giant,
wet pit-stains ring my T-shirt. I've hardly eaten in a week,
so my pants are even bigger and more homeless-man looking than usual. And then of course there's the mole, growing
and itching and taking on a personality of its own.

Have you seen a school at night? It looks like any other
institution: a prison, an asylum, an office park. In the dark,
nothing suggests learning or education there. The brick and
stone are colorless, undefined. The grass of the football field
is as black as a winter sky, and I'm happy to report that St.
Viator trounced the Sheep in last night's Homecoming game,
42–7.

I go into the school and show the chaperones at the
east wing entrance my school ID and camera, saying that
I'm reporting on the dance. They just wave me on through.
Nobody checks my backpack. Wouldn't matter if they did. I
hid all my equipment in a fund-raiser chocolate bar box and
sealed it shut.

I'm here early with the other punctual drips. The guys'
suits are no better than my funeral suit from Bonfire Night,
and the girls look too tan. I walk around, aimlessly snapping
photos. I make mental notes of the cardboard pirate chests
where the Homecoming "treasure" might be hidden. As the
gym fills up and the DJ starts spinning, I can blend in much
better. There are lots of kids studying their maps, poking

around, looking for the treasure. I poke around, too, but now I am looking for the perfect spot to hide *my* treasure.

I find exactly what I'm looking for: a chest by the bleachers against the gym's west wall. It's dark over here; too far away from the stage for people to want to dance, yet too close to the garbage cans for make-out purposes. There are some people sitting up on the bleachers, but not at this end. There are no chaperones on patrol here at the moment.

I seize my opportunity. First, I take the chocolate bar box out of my backpack, tear off the lid, and remove a small pipe packed with a chlorate mixture, and then I open the cardboard chest and carefully place the pipe inside it. Running out the end of the capped pipe is an electric fuse connected to a timer and a battery. It's more complicated than the fireworks bomb I used in the Sullivan toilet. My pipe bomb will be triggered from the battery when the timer—rigged to ignite in an hour—goes off. I push the chest slightly under the bleachers.

I stand up quickly. Though no one has seen me, anxiety floods my system. The room tilts, vibrates. I get that cold-Jell-O sensation down my spinal cord. It's not the adrenaline rush I was expecting. There is no flat affect for me here, Dr. Elliott. I don't know what this is. It grips my heart in its jaws.

I slip into the cafeteria, which is open for hanging out and photos. A "deserted island" backdrop is set up in the corner, complete with skeleton in the sand; I don't think the girls will find this romantic. I sit down at a table. I don't understand what is happening to me. I'm supposed to feel triumphant.

Students walk by me, teachers and chaperones, too . . .

nobody seems to notice me. If I were smart, I would hightail it on out of here now to distance myself from what's about to go down. But I can't move. I've read that pyros like to watch what they burn. So I guess I am going to see this thing through to the end.

I scroll through the photos on my camera: a somewhat chubby girl adjusting the strap of her dress while two girls behind her watch with mean smiles; a couple slow dancing, elbows ramrod straight, as far apart as possible; a middle-aged chaperone, someone's mom I guess, looking at a group of buff football players in their suits—her expression is wistful; McNeill pulling at his absurd mustache; girls who came stag in their pretty dresses, wallflowers in every sense; the guy that everyone knows is gay who came with the girl whom everyone knows is in love with him; a garbage can with a corsage in it.

These are probably not the kind of photos the *Vox Populi* would publish. Yeah, of course there are happy people having happy fun. I could have taken their pictures. But we already know those people are out there. Troubled people: the loners, the unloved, the bitter—that's who we should force ourselves to see.

Nikki and Reggie enter the cafeteria with some of the Checkmates. No surprise, Reggie looks cool in his suit with the embroidered skull and crossbones all over it. He even matches the theme. Nikki looks great in this jade-green, 1960s-type prom dress. Sloppy ponytail, glasses, no makeup, black Converse low-tops. She somehow looks tougher and more badass than if she were flaunting various piercings and tattoos.

I slide down in my seat. I don't want them to see me. They're having a good time joking with Reggie's chess friends. I see a group of stag girls rise from a table and walk to the entrance near Reggie and Nikki. They are mostly from the Engineering Club and the Mathletes and other nerd-girl organizations—and believe me, when I say nerd girls, it is the highest compliment, because they are not what you expect. These girls are pretty in a completely different way than the popular girls: understated, sweet. And generally nice and smart. In an alternate universe, I could be attracted to them.

In the midst of those girls I see Mila. She came stag. And first I'm glad, and second I'm blown away by her overt cuteness—her dress is white and gray with some kind of shimmery material over it, and it hits right at her knees. Even her knees are cute. I've never seen another pair like them. Her shoes are flat. Her hair is regular: two glossy black curtains on either side of her face sweeping toward her pointy chin. It's really not fair when you see the girls who have put so much effort into their appearances—the tans, the trendy dresses and stiletto heels, the fancy hair-dos, the purses and glittery makeup—and then you have Mila walk in with this knee-baring dress and regular hair and flat shoes, and she totally knocks them out. They look like wax figures next to her.

Just beyond Mila's group, an obviously drunk guy is fighting loudly with his girlfriend. She yells some incredibly filthy things at him. I see Mila raise her hands slowly, index fingers touching thumbs, framing the couple in a shot like a film director.

I want to walk over to her and be a new guy: a romantic-comedy kind of guy.

But I've rigged a bomb in the gym that is due to go off in thirty minutes.

Please don't go in there, I plead silently. *Nikki, Reggie, Mila, cute Mathlete girls, pimply Checkmates. Please, girl I saw straightening her corsage as her date scanned the room for better-looking girls, don't go in the gym. Gay guy and love-sick girl, you should stay out, too. You two always said hi to me in study hall. Please don't go by the bleachers. Yes, the rest of you—jocks, bitches, Trevor, Dylan, Jason, Rebecca, Chemistry girl whose name I don't know from Charmers Cafe, Colin McCool with your lousy threats—you all can go in. You, too, teacher chaperones: Ryndak, you overgrown sack of shit; Mr. Blankenship, sadist from Phys Ed with your impossible rope climb. You go.*

But then . . . jeez. Ms. Viola's here? She has to chaperone everything—she has no life. *Please, Ms. Viola, only teacher I have ever connected with; your anger is one of the only things that has gotten me through these last couple months. Please, do not become a civilian casualty in this war I've waged.*

This ship has sailed. I cannot undo what I've done even if I wanted to—and I do, but I don't. Something in me is breaking up.

Mila walks over to Reggie and Nikki and chats with them. Some dude from the Checkmates is trying to hit on her. It's so obvious. Then as a group, the four of them move out of the cafeteria. There is nowhere else for them to go besides the gym. The timer in the treasure chest is counting down the minutes.

I can't get up. Literally cannot move. I can actually taste the anxiety on my tongue. It's like licking a battery. What do I do? I could go in the gym and masterfully guide my friends away from that area. Right? I could lie and tell them there is some emergency, and they have to leave the gym. They'd listen to me because they—Nikki, Reggie, Mila—always listen to me. They believe everything, almost, that comes out of my mouth.

But how would I explain the explosion afterward? They'd know it was me.

And now I see what my problem is: I don't want them to know I did this. I don't want them to think of me this way: the liar, the thief, the killer. I'm rooted here, tangled in thorns, about to pull the foundation out of the ground.

I see that douche bag Trevor. He came with this girl from the newspaper staff, and he pulls her chair out for her and then gets her a cup of lemonade, and she takes it without looking at him and sets it on the table, and then takes out her phone and plays around with it. And he sits there with this miserable expression on his face, and he fixes his tie and leans in to say stuff to her every so often, and she is not into him, and it's the kind of thing that happens a million times a day, but when you see it happening to someone in front of you, even someone as revolting as Trevor, you would have to be an absolute *monster* not to feel some vestige of sympathy.

Dylan and his buddies and their dates pass by, and with them is Dylan's little sister, the freshman he pointed out to me on my first day. She has very bad skin and is not pretty—I'm sorry to say it and I'm not judging, but there it is; and she's apparently dateless and tagging along with them—probably their mother made her go because Dylan is Mr. Popularity—

and he has his hand lightly on her shoulder when she says something to him, and her whole face is a study in misery, and he replies and pats her back, like, *Come on now, it's all right*. And he looks sort of, I don't know, *human*, and his sister's posture, hunched and defeated, embodies the last fourteen months of my life, when things began to misfire in my brain and the whole universe decided it was out to get me.

I look around, here in the cafeteria, with ten minutes till ignition. Surrounded by classmates and teachers, those I know, those I don't, those I thought I knew.

These are people. Human beings. And some of them are horrible, but—and now I find myself breathing normally, not sweating—they possess hidden dimensions that maybe you can see only when you are unseen. When you are X.

I rise from my chair.

I run to the gym. The feelings racing through me—fear, excitement, confusion, victory, regret—bash into one another and break down my resistance. I am *feeling* these things. They threaten to expose me, explode me. I have only eight minutes.

In the gym lobby, Reggie and Nikki are standing by the trophy case. The plaque with Reggie's name on it is to the right; to the left is the old photo of Ms. Viola with her archery team. Before they took away the one thing she loved.

"Bud!" Nikki rushes up to me. "What are you doing here?"

"I'm only here as a reporter. I can't talk." I try to push by her.

But she latches onto my arm—hard. "Yes, you can. Look at me. Look."

I look at her. She whispers, *"I know it's you."*

"You know *what's* me?" I shake myself loose, but she grabs me again, digging in with her ragged fingernails.

"I knew it had nothing to do with Loyola Beach, the lousy football party, or the Gridiron Queen. I just didn't know till this second that you meant here. But it all makes sense."

"For the last time, I didn't write those anonymous letters!" I have *got* to go. Five minutes.

"I don't mean the letters," she says. "I mean the locker note."

I freeze.

She knows.

We stare at each other.

But I've got a bomb to defuse.

If I get to the treasure chest in time, I can grab it, run out the gym doors on the west wall, and fling it into the empty playing fields. With all the noise in the gym, nobody would hear the detonation, and nobody would get hurt. I can do it. I run through the crowd, knocking shoulders with everyone. Past the stage, past Ms. Viola holding hands with Mr. Downie, past the bleachers full of couples and wallflowers and everyone in between, to the spot where I pushed the chest underneath.

Except it isn't there.

I crawl under the bleachers, looking everywhere, but it's nowhere. I back out, whirl around. Where could it be? What is going on? Three minutes and you'd think I'd have a panic attack right now, that I'd black out or freak out or hyperventilate myself into unconsciousness. But I don't.

Behind the garbage cans, I see a couple. The girl is holding their map. The boy is holding the treasure chest. *The* treasure chest. They look like they can't wait to get their Olive Garden gift card. I hurl myself over there and try to grab the chest out of his hands.

"Hey! Back off!" he shouts.

"I'm sorry," I say, "but I really, really want to win this thing," and I rip the chest right out of his grasp. I don't know if I have time to get outside, but there's nowhere in here I can safely toss it. So I fly to the exit, glancing over my shoulder. Nikki and Reggie elbow through the crowd, not far behind me, trying to signal to me. I half turn and raise my palm, *Stop, go no farther*, then hold up one finger to indicate *Wait a minute*. I have to hold them at bay for as long as I can. I look at my hand. It is pointed like a gun. . . .

But still they come for me, and I bust through the exit doors and tear across the playing fields. My lungs are on fire because honestly I have never run this much in my life. And I realize I'm afraid to throw this thing! I won't be able to throw it far enough because I suck at throwing. So I'll just have to *escort it* as far from the school as possible. I speed-walk, trying not to jostle the chest. Most unintentional-detonation incidents among pipe-bomb builders occur when packing and assembling the bomb, not when running with it, but I don't want to take any chances. I don't know the exact millisecond when the timer is due to go off.

I hear voices behind me. I pass the track and the football stadium. Then I reach that forgotten tract of land, a parcel barely used, barely mowed. The archery field—where one teacher found her mission. A crime of injustice, taking away a good club because it makes no money. A tragedy. The scene of the crime. I'd told Nikki the school would take this field away from Ms. Viola over my dead body, but those were just words. Weren't they? I didn't mean them, not like this. I *wanted* to blow up this goddamn field for Viola, for me, but what would that solve? The school would build the new football stadium on the rubble.

But still . . . I guess . . . I will blow up this field after all.

At the far end are the targets, standing as if the archers are poised with arrows drawn. The area between is riddled with saw grass and goldenrod. I look to the stand of black locust trees at the edge of the property, the edge of our world. Voices coming closer. Nikki runs fast. Good thing she wore her Converse tonight. For a second I think maybe this was all for nothing, that the timer, or the bomb itself, is defective. But then I hear the telltale *pop*. And I lift the lid and tilt the chest.

CHAPTER TWENTY-FOUR

*P*ain and noise and heat. Red and black, like fireworks, gorgeous fireworks, in the black November sky. And the sensation of falling upward, like swimming in a riptide, thinking down is up and plunging to the cold ground instead of rising to the stars.

Ringing in my ears. Roaring. My hands are *burning.* Sticky, wet blood on my face, pooling beneath my cheek and dripping from the wounds on my hands, ebbing out into the grass and around my student ID card still connected to the lanyard around my neck. Blood covers the card and washes over BUD HESS.

The blanket of night settles on me and mercifully takes over the pain. Before I slip under, a voice in my ear—Nikki—gentle, insistent: *Bud, come back to me. Come back.*

I come to in the back of a car. Nikki sprawls on me to keep me from rolling around while she backseat drives, shouting directions at Reggie to Methodist Hospital.

"This is crazy! I don't know where I'm going," screams Reggie. "Why didn't you let me call 911?"

"If we did that, everything would be all over for him. The

school can't know about this, we couldn't have an ambulance come there. His parents would take him away forever."

"It's better than him dying, Nikki!"

"He's not going to die," she mutters through clenched teeth.

I'm not going to die. The pain is *beyond* beyond, but I know in my gut that I am okay.

I open my eyes as best as I can and croak, "If I die, you guys can have my Godzillas."

Nikki whips her head around. Her eyes are shimmering with tears. "You stupid idiot! What the hell where you doing? I could just murder you!"

I try to smile, but pain rips at my face. "I was saving you."

"Man, you should have let it explode in the gym," Reggie says. "No one would have known it was you—no one but us. And we would have covered for you."

"I couldn't." The darkness is coming back. "There were people in there."

CHAPTER TWENTY-FIVE

Know what I hate most about the hospital? No magazines. It makes me long for the good old days of Dr. Elliott's waiting room.

Suicide watch. It's so ridiculous. But Nikki and Reggie brought me into the ER, saying I got hurt setting off fireworks in a vacant lot to celebrate Homecoming weekend, and then the triage nurse asked who my doctor was and I said Dr. Elliott and she said is he your pediatrician and I said no he's my shrink and then she got a funny look on her face and things began to move in another direction pretty quickly after that.

Two days have passed since the Homecoming dance, and I have to stay here at least five days so they can be sure I am not suicidal before they release me. Seriously, five days? "Do people really go from suicidal to all-better in five days?" I asked. Because that's not how it went for me last year when I really did try to kill myself. They said no, but you can go from suicidal to not-suicidal, which is the best you can hope for.

If the hospital wants to think I tried to kill myself, let them. I know I didn't. They do know, thanks to Dr. Elliott, that I tried once, so that's the end of the conversation as far as they're concerned. Kill myself? Try the opposite: I wanted to make sure other people *lived*. Especially since I almost killed some of them.

You know what? Nobody at school has any idea about the bomb. The blast wasn't that big, though I had wanted it to be. I had imagined unleashing something terrible and shocking—a dragon, a dying star—but I think when the time came, I couldn't let myself direct it at people. I had to turn it elsewhere. So I did, and I tilted the chest. Better me than them.

Nobody followed Nikki and Reggie outside when they chased me, so nobody heard anything over the din of the music and the crowd. Plus the archery field is in such shitty condition, nobody would even notice the debris left over from the fusillade if they did go out there. After all my scheming and planning, you'd think it would feel anticlimactic to me, but it doesn't.

They let me have visitors, so that's good, depending on who the visitor is. My parents came by yesterday—not so good. My mom looked about ten years older. That's all my fault. She'd brought me my own pajamas, and she was crying. I feel a tremendous amount of weird things now and can't handle guilt on top of it all.

"Maman, I know what they're saying, but listen to me. I was not trying to kill myself. I was having recreational fun with fireworks, and it went wrong. That's *all*."

But she just cried and shook her head. She flinched when I said the words *kill myself*, as if hearing them caused her physical pain. What the hell do I know? Maybe it does.

Dad stood there mutely, tears in his eyes.

Their son is on suicide watch in the hospital, and nothing I say can change that. We are all going to have to get through this. I accepted the tranquilizer the nurse brought later without any argument.

Someone knocks at my door now. It's 3:30 in the afternoon. I don't say come in, because people tend to do what they want when you are confined to a bed.

The door swings open, and it's Nikki and Reggie. I haven't seen them since they brought me here.

Reggie flops in the chair. "This is total bullshit."

"Shut up, I think it's kinda cool," Nikki says. "Suicide watch. Adults in a tizzy. That is just chrome-plated awesome, Bud."

They laugh because they don't know the truth of it. That I have been here before, and with good reason.

I'm embarrassed to have them see me like this—in my SpongeBob pajamas, old and new cuts on my face, bandaged hands, hair a testament to time spent in a psychiatric hospital. But then, they've seen me worse.

Nikki is standing over me. I hate that, looking up at people.

"So how are you feeling?" she asks.

"I don't know."

She thinks I mean my hands and face. Yeah—they hurt. But I honestly don't know what I feel. Dr. Elliott and the psychopharmacologist treating me at Methodist agreed to put me on a different SSRI this time. When will it kick in? Who knows? Anger, exhaustion, elation, sadness, nothingness— they all pass through me. My heart is a sieve.

Reggie asks, "What do they feed you in here? You hungry? I've got some mini-Twix from Halloween."

"No, thanks," I say. Maybe I *am* in bad shape if I'm refusing junk food.

Nikki sits on the side of the bed. "Can you talk now? I mean, are there hidden cameras or something keeping watch on you in here? I've been dying to talk to you. I need some answers."

I say, "I need a lot of things."

"What do you need? I'll get it for you. I'll give it to you."

"Really? Anything I ask for, you'll give to me?" I stare at Nikki, daring her to refuse me.

Give me that part of yourself you have never given to anyone.

She wrinkles her brow and says, "Sure. If it's anything that I'm able to give."

Maybe she's just not able to feel *that way* about me. Like how I can't help the way my brain misfires. It's chemical.

I change the subject. "How did you know? How did you figure out I was the one who wrote the notes in the lockers?"

She says, "I got sidetracked by all the beach party stuff, the chocolate bar sales, all that. And when we got the notes in our lockers, I just assumed they were from Anonymous. I should have realized that no one could hate you that much—not after knowing you for only a short time anyway. The newspaper letters are still a big, fat mystery, but I don't think the author has it in for you."

Is it because Reggie is the author? I give him a long, hard look. His eyes reveal nothing.

"Okay, go on," I say.

"I knew how you felt about Viola losing the archery team to football, about Mila losing the Computer Camp trip to football. *That* had to be 'the scene of the crime'—the school, the *gym*—the scene of all the crimes: the pep rallies, the Homecoming dance and the assembly, you falling off the rope in Phys Ed, everything related to sports that eventually sucks the life out of the other clubs and the rest of us nonjocks."

"Oh," I say. It's weird being deconstructed like this as if I were some mastermind whose big plan got foiled.

"Plus the lyrics from 'Car Wash of Death.' They got stuck in my head . . . especially the part about the stranger with the engineering degree wiping down cars and being dead on his feet. It's a vivid image. The stranger, dead on his feet. Your brother. You. And that stuff in the locker note about who is dead and who is the stranger. It was too similar; I realized that you had to have written it. And if you wrote the note, then the target was *you*. Not that you would harm yourself, not the way *they* think you would, but harm yourself in another way. Isolating yourself forever. Making sure that everyone knew how they had hurt you, making sure you'd get kicked out of Magnificat. I didn't know what you had planned, but I knew it would be destructive."

Reggie hooks his long legs over the arm of the chair and slowly swings them back and forth. He says, "Well, the note sounded like Anonymous to me. I didn't even think of 'Car Wash of Death.'"

I'm not Anonymous, but I am anonymous. I'm Muslim, but not really. I'm not Badi, I'm not Bud. I don't know what I am.

Nikki takes off her glasses and studiously cleans them with her shirttail. "I don't really get how explosives work and all that, but you weren't hoping to seriously hurt people, right? You just wanted to damage stuff."

I don't want to be truthful, but I've got to start sometime.

"I wanted all this hounding and hatred of me to *stop*. I didn't know how else to *make* it stop. I did want to hurt people. But I changed my mind, Nikki. I don't know how else to say it. It was like it dawned on me, looking around that school, that nobody deserves this. Even assholes are people, too."

Dariush pokes his head into my room. "Hey, Badi, is now a good—" He catches sight of Nikki and Reggie. "Oh, I can come back."

My friends leap up at this, their first viewing of Dariush, who has reached rock-star status in their eyes. I tell my brother to come in, and Reggie offers him his chair. Nikki smoothes her hair. I wish I could laugh.

"So you're Dariush," Reggie says.

"You must be Reggie." They shake hands. I've never seen Reggie look so dorky. He's grinning like a little kid.

"Taking care of this guy?" Dariush asks, jerking his head at me.

"Trying to," Nikki answers.

We all talk for a while in a way that passes for normal in the psych ward. Then Nikki slides her eyes to Dariush and then to me and says quietly, "I need to ask you something, Bud, but maybe it can wait."

"You can say anything in front of my brother."

Reggie and Dariush look at us expectantly.

"Okay," says Nikki. "Dylan told me you tried to kill someone while you were at Sullivan. He was lying, right?"

"No."

"You didn't."

"I did," I say. "I tried to kill me."

Their mouths are actually hanging open. It's not often that I can shock people with the truth.

"This isn't the first time I've been in the psych ward. That's why I have to see a shrink—not just because I blew up a toilet. That's why I couldn't go back to Sullivan, even though I wasn't technically expelled. That's why they're keeping me here: they think I tried again, no matter what I say. I don't know when I'm coming back to school. My hands and face hurt like hell, but that's the least of my problems. I have to go back on an antidepressant and antianxiety meds and I don't want to, but I don't know how to live normally without them. I don't know what's going to happen to me."

Reggie asks, "How?" We all know what he means.

"Pills. Pills, pills, always pills, and the doctors just keep giving me more." I hate talking about this. That was the old me, and no one will let me ever forget it. Every time I think about that suicide attempt, I'm reminded that the wound is still there, and how the hell can it ever be repaired? If I were normal, I think I'd be crying by now.

I'm supposed to be feeling triumphant about saving the school—from myself—not deadened by all the mistakes I've made and how they continue to hurt people.

"I'm tired," I say, turning to the wall. "Would you guys mind going?" I look at my brother, who hasn't made a move. He doesn't know about me and the bomb at school. He thinks it really was fireworks. "Try me tomorrow, Dariush." My voice cracks. And though I'm on some wicked combo of tranquilizers, mood stabilizers, and I don't know what, if I have to talk about this one more minute, I will crack, too.

CHAPTER TWENTY-SIX

r. Elliott looks weird in this room. I am used to seeing his carefully crafted bald head and cashmere sweaters and wide-wale cords in his bonsai office, surrounded by books and low lighting.

"So, tell me what's brought you here, Bud."

"Don't you know everything?" I say. It comes out sullen, which is exactly how I feel, so I've started out on a good note by being truthful.

"I've read your admission record."

"And?"

"It says you were playing with fireworks in a vacant lot. It says the injuries sustained may or may not have been intentional. So that, coupled with your decision to abruptly stop therapy and to stop taking your medication without discussing it with anyone, concerns me."

"I swear I was not trying to kill myself. It really was an accidental explosion."

"Okay, tell me about it."

I could start the cycle of lies again, the way I did with the other doctor and with my parents. That was out of self-preservation. I couldn't tell them what really happened at school.

But I am sick of the lies, and Dr. Elliott might be able to help me. Because I think I really do need help.

I say, "When I talk to you, it's like the crypt or whatever, right?"

"The crypt?"

"The vault? The confessional? Nothing leaves this room?"

"You have my word," he says. And that's shocking. No qualifiers like "as long as you haven't broken any laws" or "as long as you aren't a danger to anyone or yourself."

So I tell him. Everything. I tell him how I wanted to do damage, not necessarily blow people up—but maybe I did, I don't know—and then changed my mind. It takes forever, because I leave nothing out.

When I'm finally done, I get out of bed and lean against the windowsill and look out at the courtyard below. I feel winded. The truth takes a lot out of you.

He says, "You didn't want to hurt your friends."

"I didn't want to hurt *anybody*."

"Why didn't you throw the chest? It could have exploded farther away from you, and perhaps it wouldn't have injured you as much."

"I wasn't sure if that would make it worse, a bigger explosion. If it just exploded near me, then I would be the only one hurt," I say. And scars can be useful reminders.

I think he believes me. Later on he has a consultation with the doctor, and they say I'm not on suicide watch anymore. It's a distinction I am happy to give up. So I'm just here in the hospital because of physical injuries, like anyone else.

My parents pick me upon Wednesday morning after Dr.

Elliott speaks with them. They seem happy to take me home. Dad took the morning off from work. Although they were told that my injuries really were the result of an accident, they're on edge. After all, they're still stuck with a son who builds explosives.

They have this big talk on the car ride home, reassuring each other that everything is okay, that since I conducted my "fireworks experiment" in a vacant lot, the Magnificat administration knows nothing of it and that there's no reason I should not go back there when my burns have healed a bit more.

"What did you tell the school about why I've been absent this week?" I ask.

Dad clears his throat. My mother crosses her arms and stares at him. "Go on, Javeed, tell him. Tell him the excuse you gave without consulting me. Tell him what you told the school office when you called Monday morning."

"Well, I had to think of something to explain the bandages on your hands and the burns on your face," he says, "so I just said we had a . . . a cooking accident. A big pot of lentil soup in the pressure cooker. You were trying to help and it exploded on you, and you tipped the pot on yourself."

"A cooking accident!" shouts Mom, turning back to me, her horror fully apparent. "In *my* kitchen! A cooking accident. And why on earth would I use a pressure cooker for lentil soup?" A look as black as thunder crosses her face, and she turns to the window, shaking her head.

I can't help it, I burst out laughing.

We get home, and I lay around like a sick person for a couple of hours. Mom makes me lunch and brings it on a tray to the living room and lets me eat it in front of the television (unheard of). It is, actually, lentil soup, and the irony is not lost on either of us.

"Ohhh, whoa . . . whoa . . . whoops," she says in mock alarm, pretending to teeter and stumble. Dad straightens his tie, announces he must get back to Abbott, and flees out the door, my mom shooting daggers at his back. Her anger is the funniest thing I've seen in ages. Maybe the meds are working after all.

Dariush comes over after lunch, and we play Trivial Pursuit and he wins. I told him everything that happened— *everything*—when he came back to see me in the hospital alone. I even showed him the Thunder Pants video on YouTube, which now has over a thousand hits and an offshoot video where they've autotuned my screaming.

By the time two o'clock rolls around, Dariush has left and I feel anxious. It's not a result of the drugs or anything. It's because for days now I have been trying to sort things out in my brain, the mystery of everything that has gone down. My mind cycles through everything I know: all the disjointed facts and hints, all the coincidences, all the subtext beneath the words. Slowly it comes together, like if you run a movie backward of something breaking apart: all the shattered pieces move toward the middle and then the picture is whole. Now there is something I need to do, and I don't want to do it.

I wait for Mom to leave for her birding class (field trip to the Harold Washington Library downtown to see a peregrine falcon nesting on the cornice), and then I load up my briefcase and backpack with some surprises—sort of tough with bandaged hands, but I manage—and sneak out to the bus stop. The little kids will go to my aunt's apartment when they get off the bus from school. Mom and Dad will never know I went out.

Forty-two minutes later, I'm standing at the entrance to the school, looking up at the clock tower, watching the sweep of the second hand. Just like my first day. The limestone pillars still look like gun turrets and guard towers to me. I think they always will. I think they are supposed to.

Then I walk in. It's after the dismissal bell, so the school has emptied out quite a bit. I checked the extracurricular schedule on the website for today: poms, archery, football, Computer Club, Religious Activities Club. On my way in, I tell Mrs. Kobunski that I'm picking up my assignments. She hands them to me, already packed into a manila envelope. Her broccoli rubber band bounces against her throat when she speaks. I notice, but it doesn't bother me.

"Oh dear, your face," she says sadly. "I spoke to your dad when he called. Are you okay?"

"I will be. Is it all right if I go to my locker? My jacket and folders are in there."

She nods. I head down the main hall. I pass the lab where the Computer Club meets, and I peek in the doorway. They're mostly laughing and goofing around, like regular people. Mila sits hunched over at a desk, her chin resting on her fists. She's not laughing. She turns to her friends every so often as if she is listening, but her eyes look blank. I don't want her to see me. She looks out the window. Below are the playing fields. Football practice is right next to archery practice. That's a recipe for disaster.

I walk the near-empty hallways. I run my fingers along

the lockers, touching the grates: openings for airing out sneakers in a permanent state of funk or lunches left over the weekend, breathing holes for people thrown in there for fun by classmates, or mail slots for notes left by an unseen hand.

The east hall is quiet. I catch my reflection in the "You Can Make a Difference" mirror. All right, I'm trying.

I hurry and make my move. . . .

When I'm done, I go out the east-hall doors and take the shortcut to the playing fields. The wind cuts through my jacket. The football coach is shouting insults at the players in an attempt to motivate them.

Ms. Viola is shepherding the archers farther and farther from the encroaching football drills. I don't think it's to keep the archers from shooting the football team; I think it's to keep the archers from being trampled by them.

For a moment I get this horrible, choked-up feeling looking at the archery field. My heart beats faster, slams against my chest. I look around, but there's nothing to show that I was ever out here that night.

I glance up at the school, at where I think the computer lab is. I think I see a figure at one of the windows. I imagine Mila is looking down here and seeing someone that reminds her of me.

Ms. Viola is wearing that padded suit again and letting the club shoot arrows at her as she runs across the field. I know they're playing with safety arrows, but doesn't it seem a little dangerous? Just because you're screwed over and sad doesn't mean you shouldn't be looking out for your kids. I watch her tearing around like a madwoman.

When I get within shooting range, I flag her down. She walks over to me. "How are you?" she asks. Her eyes travel over the damage on my face to my bandaged hands.

"Can you take a break?" I ask. "It's important."

She tells the team to do their wrist and elbow drills for a few minutes and then takes off her helmet and looks at me. I can't tell if she's genuinely crazy or just a wounded, desperate person.

"Why do you let them shoot you?" I ask.

"There's no harm in it. It's very unlikely I could really get hurt. Besides, they're having fun."

"I can't believe Principal McNeill lets you do that."

"He ignores my club, so he doesn't ever notice."

"But someone could get hurt. They're just kids. You shouldn't be doing this, encouraging them to break the safety rules or whatever. That would be like the football coach telling the team to play without helmets."

She laughs, but it sounds unhappy and faraway. "Don't compare *us* to them. Kids today need to be taught that you can flout the rules once in a while, that you *should* flout the rules."

"Yeah, but when you try to stir kids up without them really understanding the reasons why, people can get into trouble."

She stares at me. "What are you talking about, Bud?"

I don't know how to talk to adults even in normal circumstances, and this is *way* beyond normal, but I try again. "I know you're unhappy, Ms. Viola. I know the school has let you down over and over. But you shouldn't have let me become your scapegoat."

Her eyes have an unfocused glaze to them, and for the first time I think she really is unhinged.

"The newspaper letters," I say. "I know you wrote them. You're Anonymous."

Viola glances back at her archers. They're running drills, not paying attention to us.

"You let people think it was me," I say.

"I didn't know." Her voice is hoarse, pleading.

"You knew! Nikki told you herself. I was *there*."

"Bud, you must believe me: my intentions were good. All I wanted was to get people thinking, and I knew anonymous letters would seem exciting and mysterious to teenagers. I never meant to hurt you. I promise."

"But I did get hurt! I got beat up. You saw my face; you knew what was going on."

"No, no." She shakes her head, takes a deep breath. "You told me it was the trampoline, a car accident. I mean, I didn't really believe that, but I was confused by everything and couldn't seem to stop. I knew kids didn't like you, but I didn't really think you were beaten up over the *letters*. I thought they were after you because of the chocolate bars. You have to believe me."

"And what was all that bullshit about the Loyola Beach party? You didn't actually go and do anything there."

"No." She looks down sheepishly.

"You only wanted to scare them, huh?"

"I don't know. I suppose so. It infuriates me that that party goes on and nobody stops it. I didn't know what was happening with you. I . . . I thought maybe there was trouble at home or something."

"Trouble at home?" I almost spill it then, about the archery field, the bomb, my suicide attempt, my crushing depression. But I can't do it. I *won't*. Not with her. "Listen, here's what you can do: you can let the administration know it was you who wrote the letters, clear up any lingering suspicions that anybody may have that it was me."

"I would lose my job," she says, looking back at me.

"So what! You hate your job. And now that you've lost the archery team, there's nothing here for you." I hate being so rough on her—she's not a bad person, and it's not normal to talk to a teacher this way—but she is not a normal teacher.

The archers have gotten bored with their exercises, and now they're watching us. Luckily we're out of hearing range. I'm about to say that either *she* can tell McNeill or *I* will when a look of resignation passes over her face.

She says, "I've lost touch with why I became a teacher in the first place. When you came into my classroom with your quiet revolution, you inspired me. I thought I could encourage kids to view life, conformity, authority differently. But somehow it got away from me. I'm so sorry. You won't take the fall for this. I'll tell Principal McNeill."

"Tomorrow," I say.

She nods. There is a lot of pain in her eyes. I hate her and respect her all at once. And somehow I know—*I know*—that I am never going to let myself end up like that: unfulfilled, desperate, afraid, alone.

Then I turn and walk away. Life was easier when I connected with no one. Easier, but empty. Now I'm wildly caught up in other people's lives and my own feelings, and it's crazy and intense and it's scary as hell, too—to be so human, so alive.

CHAPTER TWENTY-SEVEN

On Thursday, Nikki and Reggie stop over after school and bring me homework and junk food. Reggie's brought his travel chess board and sets it up on the table so we can play.

Nikki spreads out her homework, even though I know she won't do any. Just a pretext to keep Helicopter Mom from hovering. As soon as Mom steps out of the room, Nikki leans over to me and jabs her finger into my chest. "You. Listen."

"Yeah?"

"I've been thinking about what you told us. About your suicide attempt last year. I don't know if you meant to hurt yourself at Homecoming, and you don't have to say, but if you ever pull anything like that again—I mean getting so low that you give up on coming to me for help—you won't *have* to kill yourself because I swear to God, I will do it for you. And it will be long, torturous, and painful."

"Oh. Thanks. I mean, okay," I say, feeling my skin prickle with heat. "So you care."

"Yes, I care, I freaking *care*, you stupid idiot. I love you."

I wish I understood what kind of love. "Me, too." I say it fast. The truth hurts.

She looks over her shoulder at Reggie. He returns her stare, and then turns to me and shrugs. "Hah. For real? You're crazy if you think I'm gonna say it."

I stuff a KitKat in my mouth as a distraction. "The school really never realized anything blew up on the archery field, huh?"

"Nope," says Nikki. "Dumbasses. It's always a mess out there, it rained hard the other night, and nobody but Viola, her club, and that burnout David-Earl go out there anyway."

Viola. The Kit-Kat kind of chokes me. "How are Regionals going?" I ask Reggie as we put the rooks in place.

"Great. I sent Alex Collier in my place as today's alternate."

I stop chewing. "What? There's a match today? Why aren't you there?"

He shrugs again. "I wanted to pick up a game with you. You know, we've never played. I have a feeling that you really suck, and I just want to see it in action."

"I *do* suck. You shouldn't have skipped the match today just to visit me. You're not going to earn enough points or whatever to qualify for State."

"I'll be fine—more than fine, if you want the truth. When you're as good as I am, you can afford to miss a few tourneys." He gives me a lazy grin.

Reggie skipped a day of Regionals to check up on me, to hang out with me. That's what friends do, I guess.

White goes first. I move my king pawn out two squares—not so simple with bandaged hands—and stare at the board. I want to tell them about Ms. Viola but don't know how to say it or if I should.

"How was Modern Lit today?" I ask Nikki.

"We had a sub. We read *The Stranger* to ourselves the whole time. All I could think of was the stranger in 'Car Wash of Death,' the stranger in the locker note. Kind of a coincidence that it was on Viola's syllabus, huh?"

"Not really," I say. Reggie makes his move and I continue, "She's not coming back, you know."

"What? How do you know?" Nikki asks.

I move out my bishop. "Viola wrote them. The letters. She was Anonymous."

"What?!" They both blurt out.

Mom has gone down to the laundry room, so I launch into how I snuck out yesterday and confronted her at school, the whole thing.

"Crazy bitch," says Reggie when I finish.

"She strung us along," Nikki says. "She lied to us. And she let the whole school blame you!"

"I was angry, too, but then, I don't know . . . I have wanted to do things like that myself. Uh, I *have* done things like that."

"Well, you're about a thousand times more accepting than I am," says Nikki. "Crazy bitch is right."

"I thought it was you," Reggie says to me.

"And I thought it was you," I reply. "For a while."

"Watch your queen," says Reggie. "I mean, I'm happy to whup your ass, but let's make it slightly fair."

"Did anything ever happen with the Loyola Beach party? Did they crown a Gridiron Queen?" I ask, though I know the answer.

"The same things happened that *always* happen at that party. Nobody cares," says Nikki.

"It's still not right."

"Nothing about high school is right, Bud," says Reggie.

"So when are you coming back to school?" Nikki asks.

"Maybe Monday? I don't know. It's not just my burns that have to get better. It's my . . ." I tap the side of my head.

The new meds they have me on don't kick in right away. It might take weeks for me to feel the way everyone wants me to feel. Plus I'm still on painkillers. So many pills. I get weird twinges of feeling nothing, and then surges of lingering anger, sadness. Dr. Elliott says it's normal, which is the first time that concept was ever applied to me. So I don't know if what I'm feeling at this moment is real or imaginary, but I get this stab of determination that I'm going to come back to Magnificat, and it's going to be okay. That is where my friends are. That is where I want to get myself together. It's too exhausting to move from school to school, trying to stay ahead of my past, trying to memorize the floor plans and the layout of the janitor's closet. Maybe I don't need to do that anymore.

I reveal the last bit of information I have: "So my dad bought up all my chocolate bars, plus another forty-eight boxes."

Nikki shakes her head.

Reggie says, "They can't stand to let us be who we are." I know who he means.

"Well, that explains the School Spirit ribbon they awarded you," Nikki says.

"What? Me?"

"Yeah, McNeill himself taped it to your locker this morning. You single-handedly won the free day for the junior class."

"I don't want their goddamn ribbon." This news rips through my painkiller fog. "It's not real. I'm not one of them. Tear it down," I say.

"Wait," says Nikki, "does that mean . . . did you put chocolate bars in the lockers last night? A lot of us found them this morning."

I smile, remembering my last act of subterfuge. "As many as I could carry with my oven mitts," I say, lifting my bandaged hands. "Before I left the house, I loaded up my backpack and briefcase with chocolate bars. I told Mrs. Kobunski I needed to get some things out of my locker, and nobody was around to see what I was doing in the hallways. I also left one on Ms. Viola's desk as a farewell present. It was nothing. I've had all the locker combos for ages."

"The locker combos? How?" Reggie demands.

Nikki says, "Hold on. Let me get this straight: you have the alarm codes and all the locker combos. And yet you never stole anything from school."

Reggie practically shouts, "You have the *alarm codes*?"

"It's a long story," I tell him. "Anyway, I stole this Black-Berry device from the front office that has every code and administrative password. I decided to leave it in the boiler room, though, yesterday. And I took some candy and a mini-stapler and a USB drive that proved worthless—"

Nikki interrupts. "Yeah, but I mean money, valuables, personal stuff from people."

"I stole three bucks from Kobunski's drawer. I feel pretty cut-up about that."

She stares at me. "You could have broken into people's lockers to steal anything. You could have broken in to vandalize the school. But you broke in to *give* people things."

"You know I prefer to use my powers for good, not evil."

Reggie looks down at the chessboard. Then he says, "Oh." He jerks his head up in surprise. "Moving your bishop and queen around like that. I thought you didn't know how to play chess. I didn't think you knew what you were doing."

I move my queen diagonally two squares and take the pawn in front of his bishop. His king has nowhere to run.

"The four-move checkmate," Reggie says. "I can't believe I fell for it."

He offers me his hand, and we shake. Damn, it feels good to win once in a while.

CHAPTER TWENTY-EIGHT

Friday. The wind is kicking up something fierce, but it's still one of those great fall days. I have nothing to do, so I decide to ask the neighbors if I can take Rex for a walk. I did it yesterday, too. I say I need the exercise, which is true, but I like walking with him. He veers constantly, like his stability is off.

"You chemically imbalanced, too, boy?" I ask, rubbing his ears.

I'll say this for him: he knows his way around the block. He likes to scoot down the alley between Lunt and Estes, where there must be some good-smelling garbage. When I ring the hippies' doorbell, the howl that goes up from inside the building is awe inspiring. It's like he knows it's me out here. Waiting to see where he'll take me.

When Rex and I get back from our walk, I see someone sitting on our front steps. I let the dog lead the way, as if the sight of his sagging mouth, stumbling gait, and excessive salivation would scare off anyone. But there is no need for caution. It's Mila. She stands up when I approach. There's a weird banging in my chest, and I realize it's just my heart beating.

"Hi," I say.

She walks down the steps, her eyes never leaving my face. "I came to see how you're doing. I heard you spilled soup on yourself."

"Er . . . yeah. Thanks, I'm doing better."

She keeps walking until she is toe-to-toe with me. "Your face looks so painful. I'm sorry."

"At least the burns detract from my mole."

"I don't know what you're talking about."

I touch my cheek out of habit, but all I feel are scabs.

She looks at me expectantly. I feel bad for lying to her about my injuries, but this isn't a conversation I can have now, not on the sidewalk with Rex drooling at my side.

"How did you know where I live?"

"I asked Nikki. Your mom told me you were out walking the neighbor's dog."

We both look at Rex, who farts and then sits on my foot.

Mila sighs. "Are you going to tell me what's going on? I don't believe you burned yourself with soup. When are you coming back to school?"

"I don't know."

"What's the matter? *What* is going on?"

"Nothing, really," I say.

"Why do you have to be mysterious?"

I don't.

"Something bad happened to me last year, Mila, and I can't explain it yet because it's painful and humiliating to talk about. And since last year—or maybe longer, I don't know—I've just been wired wrong, and I can't fix it myself because it's part of my *pathology*. Do you know what that means?"

"SAT word. The study of disease? Or something abnormal—whatever *normal* means."

I grin in spite of myself. "Well, yeah. Except it's my brain that's not normal. I'm getting help because I can't handle the everyday stresses that regular people can. I imagine things are a certain way, but everyone else sees things the opposite way."

She scuffs the toe of her sneaker on the sidewalk, and then she says, "*I* like the way you see things. I basically just like *you*."

If we were in a movie, this would be the time for me to kiss her or for her to leap into my arms. But this is barely real life. I like her, too, but I can't say it. Do I like her like I *like* Nikki? Honestly, I don't know yet.

"I could come back another time," she says. "My parents grounded me because of the chocolate bars, but they let me go to Computer Club. I could ditch once in a while and come see you instead."

"Okay," I say.

I look down to nudge Rex, but he's gone. I whirl around. Where can he be? I'm still holding the leash.

"Where'd the dog go?"

Mila says, "He was here just a minute ago. He can't have gone far."

We're about to embark on a chase down Lunt when suddenly she stops and points to the hippies' front porch. Rex is there on the top step, calmly waiting for someone to let him in. I don't know how he got the gate open.

"Oh *good*," I say. "He found his way home."

Mila laughs. "It's only one door down. How hard is it for

a dog to get lost when he's standing right in front of his own house?"

I don't even mean to—I *swear* it—but I end up holding her hand and saying "You'd be surprised."

It's quiet in the apartment. Dad comes home early from work again—that makes three times this week. When he gets in, the first thing he does is check on me. He pokes his head in my room and says, *"Pesar,* are you busy?"

Pesar. Son. I haven't heard that word around the house in a long time.

"No, you up for a game?" We've been playing a lot of chess since I came home from the hospital.

I follow him out to the living room. I set up the board, and he gets us a snack. This is a big deal, him getting the food instead of bellowing for Mom or one of us. He comes out with some Madar Biscuits because dumping a box of cookies on a plate is all he can manage in the kitchen. The cookies are printed with the Persian characters for *madar,* which means "mother" in Farsi. Everyone in our family is in love with these cookies.

As we begin to play, I tell him I beat Reggie this week.

"The black? He plays?"

"Yes, he plays. And he's great. He'll be going to State this year for the chess championship. He'll probably get a full ride to college."

His eyebrows lift. "A chess scholarship? I had no idea of such things. And you beat him? Perhaps you could also—"

"Baba."

"What?"

I laugh. "Just take your turn."

He lets it go. We play for an hour and I win again.

Mom is sitting at the front window with her binoculars and *Stokes Beginner's Guide to Birds: Eastern Region* open on the arm of the chair.

I look out the window. I see a flock of birds in V formation in the sky.

"Geese heading south for the winter," I say.

"*Branta canadensis*," she says. "And they don't migrate south. They just move to slightly less frigid climates."

"What's the point of that?"

"It's all they need."

I lean in toward the glass, my gaze following the birds. I want to watch them, to see where they go. But they're moving away from me.

"Did that girl find you?"

"Yes," I say, "she did."

"Good." She shifts in the chair, looking for another unsuspecting bird to watch.

"Ever spy on people with your binoculars, Mom? You know, by accident?"

"On purpose, too," she says, smiling. She puts down the binoculars and reaches up to my face. Her fingers sweep over the burns, unafraid to touch them.

In my room, King Sargon is in his usual spot. I climb up on the bed next to him, scratch him a little behind his ears, and listen to the sounds of the neighborhood: car alarms, kids yelling and playing some game outside, Mexican pop music. I take my journal out of my nightstand drawer. I haven't been able to write in it for a long time.

I put down what happened last year, what happened this fall. It's a lot. It takes me hours. Up there on my wall, Albert

Einstein sticks his tongue out at me. I end my journal entry with a famous quote of his: "Learn from yesterday, live for today, hope for tomorrow." Pretty corny, but it fits. I close the journal—that's enough for one day. I put it away in my night-stand drawer. I'm about to turn out the light, but first I go back to the drawer to make sure the slip of paper with Hes-samizadeh, my name, is there where it belongs, with all the stuff I've chosen to keep.

It is.

THE END

16543859R00166

Made in the USA
Charleston, SC
27 December 2012